Quite Contrary

Also by Stephen Dixon

No Relief
Work
Too Late

Quite Contrary

The Mary and Newt Story

Stephen Dixon

HARPER & ROW PUBLISHERS

New York, Hagerstown, San Francisco, London

Grateful acknowledgment is made to the following publications for permission to reprint the following stories in this volume, all of which appear in somewhat different form:

"Man of Letters" appeared originally in *Upstart Magazine*. "Prolog" appeared originally in *Story Quarterly*. "Conclusions" appeared originally in *The Paris Review*. "Parents" appeared originally in *The Antioch Review*. "Mary Wants to Sleep" appeared originally in *Chouteau Review*, Kansas City, Missouri. "Newt Likes the House Neat" appeared originally in *Viva* Magazine.

FIRST EDITION

Designer: Stephanie Winkler

Library of Congress Cataloging in Publication Data

Dixon, Stephen, 1936–
  Quite Contary.
  I. Title.
PZ4. D6217Qi   [PS3554.I92]   813'.5'4   78–20202
ISBN 0–06–011072–4

79 80 81 82 83 10 9 8 7 6 5 4 3 2 1

To my mother

Contents

The Return

Someone rang my bell. You can't tick back in this building to let the ringer in and there's no intercom. So I went out to the hallway and yelled "Coming" down the stairwell and ran down the two flights of stairs.

Mary, grinning and waving at me through the glass half of the vestibule door. Her hair up, in a sheer shirt. I waved back, opened the door, said "Beeg surprise" and she said "That's my middle names" and I said "Well look it here, all my gear" and she said "Come on, don't be unfaithful: the lips" and we quickly kissed. She'd brought back my things: clothes, books, records, work materials, probably somewhere in there my two-cup espresso pot and toilet articles. I said "Like to come upstairs a minute before you go?"

"Sure. Let me park first." She left. It took me three trips to haul it all to my apartment. I started putting away the clothes. There was a note on top of the shopping bag of books. It said "It seems so terminal, three weeks and no word from you. I find it kind of sad but nothing either of us can do. I wish the timing had been right for us—you knew better than me last fall and then spring that I had to be off on my own. I hope it doesn't seem too cold my carting back your estate this way. Your keys I used to lock up your place and have thrown under the door. Maybe you've already kicked them clear down your hall into the coat closet like a soccer ball goal. If only we could see each other when we wanted to and have fun without it getting so gripping and glum. But what you expected from me was much more than I could give. It became a pact like I had to live up to—to be like it was. I couldn't—it isn't

—you saw and I can't keep you diddling around waiting for me to go through all the living I have to before I'm ready for a more continuous thing with someone like you. So hey. Maybe another day. Okay, boss?"

I ran downstairs, looked for her both ways in front of my building. Ran in the direction her car went to Columbus Avenue and stayed on the corner there looking all four ways for her, gave up after a few minutes and started home.

"Warm day for May," a super I know said.

"I'm only sweating because I was running."

"Me it's because of the weather."

"Newt?" She was coming from the park corner. I walked to her. She waited for a few cars to pass before crossing the sidestreet. I ran to her and she to me. We kissed and hugged, stayed enlaced like that till I said "Movies are better than ever."

"No *versteht.*"

"Your note. I didn't think you were coming back."

"Oh, my note. I wrote it last night. I feel a bit differently today. Though I still think I need a few months break from you."

"So go. No hard feelings or knocks. But you have to shove off right away?"

"Want to walk in the park first? It looked beautiful when I parked."

"My door's unlocked. And I'm still in my bare feet."

Arm and arm back to my building, hand in hand up the stairs. Socks and shoes on. Socks off, just my sandals on. Just sneakers: wasn't warm enough for only sandals and I could never see myself wearing sandals with socks. Mary drank a glass of milk and re-toasted and ate an old buttered toasted roll I'd forgotten about in the stove yesterday. Then we left the building. The landlord, when I apologized, said she wasn't worried I hadn't paid her the gas, electricity and rent. Climbed over the park wall and were on a bench embracing again when a woman I know biked by.

"Hello, Newt."

"Hi," I said.

"Hi, New," her son on the baby seat said.

"Hello, Jim." I hadn't even seen him.

"I got money," he yelled, his mom still pedaling away. The bill blew out of his hand and I stepped on it before it rolled into the lake.

"Hey, Barb—stop," I said. They were gone. "A five. This is our lucky day."

"Do you think I cut myself off from you intentionally and over-dramatize our incompatibilities and then that very cut I made just to get back to the same intensity we had?"

"We might."

"I think I do and if it's true that's sick of me. You're the center of my life. Everything revolves around you."

"I didn't want to ask. But it's all your fellow satellites. Oh well —like to have dinner with me tonight?"

"I'd rather go to a movie and after that a snack. And then we'll be good friends again and I'll go home alone—is that all right for tonight?"

First she had to return some class notes to a classmate for a film course she's taking at the New School. We drove downtown. I said I'd wait outside. She said "Come on in, it won't take long."

The man was waiting for her in the student lounge. He walked over smiling. I walked toward him with her and she dropped my hand and I veered to the side past him into the cafeteria. I wanted to eat an apple. The sign said it cost thirty-five cents. "Thirty-five for an apple?" I said to the cashier, apple in my hand. "This is supposed to be a nonprofit cafeteria."

"If we were selling them from a crate outside it'd maybe cost a quarter. But thirty-five is what it comes to when you take in the upkeep of the place and personnel plus the apple."

I put the apple back and got an orange. Its price wasn't listed. "Forty cents," he said. "That's a Haifa."

I put it back and got a bag of dry roasted peanuts for fifteen cents.

"That seems fair," I said. "About one and a third peanut per penny."

Mary was still in the middle of the lounge talking to the man.

Both laughing, Mary clapping her hands once when she particularly broke up at something either of them had said. The lounge was carpeted and most people sat on the floor, their backs against someone else's back or the wall. I sat on a chair. A man came up to a woman sitting on the chair next to mine and said "Hi, how are you?"

"If you want to know," she said, "I'm doggedly grading exams."

"Maybe I can help you." He sat down next to her. "What's that?" He bent back the test paper to see. "Marx? You're in luck. Marx and Freud are my two specialties."

"Bullshit. They're everybody's here." She gave the paper an A.

"Not getting the best of vibes from you, sis. What's your name?"

"You don't know? I'm supposed to be your sis. But you really want to be of some help to me, take off."

"Sis as in sisterhood. What about a coffee then? Or a beer? They sell it at the caf now."

"What the hell," and she got up and went with him to the cafeteria. Another couple came over. They were very welldressed for this lounge: tie, suit, long pressed dress. He sat, she squatted on the floor. He said "Hiee kwahwahha." She asked how to spell it. He spelled kwahwahha. She wrote it down in her notebook.

"Then that's it?" she said.

"Kwahwahha. What could be after that?"

"Too true." He stood up and she took his seat.

"I'll see you this weekend perhaps?" He gave her what looked like a business card. "This is an excellent place to go Friday and Saturdays around half past nine. I'll be there both nights."

"Not cheap?"

"No, nice. Lots of good African girls go there. Fine music. Topnotch dance. Ethno food that you can't get here."

"Maybe Saturday then. Friday I have to have dinner with the people. If I don't, they write home."

"Good. Then you are being looked after." They shook hands. He left. She opened a book and uncapped a Magic Marker. Mary was still talking and laughing with the man in the middle of the lounge.

He took the class notes from her, flipped through to a page, looked serious, sneezed and began jabbing his palm into his indexfinger. She offered him his hanky. I went back to the cafeteria, got an apple and brought it to the same cashier. "No price rise since the last time?" I said.

"Why make a big deal of it? Money's paper to burn these days. As Marx said—"

"Marx said 'Money's paper to burn these days' or 'is paper to burn'?"

"Man, you're either a hostile type or got a deep-seated gripe. Anyway, as you well know, Marx didn't say it: I did. Though obviously hordes of people said it before me and even Marx might have said it, for it's an ancient cliché: I bet anteceding the Greeks. But what I'm saying Marx said about money that applies to this particular fiscal business of your apple here is—"

"Would you two please continue your political powwow after I've paid?" the customer behind me said. Pointed beard, love beads, long gray sideburns, cultivated curls down his neck and mod clothes: looked like a philosophy prof to me or M.D. analyst. I paid, he paid. Ry-Krisp and cottage cheese was all he was eating. The cashier saluted me with his paper cup of beer. Three or four dogs wove around the room. I deliberately sat down at the table next to the man and woman who had gone into this cafeteria before for a coffee or beer.

"You're a T.A.?" the man said.

"That's right," she said. "A teaching assistant."

"Don't have to tell me what the initials stand for. What I'm asking is what you do as one."

"Correct papers and proctor exams and such. And in rare emergencies make sudden plane reservations for my professor and subsequent apologies to his wife and take over his class and be appreciated by his students more than he ever could."

"That's all? How'd you get such a cushy breeze—brushing your teeth every morning and your hair a hundred strokes a day?"

"Is that literary crit of my breath and disheveled hairdo?"

"Hold on. I meant it takes nothing out of the extraordinary to get that position, right?"

"If you're a grad student with good grades and proven poverty, you can become a T.A. It's not a glamorous job."

"It is to me."

"Grief. Look at your eyes. Haven't you anything else on that mind?"

"I think it's sort of exciting to think the thoughts I do and to be able to emotionally and physically fulfill them rather than just conceive them. Would you, pardon my tongue, I mean my language, consent to sharing a repast with me later on?"

"I might if we go Dutch."

"No other way, sis, no other way."

They drank up and left. "My exam papers," she shouted at the door.

"Leave them."

"You totally crazed?" She came back and also got her sweater off the back of the chair.

From my table I could see Mary still listening to the man in the middle of the lounge. Point 44, his finger jabbed, points 45, 6 or 7. I cut my apple into quarters, cored the quartered core, peeled each piece and sliced them in half, put a couple of seeds in my mouth to see if they could be ground fine enough by the molars for me to swallow, as the entire apple excluding stem and tree supposedly went into those All Natural Swiss or American-cum-Swiss dried breakfast cereals that by the month seemed progressively more popular and expensive and so always out of reach of what I thought I could afford. But the seeds were too bitter to grind further, so I spit them into my hand when there was still something of substance to spit out rather than lose them below my gums, and only ate the mesocarp.

Mary standing beside me: "Where were you? I've been looking all over the place. I imagined you had a change of mind about me or us and beat it home."

"Sorry. Thought you saw me circling around and then come in

here. I tried to make myself obvious: waving, doing a junior fan dance. Want something? Coffee or eighth of an apple with beer?"

"We might be late for the movie. Mind if we go?"

We drove uptown to the theater and got stuck in a long traffic tie-up.

"I knew I should have taken First instead of Third," she said, "or Second instead of Lex. What avenue are we on? Look at that guy," motioning to a man waiting for the light to change or just standing there through several greens and reds. He was in a shiny plum jumpsuit and bowler, orange platform shoes with silver heels and soles, by his side a heeling overgrown borzoi. "They're both beautiful."

"I don't know," I said.

"At least he's interesting and his dog's beautiful."

"How do we know it's his dog? They don't look alike and she's unleashed."

"You never especially cared for people with real street flair—not a notable or nadiral flaw of yours, just an impression I re-get. Because how can you not think it's what first and foremostly makes this city what it is?"

"Right now I think, feel, sense and intuit nothing but riding out of this sticky triffic jam."

"Whew, are you ever pissed. You sinking into one of your male menstrual moods?"

"No, I'm going to come out of one."

"That's my man." She grabbed my hand. Let go to slip into gear when the tie-up about ten blocks ahead started to move. "Oy vay ve vamoose on our una and only luf day." Once in second, she lifted my same hand and kissed and licked the fingernails and tips. "If you ever remembered a poem in your life other than 'O Captain! My Captain!' or 'The Man with the Hoe,' could you recite it to me now?"

"Ummm . . . Roses are you, violets are me, irises I guess are just irises or irides just as daisies could be dazzlers or marguerites. No."

"Why not? It doesn't rhyme."

We got to the theater, parked in front and found we had an hour before the movie began. "Let's nosh somewhere," Mary said, "but not one of those swinging East Side hamburger joints where the French-fried onion rings come to the customer kitchen-unfrozen and factory-made."

We settled on a small luncheonette because its door was open to let in the air, the door was being held open by a beveled wood block, this stop seemed to have been chopped by a non-axman's whacks, a cat sat at the window, an old bladed fan revolved on the last stool, lottery tickets and Bromo-Seltzers were sold, Greek music was playing on a radio and it looked like an eatery out of the early American forties, which was the period, despite its great war and other collapses and aftermaths, that Mary would most love to have lived through other than late Olmec and seventh century Damascus under the Omayyad caliphs.

We sat at the counter. The man on my right read a scratch sheet and actually said to a counterman "Who do you like in the fifth?" The two countermen looked Mary up and down, crossways and cornerwise, then tried to eye each other hugger-muggerly to say they liked what they saw.

Mary said "Ah, Greeks" and said something like "Kalimara" to them and shook their hands.

One of them said "Ah, you speak the Greek" and spoke back to her in Greek. She said something else in Greek and they looked impressed and spoke to one another in Greek, and to me she said "What I just told them meant 'You speak much too fast for me in Greek and I can't understand a word you said.'"

"See anything that looks good?" I said.

"Let's see. You make the soup here?" she said to one of the countermen, and he said "Yes, soup, straight from home."

"You mean you or someone else makes it home and brings it here or you make it here yourself?" and he said "Yes, I make it here—we, my brother and I. Good soup. Lentil, plenty of lentils."

We ordered one bowl of soup with two tablespoons, a side dish of French fried onion rings, because they also came from home and along with the cheese blintz were Mary's two quests for food perfection in life, and a Western omelet, though on a wall sign it said San Diego omelet. I told her that in California the Western was called a Denver. "I don't know what it's called in Denver— maybe an Albuquerque. Though maybe by some luck a Denver's called a Denver in Denver and Albuquerque, and the naming journey for this kind of omelet could end."

"Now that's what I meant the last time we split about your intellectualizing the hell out of almost anything. Why can't you just accept their San Diego for our Western or at least stop at what it's called in California?"

"I don't want to mislead you or go any further with this when it's obvious I should, but as far as I know it's only in San Francisco that it's called a Denver. In Oakland it might be called an Orange County and in Whittier or Sierra Madre, let's say—but you're right," when she gave me a look to stop, "I'm probably only playing these word games to draw attention to myself. And maybe now talking about drawing attention to myself because I want to draw attention away from the countermen to myself." But she was speaking in Greek to the younger counterman again, who was beating our omelet eggs into the sautéed vegetables as he sang along to the radio song.

"What?" he said and she asked for the call letters of the radio station and hours it plays Greek music, which she jotted down in her memobook, and also "Where can someone like myself go dancing and drinking in a real Greek place in New York? I was in Samos last summer and haven't found anything like those tavernas they have there."

"In Astoria, that's where all the best Greeks live." He gave her the names and addresses of three places in Astoria where she could eat good Greek food at no unfair prices and dance on a big floor to the best live Greek music in America—"I swear to you. You like retsina?"

"No."

"The wine? No? Ah, retsina," and he kissed his spatula. "To me it's the best."

We got our food and shared it. Mary said the onions were only so-so. "At most a C plus. I have no money," she said, and I paid.

"Thank you," she said, shaking the hands of the countermen and the man sitting beside her, still doing arithmetic and circumscribing and scratching out horses. The younger counterman said to her "My brother, he's married. But me, I like to have fun and dress up and go dancing. So maybe I see you at the Delphi one Saturday night. If I do, my name's Ted and I say hello."

"Please do."

We went to the movie theater. Mary had to go to the ladiesroom and I went into the theater to get two seats. It was like walking into a funeral chapel minutes before the service began. The room was small and crowded, the recorded music low and funereal. A black curtain drooped over the screen to the floor. The audience was on an average much older than in any movie theater I'd been to recently and conservatively dressed and groomed and most had serious expressions and spoke in hushed tones.

"Joan?" a man said, looking for a seat and spotting a woman he knew sitting in the seat next to the one I was holding for Mary.

"Bud, how are you?"

"Great, and you?"

They talked for a minute, about last winter on the Island, Rhona and Tony and Bud's baby and Joan's kids. Everybody was fine. He wasn't renting the same cottage this summer. Business as in all retail stores these days was slow. The White House? Don't even mention it. She was doing the lighting and costumes for a new show this fall and in every which way had spent the happiest six months of her life. "Is that seat available?" he said to her.

"I don't know," Joan said. They both looked at me.

"It's taken," I said. "And I know what you're next going to ask me, and I'd rather not." I just didn't want to move over one seat and be against the wall and possibly out of sight of part of the screen, which I still couldn't see because of that black pall.

Bud said he hoped to see her later and got a seat up front. Mary came down the aisle waving at me waving at her just as the lights began to dim.

"Lots of women with urinary problems and only one stall. And looks like you might have had a tough time saving my seat," and I went into the incident about not moving over one.

"You should have. For how do you know you'll miss part of the screen?"

"I just feel it."

The curtain rose on an award-winning Slovakian cartoon. It seemed everyone found it funny but us. "Looks like you were right about the screen," Mary said. "But you still should have moved over one, as at the time you didn't know you were right and they wanted to sit as a deuce. But no big thing," and she took my hands, rested her head against my shoulder and stayed that way throughout the show.

Walking up the aisle, she said "When have we seen an audience like this? They all look like the radicals and revolutionaries of the thirties and forties who are now very to excessively successful in whatever they never set out to be." The film was by Jean Renoir —his last, we overheard.

"I have to make a phone call," she said outside. I remembered the Greek place had a pay phone on the wall. It was on the next block. We went back. The chairs stood on the tables and the brother was gone and Ted was mopping the floor. He saw us looking at him through the outside gate and waved. Mary made motions of dialing and speaking into a receiver and cupped her hands in prayer and looked heavenward. Sure, Ted said. He unlocked. The music was blues-oriented rock. She went inside and he relocked the door and she made her call. A couple walked by, with the woman saying "The truth will always surface if you let it" and the man said "Yes?" and she said "Yes" and darted into the street to flag down a bus. "Let's take a cab," he said, but she was already in the bus and he followed her.

After the phone call, Mary talked with Ted for about five minutes. They laughed, he took a pencil off his ear, put it back without using it, patted her arm as she left. "Ciao, Mary. Hello," he said to me, shutting the door.

"He wants me to go to the Delphi with him any day I will please myself, as he put it, though it has to be in the next three months. Otherwise, he'll be unfree."

"You consent?"

"He's cute, though too much the smoothie for me, but I said let's leave it to chance. I meant it, for I never know."

"Get through your call?"

"I had a date at ten but had to break it."

"Two people passed when you were in there," I said, but she cut in "Where'd we leave the car? I always forget."

I pointed. We walked. She said "Your two people before" and I shook my head. I was thinking about her phone call and Ted. Other than for a long-standing friendship, I hadn't seen another woman in the year and a half I'd known Mary. No, once, when she was in Greece and a week or so after she wrote me from there saying she wanted to continue to be unattached from a man, but both that woman and I were drunk and didn't much care for each other before we met in the bar or in bed. "This is one of our main problems," Mary had often said in different ways. "Your external world is too small for me"—a few months back. "I shrink from the pressure of your intensity," or the other way around, "to find space alone for myself and for others," she wrote a while ago. Last night I wrote her a postcard that said "It now seems clear to me what you want for yourself and from me and what you want me to want for myself and from you, and I now finally know there's no solution to it and so no future for us and I also regret it took so long for me to find all this out." I wrote this, in slightly different versions, on six postcards before I was satisfied with the writing and the way the words looked, and mailed the sixth card and dumped the rest when I went for my morning run.

We reached the car. It was still light out. "You drive," she said. "I'm tired of the wheel."

"Let's walk along the river first."

"I like your idealism."

We walked down to the East River, found there was no way to walk along the river. A raised highway. Nothing for pedestrians. A high chain-link fence with garage-parked cars behind it giving us a broken-up view of the river but blocking our way. "Let's go back," I said. At the time she was talking about shirts. Walking down to the river we had talked about the revival of cuffs in men's pants. I think the conversation had started with her remarks about being tired of the steering wheel and pleased with my old-fashioned idealism. She said that when she was married she had to iron five shirts a week for her husband, more if he was covering a weekend story out of town. "It also depended on the season. Savannah during one week was worth twelve. That was before wash-and-wear shirts that really looked and felt like broadcloth. I mean oxford. Myles was never a broadcloth man."

"You must have hated ironing."

"No, it was kind of peaceful. Mandolin music on: I could really think."

Just then a man walked by, stopped, turned to her. "Aren't you," he said, pointing, "Mary?" She didn't recognize him. "We went to high school together. At least my boys' school went to dances at your girls' school and vice versa. Rick Hallmark." He put his laundry bags down. "Where Myles used to go."

"Now I know. I was just talking about him. How I used to iron his oxford button-downs five to twelve times a week. Don't ask. He's fine. Writing books, caulking boats. Don't say. You haven't seen him since you both graduated high school."

"Right. I'm still friends with Lance Boyle though. Remember the Terrorful Trio—L, M and I? You were like our mascot."

"Thanks lots."

"Well you were the only girl who was a steady attachment to our trio."

"That's what most men think women and children are. Attachments."

"Steady," I said.

"I'm sorry. Newton Leeb: Rick Hallmick."

"That's right," he said, winking at Mary. "Gave you me wrong name." We shook hands.

"How come you didn't shake hands with me?" she said.

"I will." They shook hands. "And no offense meant before. All I was saying was that Myles was the only one of us who had the same girl for three years."

"You mean he was the only one getting steadily laid. And sixteen years, not three."

"Sixteen? Well, if you see Myles, give him the mick's regards." He picked up his bags and left.

"I hate bumping into people from the gay olden days," she said. "Those times were too great. Race race race," and she ran off and let me catch up and we raced back to the car and she let me win. "You're getting too leaden. What you need like Mick had is a quick marriage, child and divorce in three easy lesions with someone else. That'll take off a big load."

We got in the car. "Where to, my lovey?" she said. "I'd like someplace I've never been before."

"Let's scout." I drove. "There's Maxwell Plums."

"I've never been there. You? Then let's." We parked a couple blocks away and started to walk back. We passed a candystore with a newsstand outside. She picked up a copy of *Screw,* opened to a photo of a woman on her back with her mouth taking two men, who you couldn't see—just their penises from two sides—and her vagina another man, who also couldn't be seen except for his penis. "God, there really is no censorship anymore," and she paid for the paper and turned to the personals. "Three other things I've never done before is read and buy one of these rags and answer one of their ads. Now what's my pleasure? Gentle genital massage? Group climax control?"

We went to Plums. "Too crowded and gaudy," she said. "Look at those obscene goblets."

"It is a bit flashy, but let's have one beer at the bar."

"I don't want to. And why should you when nine out of the ten men there are men. Let's leave."

"You can be too bossy sometimes."

"I was born under the sign of the lioness, so what do you expect?"

"Leaving?" a man coming in with some other men said to Mary and she said "Yes we are" and he said "Sorry about that."

We looked for another place in the neighborhood. They were all too crowded or smoky and seemed like Plums, though less gaudy and no goblets. Through the window of one of them I saw the couple from a few hours ago. The T.A. and the man. Sitting at a table, drinking beers, his hand over hers. He spoke. She pulled her hand away and put it on her lap, but didn't look annoyed. He laughed, lit a short stogy and spoke. She smiled, put her hand back on the table and stroked his wrist. I tapped the window from the street. They looked. I said "Hi" and waved. You know him? their expressions asked of one another.

"You know them?" Mary said.

"From your school before. But only to overhear and watch."

Mary, with her indexfinger, made a screwing motion at my temple for them and they laughed.

"That wasn't nice," I said.

"I'm sorry. I also make mistakes." She made the same screwing motion to her own temple and the couple laughed and made screwing motions to their temples and the waiter picking up the empties after he set down two new steins made the motion to his temple, but I kept my hands at my sides and only watched.

In the car Mary said "Let's drive over the bridge to the Brooklyn Boondocks."

"Too far."

"Then the Boondocks downtown. Then the old place." That was a bar on the West Side three blocks from where I lived. We'd been there a hundred times together. We got a table in the glass-enclosed patio that jutted out onto the sidewalk. Mary wanted sangria for a change. But the only sangria they had came in big pitchers, the waitress said. "I still want sangria but not a pitcher of it," Mary said.

One of the two women sitting at the next table said "Why don't you take some of ours, as we won't be drinking through more than half of it. We didn't know we were getting so much."

"I got a great idea," Mary said.

"Good," the woman said. "I love great ideas."

"Why don't we order a glass of red and white wine and then you can sit here with us and we can add our wine to your pitcher and we'll all drink wined-up sangria together."

"That is a good idea," the woman said. "Done."

Our wine came. "Come on over," Mary said to them. We also ordered an avocado salad and a cheese, fruit and bread board. "Now you have to take some of these too."

"Honey. See this waistline?" the woman said. "Or this clothesline? Well that isn't slimness. That isn't even unpleasant plumpness. That's big blubbery fat, so thanks but no."

We poured our wine in their pitcher and toasted to "continuing great ideas and camaraderieship." We talked about politics, city and federal. Then Lucille, the one who wouldn't take any food, said to Mary "Okay. You sound like a liberal and that's good, I'm not saying no. But what would your folks say to seeing you sitting here with two blacks?"

"I didn't know either of you were black," Mary said.

"I don't quite get the point of what you said, or rather why you're saying it," I said to Lucille. "It doesn't seem to relate to what we were speaking about."

"It's a point, can't that be enough? Now you know, period. But what would your folks say, Mary?"

"Probably nada. Or my father would say 'Pour your mom and I a glass of that fruit punch, M & M. We want to partake a taste of it.' And if they were here, then realistically there would have been enough of us to order a pitcher just for them and Newt and I, and then the four of us now would never be sitting here like this. So you win and lose."

Terry, the other woman, said "Screw color. Screw all race rela-
tions except the sleepytime kind." Lucille looked reprovingly at
her. "That's right, baby. Screw all that crap. I say have fun, have
fun. And these are young people. They don't define you by your
shades and hues."

"I'm not young," I said.

"Well your girl's young. And you look young. Don't give me a
hard time. You look good. Accept it." She got up. She'd gotten up
every five minutes or so to phone someone. When she came back
she said "That son of a b's still not home. Where in hell is he? He
knows I'm not stepping a foot in our flat unless he's there first."

We talked about street and building crime, cities where there
was street peace. About what an exciting, occasionally harrowing
but always diversified city New York was. As an example Mary
mentioned the Continental Baths, which was a few blocks from
here. "You two should go," she told the women. "I was there this
Saturday. That's the one night they open it for both sexes. But
everybody there was so into him- or herself that it turned out to
be almost antisex, despite half the guys being gay."

"Did you take a bath?" Terry says.

"A swim. They have a big pool. You sit around it in your bathing
suit or clothes and eat and drink and watch the entertainment,
which can be good: a very Great Gatsby singer type and female
comedienne. But it gets so stuffy inside that we stripped down and
dived into the pool nude."

"They don't mind?" I said.

"They don't encourage you. But nobody there was going to be
so un-twenties to admit with mouth or glance to being concerned.
You ought to take an overnight or weekend room there just to see
what goes on. I would if I were a man and especially one in your
profession."

"I don't think I want to."

"What do you do?" Terry says.

"Nothing much."

We got into the subject of romantic love. Men and men. "Sure, lots of them seemed like they were in love and really making it," Mary said. Women and women and then women and men. Lucille said she was a heterosexual to the nth degree and then some, "but never in my life, and I'm over forty, honey, have I ever felt what it is they say is love at the exact time a man was feeling it for me. That high feeling like too much caffeine in your too many coffees, but softer—like rolling. Either he's up there and I'm not or I am for him and he's somewhere else, but never love with any of its most extreme advantages."

I said "We've had that high-flying feeling lots of times together" and Mary looked at me and then nodded and said "You're right, we have."

"Then you're lucky," Lucille said. "But I've been married and with live-in lovers and the best of men and everything, but not once. I never told you this," she said to Terry.

"No, and I'm really flabbergasted to hear it."

"It's the truth. I don't lie."

"I know, dear, which makes it more amazing. You wouldn't say it 'less it was."

"I can't lie either," Mary said. "I try but find it impossible to lie to anyone about anything, even to my own daughter when it's damn well the best thing for her."

"You've a daughter?" Terry said. "You look too young to have a child."

"I've two children, a daughter and a son. The girl's twelve."

"Twelve? That's unbelievable," Lucille said.

"Her son's fourteen," I said.

"I absolutely don't believe it."

"Why? It just means I married young."

"Honey, if they were sitting next to you now and both of them had your puss stamped on them and were calling you mommy, I still wouldn't believe it."

"They yours too?" Terry said to me, "or you two aren't married?"

"No, by somebody else," Mary said. "The son's with the father and Linetta's with me."

"That's too bad."

"It works out. We exchange them weekends and then some long weekends and two weeks a summer each of us gets them both. It also forced me to get my own digs and job and hack it out on my own."

Lowell, my closest friend, came into the bar. "Hey, schmoozer," I said, and his eyes bounced back and forth between Mary and me. He came over, eyes raised translatably for me, as a few days ago I drank at this same table with him and said that Mary and I were "this time really through" and he said then "Nah, you two are never really through. You're a pair: Tom and Jerry, Biff and Bang. You just tell yourselves you're through to make your sex better and your lives more mythic and poetic and to repeatedly renew those first two beatific weeks you went through."

He sat, we shook hands, he kissed Mary's cheek. I introduced him to Lucille and Terry and straightaway he was talking about shares and losses, that platinum was the best investment bet for today and silver the worst but in the long run it was still gold. Lowell was deeply into gold. He bought gold coins and whatever else there was to buy of gold and sold them when the market went up or down or both, I forget which. And I never knew what market he was talking about because he'd said the gold market was controlled by the oil and stock markets, which were influenced by the grain and livestock and cotton markets, which in turn controlled the fish, farmers and flea markets, and so forth. "Buy it," he said of something now, "and you'll double your dough in a month or maybe two. But while your savings are losing, my gold shares are soaring." After about fifteen minutes of his almost nonstop lecture on investments and the interconnection of the world's economy right down to a Berber's dung stove, Mary tugged at my sleeve and looked at the door and I paid up. Lowell stayed behind with the two women. Before I left, Lucille whispered to me "I'm flashing on your cat. He's a whiz."

"I better be getting," Mary said outside. "I don't want to leave Linetta alone too long and there's my job tomorrow."

"I thought we might have an hour in my apartment before you left."

"Drive up with me then. But you can't bring anything except what you have on."

"If I'm staying for a day or two I've got to take my jogging sneakers and work materials along."

"But no shopping bags filled with bagels and food. Linetta and I buy groceries too. Just one bag with everything in it to wear and work with and the only thing for your mouth being your toothbrush."

We drove to my building. I went upstairs, packed a few clothes, work materials and a bread my cousin Harriet had baked for me and I'd frozen and went back to the car. "Could you drive?" she said. "I'm bushed." On the West Side Highway she said "Mind if I sleep?"

"No, sleep, please. Just take it easy, you're tired." I stroked her forehead. She rested her head on my lap, tucked up her legs, rubbed her cheek against my penis through the pants leg. The lights of the bridge woke her up. "I don't know how I could have said I was no longer in love with you that last time we drove in. I want things both ways. Tide's turning again—I swear. Though I still think we need a long separation. Maybe half a year."

"Before you said only a few months."

"Maybe even a year. I need that time to be out on my own and in the marketplace to see what I'm valued at there."

She went back to sleep. Half an hour later I pulled up in back of the house she rented and shook her. "God," she said, "it's like being a kid again and waking up when we arrived after a long drive with my parents and grandma."

There was a note from Linetta: "Peter, Buzzy and a clown named Schnitzer called. Peter said save all day Saturday, Schnitzer said when I told him what Peter said, DISCO FRIDAY

NIGHT? He told me to write that in capital letters and his name in a Switzerland accent."

Linetta came downstairs. "I'm hungry, tired and thirsty and I don't feel too well."

"Hi, Linetta," I said.

"Hi. I didn't think I'd see you again."

"Things happened."

"What happened?"

"I'm here."

"Yeah, I can see you're here, but how come?"

"Things happened. And I missed your sweet face."

"Yeah, and if it makes you feel any happier, I missed you too."

"What's bothering you, darling?" Mary said. "Stomach?"

"Oh yeah, I said I was sick. All I need is a glass of milk and something."

I poured her a glass. "Want me to warm it for you?"

"She knows how to warm it," Mary said.

"No, not warm. But I'd like some powdered chocolate in it."

"We don't have any," Mary said.

"You didn't bring any of that Dutch stuff with you this time?" Linetta said to me.

"No, and no bagels."

"Then just toast, please." I made her toast. "Tell me a story?"

"You can't go to bed without stories yet?" Mary said.

"Come on, Mom, I read. But you know I still like stories read to me sometimes."

"Sure, I'll read you one," I said.

"And carry me to my room?"

"What is he, your slave?" Mary said.

"Yes, my slave."

"I'm her slave," I said. I got down, grabbed her around from behind to carry her piggyback.

"Not that way. On your shoulders."

I hoisted her to my shoulders, carried her upstairs. "Watch your head, chickadee," I said as we passed through her doorway.

"Now throw me on the bed, slave." I dropped her on the bed. "I said throw, slave." I picked her up and threw her on the bed. "Now cover me, slave." I covered her. "Now tell me a story, slave."

"You said read."

"Tell. I'm afraid you don't read well, slave."

I told her a story about a cat that its owner tried to get rid of by leaving it in New York and then flying home to California. But the cat walked and ran all the way back across the country. Took several months to make the trip. But it found its way home.

"That's exactly the Lassie story," she said. "Though Lassie was a collie."

"No, Lassie was a cat that only looked like a collie. You see, Lassie was so big and looked so much like a collie that its owner, after many protests from neighbors and city officials about having this big scary cat around, told everyone that Lassie was really a big collie, and then quickly taught Lassie how to growl and defile the streets and slop up its food like one. But someone got wind of the truth and that's why the owner flew with Lassie to New York and abandoned her at the airport there and hopped the next flight back to California. Anyway, when Lassie the cat finally reached its home in California, there was a note left it by the woman which said 'Dear Pussydog. I knew you were too clever and persevering and devoted a cat not to make it back here, so I decided to emigrate to Australia. Tough lucky, baby, and goodbye.'"

"Lousy owner. But at least the story's better."

"But Lassie wasn't upset or even discouraged. She just jumped into the Pacific and swam to Australia."

"That's ridiculous. Cats can't swim that well."

"This one could. Remember, she's Lassie. But actually, she got on a log a couple miles out in the ocean and stayed on it, for food scooping up fish from the sea again like a real cat would, till it reached Australia."

"Where she had a reunion with that former lousy owner."

"No."

"Good. Goodnight. I'm tired."

I kissed her, shut off the light and went into Mary's room. She was in bed.

"Can you do one more small favor for me, please?" she said. "Give me a mini midnight special?"

I started to massage her back. "Anybody able to give you as good a massage or back rub in the last few weeks?"

She shook her head.

"You've asked?"

"No more questions."

"They volunteered?"

"That part of my private life's my own, sweetheart. Please?"

I massaged her neck, feet, arms, each of her fingers, her buttocks and thighs. Then we made love and after that got under the covers.

"It's so warm in here," she said. "But I just can't part with the comforter you gave me."

"I can open the windows."

"Good idea."

I opened the windows. I got back in bed, under the comforter, shut off the ceiling light by pulling down on the string with my big and second toe. Then we made love again and held one another till the alarm woke us the next morning and I shut it off and Mary jumped out of bed.

Mary Wants
to Sleep

She starts upstairs. It's around ten. I'm reading downstairs.

"Should I shampoo tonight or early tomorrow morning?" she says, halfway up.

"Tonight, so I can nuzzle into your hair when you're sleeping."

"No, tomorrow morning. I just don't have the strength."

"You going right to sleep then?"

"I'll read for a while first."

She continues upstairs. I want to follow her, but I stay where I am. Give her time to wash, undress, get in bed and involved with her book. I don't want her to think I'm running up right after her. That because she said she was going to sleep soon, I have to get in bed and talk and try to make love with her before she's too tired to or asleep. I want my going upstairs to look natural, in other words.

I read for about ten minutes more. Then I yawn. An unnatural yawn—forced, like a couple of my loud page turnings, so she could hear it—till it becomes natural. I shut off the downstairs lights. Another glass of wine? I'd like to, and ordinary nights I'd take it upstairs with me, offer her some to sip, which she might say will make her sleep better. But the wine will put her off. She'll think I drink too much. She might say something about need. Mine on the wine, which might lead to mine on her, hers on no one, how she didn't want anyone except her children needing her and then maybe only when they had to be listened to or were pushing or pressing too hard and needed someone to react against.

I go upstairs. Light's on. She's in bed reading. Middle of the bed. Scarf around her head. It means she thinks her hair's filthy. She'll move when I climb in. Mary: hold out your arms, ask for one of my hug-a-bugs. She's wearing a nightgown. Usually she wears nothing. It's an old gown, an ankle-length muslin one that's not pleasant to touch. Her mother's and before that her paternal grandmother's and a relative's even before that, a great-grand-aunt's. It's a fairly warm spring night. But maybe she is cold or it's to serve as a reminder of her mother or her American ancestry or as some sort of physical or psychological protection against me when I get in bed, and maybe all five or was that four? She knows I'm coming to bed. I came up with my book. I put it on the floor next to what has come to be called my side of the bed. Nine out of ten times I'll sleep there. One of the things I once found on my street and wanted to give to her was an old oak table for that side. She said "No room, keep it for your place." She looks up from her book. Smiles, I smile, I go in the bathroom right outside the bed-room, brush my teeth, wash my face, urinate, squeeze the last drops free, put some water on the glans in case it smells unclean, dry it with a toilet tissue, wash my hands. I go in the bedroom and start to undress. Linetta talks in her sleep from the next room. I listen. Garbled words. Then recognizable ones and silence.

"You hear what Linetta just said in her sleep?" I say.

"No, what?"

"Dandy lions. Tiger's milk."

"All there is?" She thinks. "The puffballs she was blowing about the back today to give us more flowers and you salad leaves. And the tiger's milk I think Cindy might have tried to feed her today because she thinks Linnie's a little languid and growing too fast and thin."

She reads, turns a page, frowns and goes back to the bottom of the previous page, then to the top of the unread page she turned to before and laughs and shakes her head, impressed at what she's read.

"Anything funny?" I say.

"Not everyone might think so."

"Are those huge grapefruits downstairs Martha's big Bahamian surprise?"

"Yes, did you have one?"

"There were only two. I thought you and Linetta might want them."

"You can have half of one or even a whole. You want one now, go and take it."

"They didn't look that ripe."

"She said to get them she had to stand on Cy's shoulders and stretch over an electric fence on the road and club them off a tree."

"Maybe that's why they don't look ripe. Big as they are, not ready yet and no body-building and coloring ethylene for the trip north. Stolen grapefruits. Hate to be a prude, but do you approve?"

Only now, since she started reading again, does she look up. "She picked them, so what do you want from me?"

"But you got the booty."

"Snooty booty. Rich man's citrus land, she said, so no great loss." Back to her book.

"Something about that woman reminds me of someone."

"Sounds like she reminds you of someone you don't like."

"It's just she's so vague, frivolous and almost vacuous, and not even the least concerned about her unconcernedness about all of this. Running on about skinnydipping in her pater's bedroom pool there, sunbathing all day and later inside at night with special infrared pool lights. All those rings on her fingers and necklaces on her breasts and sparkles on her toenails, and everytime I see her, wearing a new pair of the most up-to-date eye and lip finishers and shoes. She in fact does remind me of my cousin Blondie and most of her parvenu to old-time well-to-do friends."

"Martha's okay. She feels, has a generous heart and good mind. I wouldn't put her down."

"I'm not saying I don't like or disapprove of her."

"You're not?" She looks up. "Then that's your behemothian surprise about Martha to me. So she has money, does different things and has a good time. What of it?"

"But that's it. She doesn't do different things, only original repeats or exploitative feats that nobody else could afford, to shock us. Oh, I don't know why I feel like this about her. I'm probably only railing at her in place of something I got against myself. But that pet seal in her bathtub. Those rare macaws encaged in a space big enough for a single baby pewee, because it's an antique. Though you're right. I should at least appreciate her for her theatrical and topical value, get to know her better and give her her due as she no doubt does to me."

"No, I don't think you two would hit it off." Back to her book.

I get in bed. "Was it really only last night that I broke down like that and cried?"

"You mean because it seems so long ago?"

"I can hardly believe it. I suppose that's typical of someone after a long volcanic cry. Or maybe it's just another thing I don't want to reflect on and for the same reason that I dumped on Martha, so I'm pushing it days out of the way. What do you think?"

"Let me finish the page. It's the end of the story."

We read. It's a short page. Last story of a collection. She holds the book. In it, a man comes through a forest after a week's journey by foot, sees his house, doesn't know how he could be there since by his calculations he should still be a few hundred miles from it, knocks, nobody answers, calls out, nobody comes, opens the door, sees the woman he loved and who he was taken from years before by the ruler's men and who he'd thought dead, whispers her name, she walks to him with her arms out, he sees a child coming out of their bedroom, asks who it is, she says hers and his, he holds her, she puts her head on his shoulder, he kisses her neck, she says yes, he says for what? she says to his marriage proposal several years before which she couldn't answer then because simultaneously he was suddenly blindfolded and bound and she gagged and held down, he says "I forgot, but of course, darling, yes."

"Seems like a very nice sort of story," I say. "Medieval romance?"

"Bizarre. Absolutely A to Izzard weird. I don't understand it. That couple and child were never in the story till the top of this page."

"I want to read it." She gives me the book. "Tomorrow, I mean. It's been a full day."

"Very full. And nice. Teaching. Being observed. Good conference with my assistant principal. Driving home along the burgeoning and blooming river route. Walking with you. That was a nice walk. Transplanting. Gardening. Grading papers and seeing my and their hard-earned results. Linetta in a delicious mood for a change. Hurray! And super supper, Newt. Thank you for that. And now blotto in bed. That's why I couldn't shampoo. Too full a day. I'm one-third after-dinner wined, perfectly contented and bushed."

"I kept you from a lot of sleep last night with my fleeting breakdown."

"Well now I'm going to get myself some sleep."

"You're not feeling romantic?"

"No chance." She takes off the scarf and nightgown and drops them on the floor. "You want to read?"

I kiss her arm. "No."

"Good. Mind if I shut off the light?"

"Shut it."

She shuts off the light, turns her back to me, moves a few inches further away from me and says "Goodnight, lovey."

"Christ."

"What?"

"I'm not that sleepy."

"And I'm not feeling that way. I can't manufacture it and I won't be forced."

"At least give me a kiss."

"I don't like it when you beg."

"Then don't make me beg."

"You make you beg. But I don't even like to talk about it this way and I'm too tired to tell you why."

"Then let's drop it."

"Good idea. Now I really have to get some sleep, Newt. It's been a long and I now see exhausting two days."

It's dark. No moon. Stars? I look. No stars. I can barely see the trees against the sky. She turns over and her face comes down near mine. I can tell by her breath. Her mouth must be only a couple inches away. Our knees touch. Accident on her part? I put my left foot on one of hers, bend over her and kiss her lips.

"Night, lovey," she says. The knees stay.

If she'd just snuggle up to me now. Rest her head on my shoulder and chest. Let me hold her. That would suffice. We wouldn't need words. Best nights and morning afters were the ones where we fell asleep and held each other till dawn like that. "Snuggle up a—"

"What?" She jumped. I'd startled her. "What? I was almost asleep."

"I'm sorry. All I was saying was snuggle up a little closer, will ya, huh?"

"I don't want to. I'm comfortable where I am." She pulls her foot out from under mine. Our knees came apart when she jumped. I get out of bed.

"I guess I'm not tired enough for sleep after all and do want to read," I say.

"Not here, please?"

"Wasn't going to. Goodnight."

I put on my pants and shirt and go downstairs and turn on the light and sit in the rocking chair and rock and rock till I realize the rocking squeaks might be keeping her from sleep. I stand and go upstairs and get my book off the floor and go downstairs and sit on the couch and read. The cat leaps on my lap out of nowhere, terrifying me. I throw it off, say "Say you're sorry." It licks its landing paws. I don't want to read. Book: cultural psychology. Interesting in a self-analytical way during the day, but now trying. Maybe I should read her book—that story. But I don't want to read. Even an Elizabethan poem? No. I go upstairs, get my wallet, slip into my moccasins, go downstairs, turn off the light and open the door. The cowbell on the door's outside makes a long clang and then keeps clinging. I grab the bell to hush it and it clangs again. I'll remember to sneak up and grab the clapper next time I'm walking in, and if I walk out again tonight, to open the door very slowly. I'm sure, if she's not asleep, she thinks I'm making this noise to draw attention to my leaving. If we get in another spat soon, she'll mention the bell. "You deliberately . . . so I'd know how mad you were . . . out of bitterness to me . . . spoiled child," etcetera, though probably not. Why do I project so much? That could be what's ruining or ruined this relationship, besides my flashflood temper, petulance and jealousy, and other things. I start down the hill. Maybe when I return, projectionless, she'll snuggle up to me. Put her head—yes. Knees click-click. Feet on feet or foot, bodies aligned, occasionally a kiss and hair sniff before we're sleeping dreamily, no words, none, not that we couldn't use many.

Down the steep hill. We walked down it around this same time a few months ago when we couldn't sleep. Too much coffee for her (one demitasse at dinner), not enough wine or beer or too early for me (ten). On our backs then: "Yes?" "Yes." Got out of bed, dressed. After making love? I don't remember. But we saw fireworks across the river that night, in the sky a police helicopter's spotlight probing our shore and river road for something amiss, on our side of the river a visiting American warship docked at the end of a pleasure-craft harbor, festoonery of bra-like lights stem to stern or is it port to starboard? our favorite local bar filled with lit sailors.

Still braking myself down this steep hill. "You remember just about everything," she'd say now, things being different. Next night we broke. Also outside that night a sousing cracking thunderstorm. Morning after the drench I went home by bus and underground. Two weeks ago we came together by chance on a city street. Looked like her, from the back: same black hair brushed smoothly down to her shoulder blades, sort of stocky legs, pinched waist, height, arms, shoulders, shoulder bag, size of head and backside all the same it seemed, though uncustomary clothes never before seen by me: a skirt and Dr. Scholl's shoes. "Howdy, Ms.?" I said, taking a slight chance for I still hadn't seen her face. "Newt. I don't know if I like this." Wary. Thought I might have been following her. Wasn't. We walked. Bench sat. Fukienese feast. Went home with her that night. That's when I started my unnatural act of not pushing myself on her. Of disappearing several times a day when I didn't need or want to and often without warning but which I felt she'd like. She did. Letting her do things for me that I usually refused, such as making my breakfast and morning coffee and putting my soiled clothes in her and Linetta's wash. I bused back to the city three days later, leaving behind a bogus note chalked on the kitchen blackboard in rainbow colors explaining I wanted to work in my flat as there were some things I had to do that could only be done there. Called the next day and she said I was right to go and that she kind of missed me last night. Returned the following day and developed my new role: impassiveness in place of passion and perturbation, making myself readily unavailable most of the day, often pretending she wasn't there and making her repeat things to me as if I didn't hear or was too engrossed in something at the time to listen, not swiveling around in my chair when I was reading and she was coming downstairs, and being a bit staid, logical and straightforward to her daughter rather than playful, digressive and unserious, and also to her son Timon who arrived last Friday from where he lived with his father and called himself our weekend houseguest. Then returning to the city on my own again. Same thing: devious note, day later I called, Mary saying she liked our recent inter-independence and lack of tension together, back I bused, ho-hum, and I thought she was really warming up to the new cool me. Taking my hand or arm or both when we walked. Smoothing out my forehead furrows. Asking me to do the shopping and laundry with her. Suddenly throwing her arms around me in front of our spinning clothes. Treating me to seaside lobster. Lovey-dovey every nighty with no prompting from me. Till a party two nights ago when I noticed a man there deep in solemn conversation with her and then I saw him tailing her from room to room and when I looked for his female companion I found he hadn't come with one or left any home. And then I saw Mary and him playing one of Linetta's games which required them to press and slap each other's hands while in turns calling out countries alphabetically and then the man perched on Mary's knees while both of them were having their palms read simultaneously by hired professional readers. And I later said "Who's the man?" and she said "Which one?" and I said "The tall curly-haired handsome one with the thick mustache and beige suede jacket" and she said "An old friend" and I said "Someone you were pretty close to when we were split up?" and she said "Yes, I've slept with Michael once or twice though not in the last few weeks" and I said "That's not what I asked" and she said "I thought it was implicitly implied" and I said "Look it, if you want to be or sleep with him tonight or anything, don't let me stop you, I'll just ride back to the city with one of the guests" and she said "Memory keeps failing me, but have I ever asked you before if I could leave the room to take a pee?" and I said "I don't think your analogy works" and she said "Maybe by implication or rigorous thought or some mnemonic device on your part it might" and I said "Just wanted you to know how I feel about you two, that's all" and she said "Very cavalier of you, sir, but how can I believe you?" and I walked away and later saw them lying on a mattress on the floor with several other people, all of them sharing glasses of different-colored wine and a single cigarette, though I'd never seen Mary smoke before, Michael's head on her belly and his body perpendicular to hers and Mary with her head up against someone's bare feet, and I walked out of the room and stumped back and said "Mary?" and they both looked up but the lively talk around us continued and she said "What?" and I said "What is this?" and she said "What is this what?" and looked at Michael and shrugged and he, holding a filled glass in one hand, put another glass down and closed his eyes and dragged on the cigarette and then tried passing it to her and she shook her head but he continued to hold it out for her as his eyes were still closed. I left the room and waited for her to come out and then went back in and said a little louder "Mary?" and she said "What, Newt, what?" and the conversation and laughter around us all but stopped and I said "I'd like to speak to you" and she said "About what?" and I said "The hors d'oeuvres" and she got up, Michael's head sliding off her to the pillow she quickly provided for it, and met me in the next room and I said "Your attachment or growing closeness to this man and just that you admitted to once or twice making love to him and that I didn't know about it before is beginning to bug me and I think we have to take a long walk now to talk it all out" and she said "You're the one I came here with and expect to leave with and who for the past weeks I thought everything was beginning to revolve around again for me, but I can now see that possibility was impossible and it's all falling to pieces again, isn't it?" and I said "I'll stop, let's go back inside" and she said "Lovey, it's too late" and I said "It was all very dumb and unfair of me and I guess I better find a ride back to the city now" and she said "Dumb, yes, and also yes that I liked you much better in the nonhassling and uninterfering way you've recently been, but I should have known no personality can change like that in a month and that you were faking it all, right?" and I said "In my attitude to you, almost everything" and she said "I wish for Christsakes you would have told me and saved us both a bag of soap bubbles" and grabbed the hand of a mutual friend flitting past and started gabbing with him about their daughters' science teacher, and later we went home and cooked separate snacks and never touched one another and slept in different rooms, despite my repeated mentioning that as fierce as my folks' arguments were, they always ended them for the interim when they went to bed together, and Michael wound up sleeping in the gazebo with the hostess, and the host, we learned the next day, in a motel with his daughter's college roommate, and the daughter in her parents' bedroom with the bartender, who was the roommate's brother and had known the daughter for a week and proposed and got engaged to her that night.

Next day I awoke with a note on my chest saying "Though you can sleep in my bed tonight if you like, please, though not out of any fakery, try and stay away from me for the day, as I've a lot of conclusions to come to and decisions to make."

Last night, about an hour into bed, I woke up and started to shake and then cry uncontrollably and continued to cry long after Mary asked me if this was just another conniving game I was playing to keep her awake and then held me and kept patting my back as if trying to burp me, but I could give no sensible explanation why I continued to cry. I said things like "Suddenly I was seeing myself with all my masks off and maybe that's what's making me cry" (and after each of my explanations I'd blubber and weep) . . . "But it could also be my dead parents and brother and sister whose faces I still see passing through my head as if on the same rotating slow-motion tape . . . But I also feel it's somehow tied in with some sudden realization of my own mortality and repressed fear of severe sickness and death . . . And also what a sonofabitch and fraud I've been to you and Timon and Lin and just about everyone I know including all my good friends . . . That I suddenly feel I really have no friends, good, bad, strong or weak . . . And that I'm actually a foolish ludicrous loner and mope without any pride in my past and hope for myself and future associations and work at thirty-eight . . . But I also feel it could be just the contrary to all of those and that I'm bawling because I can't take seriously anything I or anyone says or does and that I haven't for twenty years . . ." and on and on the explanations and crying went, till she said after about an hour of this "I'm exhausted, Newt. You must be too. Crying can be very enervating. So let's call it a night now and talk about it some more tomorrow if you want, okay?" and she flipped over the wet pillows, shut off the light, patted my back a last time and said "Sleep, Newt—now I said to sleep" and we both soon fell asleep.

Now I'm in a bar, one of the three on the one store street in her town. The people at the bar are mostly watching a television program called *Shaft.* Several other customers are at the pool table playing for cheeseburgers and pitchers of beer. A commercial cuts into *Shaft* just as it appears he's about to get shot by a multimillionaire loanshark's private firing squad composed of robots. The young woman next to me says "Is this the movie *Shaft* or the TV show?"

"I don't know," I say. "Till tonight I didn't know there was either."

"Did you see *The Sting?*"

"No."

"You didn't see *The Sting?*"

"No."

"It won all the awards. It's fantastic."

"I plan to."

"Did you see *The Sting?*" she says to the man on the other side of me.

"Great," he says.

"Did the ending completely fool you too?"

"Sure did."

"Is this the TV program *Shaft* or the original movie?"

"TV," he says, trying to watch the end of it.

I have a couple more beers. Shaft escaped. The news is on. I've been here a half hour. I want to wait for the weather. I leave. I climb the hill. At one point I get so tired I have to sit on the ground. I go to her house, hold the cowbell clapper as I open the door, close the door slowly, go to her room, take off my clothes, get in bed. She stirs.

"Couldn't sleep," I say.

"Wha?"

"And now I can't sleep."

"I can if you don't talk anymore."

"Come on, Em, don't give me that."

"Newt. I'm tired. Can't you tell? What's the time?"

"I don't know."

"You know. It's late."

I get out of bed and go to the bathroom, though I don't have to. I look for the moon, go into Linetta's room and try and make out what she's saying in her sleep. "Morons . . . brick balls . . ." I get back in bed, facing Mary's back, and curl up with her. She moves away.

"Love," I say. If she heard me, she doesn't say anything.

Tomorrow morning before she leaves for work we'll have another argument. I know what I'll say. She'll say "You know I hate arguing before I go to work. It kills my whole day. Please don't make a mountain out of a molehill. I told you once I was going to see other men. As friends. And if it turns out, as lovers. You should see other women. Just other people then. But don't put it all on me. It's too much." She's said things like that before. I'll then say something I'll regret and she'll get very upset with me and maybe cry and then she'll say "No, this will never work, it can't" and she'll ask me to leave for good and then she'll go to work and I'll have to get on the bus back to the city and I'll leave a note that I'm going because she wants me to and that I don't know when I'll ever see her again if I ever again see her again. It's so complicated. The note, sealed in an envelope, will read a little differently than that. She's right. I do depend too much on her for affection and attention. I shouldn't. I have to try not to. But I see no way how.

I close my eyes and try to sleep. I can't. I go downstairs and try to read. I can't. I drink several glasses of wine and feel much sleepier now and go back to bed, but I can't sleep. I move around. It's the last thing I should do. But I want her to hear me and say "Something must be really disturbing you, Newt—what's wrong?" I want her to hold me and say "Lovey, it's all right. I love you and everything still only revolves around you."

But she says "Newt. I'm not going to give you much of a choice. You have to either fall asleep immediately or not move an inch around in bed or just leave this room and sleep somewhere else tonight. If you insist on making noises in whatever room you move to, then you'll have to leave the house."

I say "Screw off" and she says "Will you get lost?" and I push her off the bed with my feet. From the floor she says "That's it. That's the last time. Now I don't want to have to get crazy or angrier than I am and have Linetta hear another word of this, so please get the hell out of here for good" and I get dressed and leave the house.

Parents

I say "What do you say we see my father today?" and she says "Your father?" and I say "Yeah, don't worry, you want to see him?" and she says "Okay by me, where is he?" "Downtown." "Where downtown?" "Just downtown." "You want to lead me blindfolded or like a blind person, that it?" "Just cover your eyes. That'll do."

She covers her eyes with her hands. "I can't see."

"Just keep them shut then."

Takes her hands away but keeps her eyes shut. I don't know if they're completely shut. I remember. I recall. As a boy I used to say I'd keep my eyes shut tight, but opened the little slits very slowly to see things finally blurredly but to see them and no one who asked me to keep them shut seemed to realize I could see when I said my eyes were tightly shut. They'd say "Eyes still shut tight?" and I'd say yes. Then they'd hide something while I watched through opened slits. "Now open your eyes and tell me where it is," or if it had been placed in front of me, "how you like it." I'd pretend to look for it, find it, be surprised.

"Eyes still shut tight?" I say.

"You want to take me there without telling me exactly where, that it?"

I nod.

"That it?"

"You didn't see me nod?"

"Yes, since I can't tell a lie to any small extent. Blindfold me. That's the only way I'll keep the truth."

I tie a hanky around her eyes. "Can't see?" She nods. I swish my hands across her eyes. No wince. She can't see. Or else there's something I found out about her I hadn't till now known. "I know you whisked me," she says, "though I don't know with what."

We leave the apartment. Hand leading hand always two steps in front of her going downstairs. "Maybe you ought to pull up the blindfold for the steps."

"No, I want this to be a real blind person's trip all the way. Lead." I lead. Outside, my landlord's pulling in the empty garbage cans.

"She burned?" Mrs. Rorng says.

"Blind, though we're not making fun."

"Morning, Mrs. Rorng," Mary says.

"Can't see but she can hear, huh? Cute. Two lovebirds. Two cute kids. Really, two cute lovebird kids." I'm thirty-eight. I don't know how old Mary is but her oldest child's fourteen. "Though I'm glad it's not two indispositions. But it's in the air. Lovebirds and lots of other birds flying all over and sometimes through my hair. Go. Have a find."

Trying to upset Mary's sense of direction, I spin her around several times, then point her toward the park and give her back a push. She walks. "Park's smelling nice," she says.

"Already other senses taking over," I say.

Puts out her hands. "Feels like it's going to snow."

"You can really tell?"

"The cold. The wet. Yes," though middle of June. We go into the subway station. She pulls out a dollar, gets two tokens and change. "You gave her a fiver." "No I didn't. I only had on me one one." Puts the tokens in two turnstile slots and we go through. Downstairs to the downtown trains.

"Maybe for safety sake you should take off the fold or at least push it up a little and open your eyes to seeing slits. Nobody has to know you can see. I'll even try and believe you can't. I'll tell myself she's blind, poor child, can't see, what a shame. Repeatedly till we reach the station and walk up the stairs from the platform my dad always gets off at and walks up from to get to his dental office."

"Just lead." I lead. Hand in hand we stand on the platform waiting for the train. "Snap snap," from a platform bench. Person chewing gum. "Smell the gum?" Mary says. "I can almost taste it. Wrigley's. Spearmint. Two sticks. Freshly stuck in mouth. Pack recently made and wrapped."

Person reading *Photoplay.* I also read the story in that magazine. "Famous Actress Unwet." No, Unwed. Mother. "Famous actress unwed mother," I tell Mary.

"Who is this unwed famous father?" famous actress says. "Possibly a Hollywood actor? I will tell you who it is. It is none of your business."

"Pity you can't read, Mary. Good article here."

"Newspaper?"

"So you are blind as a bat."

"Bats aren't blind."

"Bats haven't eyes."

"Bats have eyes."

"Bats have eyes?"

"And are insectivorous and the only true mammals capable of true flight."

"Sure you're not mistaking them for batboys? Batons? The ists who toss those ons?"

"My being blind has perhaps given you bats in your belfry, sir. But hold me. I hear something." "I don't, except for your talking." "Long train coming our way on the nearest track." "I see it now too. The local." "Can only be the local at this only local stop." Local stops. We get on. Nearly full car. Reading, standing, sitting, looking the way people usually do in a subway car at a certain hour on a certain train heading in a certain direction from certain areas on a weekday during a regular workday which Mary didn't take today because she called in sick to be with me and which I didn't take as I no gots. Several stops. Nobody seems to really notice her. "Head wound?" someone says. "Joking?" person with him says. But they're speaking about a war photo in a newspaper. We get off. I lead her out of subway and station.

"That's where the old Met used to sing," I say.

"I can hear the conductor conducting, the orchestra orchestrating."

"Across the street: my dad's office."

"How you think he'll react to your going out with a blind girl?"

"People's afflictions never bother him much. He deals with them all day. Bad tooth, he fixes it. Can't: extracts. That's not to say another dentist couldn't fix it, and if he couldn't, would extract, and if he wouldn't, send the patient to another dentist who could, and only as a last resort, to a dental surgeon to extract. But if my father can't fix: extracts. So he deals with people's afflictions all during his working day and at night at home when he talks on the phone to patients with dental problems, such as why their teeth were extracted when it's possible they shouldn't have been or at least not before he took x-rays to see that they positively couldn't be saved. But he makes up for it in the long run I heard his waitingroom patients say by making great plates for them they can be proud of, or as proud as people can be of their plates, no matter how great. But here's his building entrance, there's his mailbox. Two-story run-down structure with his office on the top floor. Long steep flight up and then left twenty average-length steps to his door. Somewhere beyond it my short father, round of stomach and head. Soft face, little hair, legs thin, strong arms and chin, soap-scented hands, pruned nails, greatest pride is in his wrists. Usually of good humor, shined shoes, saggy socks, urine-stained fly and food-tainted tie and shirt smelling from hard work and in a dental smock, which more than likely not has several blood drops on it if in the last week he came up against a patient with a tooth or teeth he couldn't fix, which more than likely not he had."

We start upstairs. Halfway there I say "I forgot his coffee and cake. Usually I bring him a schnecken or Danish and light container of coffee. Not light container, but container of . . . I'm going downstairs for it. If I don't, he'll send me downstairs for it. It's a dairy cafeteria, known for its pastries and free seltzer, only a couple blocks away."

"Isn't that carrying things too far? No? Yes? All right. I'll wait here. In the dark. Sitting on the spitting steps. But no guarantee I'll be here when you get back."

"Soviet."

"So?"

"So take the so out of Soviet and you don't get USA."

"But that's yesterday and today. Tomorrow we don't know. But you're much too apolitical a person to be making attacks and statements like that anyway. Viet."

I go to Dubrow's. Same counterman of years ago still works there. Or maybe he's been away for the same number of years, days and hours that I have and only started reworking here a minute ago today. "Hi," I say.

"Hello."

"You don't remember me?"

"Come to think of it, not completely."

"Newton Leeb, Dr. Leeb's boy. He treated you. Gave you first-class dental service at third-class prices and second-class sanitary conditions and pay when you want to, my pal, and advice that you walk downstairs from his office very slowly after he's filled one of your teeth for fear the filling will pop out."

"Now I know."

"So how are your teeth?"

"My teeth are doing fine, thanks, and yours? Come to think of it, nobody ever fixed them like your dad, the old Doc, or at least for as cheap."

"He was a great dentist, right?"

"Wrong. Only so-so. But we had great times up there. All those kibitzers in his office. Bookies, cardsharps, horseplayers, thieves, talkers, con guys, cops on the take, the works. A real place. A real place. You got a number? Forget it. What'll you have?"

"Light container of coffee and schnecken to go. No, container of light coffee and Danish. Sorry again. Container of light coffee and schnecken."

"Just like Doc. Always either schnecken or Danish but coffee

light. Years and years when I went to his office I brought him one
on the house and also a couple coffees and container of seltzer,
because that's what he liked best for his thirst and which we never
then sent out. Manager would see me and say 'Two for Doc, both
Danish and schnecken both and tell him with my compliments,'
just as he always did except for the seltzer as he was a patient of
your pop's too."

"That must be when Dad brings home with him a schnecken or
Danish wrapped in the wax paper he took his sandwich in that
morning that he'd made the previous evening out of leftovers for
tomorrow's lunch."

"You mean must have been when, for both your mother and
Doc drove or dove over some cliff overseas is what I heard, though
it wasn't in the obits themselves."

"I can't tell a lie to even the smallest extent: that's not true."

He gives me the schnecken and coffee in a bag with a look.
Everyone knows that look. Maybe babies don't but most adults do.
It must be the same look in every language, all societies, round the
globe, maybe on other planets also and perhaps even chimpanzees
and orangutans and every anthropoid ape give that look too. That
hey what's with this guy or ape kind of look.

"So long," I say. His answer: still the look.

Mary waited. Blindfold's off. I say "Maybe it isn't necessary now
to go." She walks upstairs. "Blindfold," she says, "I had to use for
my nose, eyes and mouth during a sudden sneezing and coughing
seizure. Besides, after everything you said about your father, I
thought I'd go over better with him if I uncovered my sight." I say
"Mary, I said maybe it isn't necessary for us to go see him and his
office now." She pats her ears, sticks her fingers in to pop them,
says "Me thinks my hearing's gone plop. Lose one, gain another,
or vice versa." I follow her. Top, we go the twenty average-length
steps. Electrolysis, the office door says. I knock. Same tiny sign
under the jamb bell says ring bell and walk in, but the bell never
worked and the door's locked.

He's changed. Pencil-thin mustache. Who'd believe it from

him? But all for the better I'd say. Grown too. Lost weight. Nose
job and new shoes. But same white smock, no blood, no extractions
this week or just put a clean one on. Lots of hair now too: wavy
black combed straight back. Woman in the waitingroom reading
a recent issue of a woman's magazine. Must be hers because he
never had anything before but dental journals and religious tracts
religious people dropped off. He says "Yes?" and examines my
face, Mary's face. I hand him the bag and he says "I didn't order
anything" and I say "I thought I'd bring you something nevertheless." He opens the bag. Little to the right is the alcove where he
eats and phones and a couple of his bookie friends phone and
diplomas and pictures of his parents and wife on the desk and walls
but no radio now or it's off with its tinny sounds of semiclassical
music and news. Treatment room facing it with his dental chair
and revolving bracket table and foot pedal drill and foot pedal sink
I liked to play with with my feet or on my knees with my hands
and which was always in need of a washer and so always ran.

Mary elbows me. I say to him "I want you to meet." She sticks
out her hand. They shake. Also kisses his cheek. "Well now," he
says, "nice to meet you." Then a stern look at me when I'm looking
at him and Mary's looking around the room. Later at home he'll
say "Is she not of our faith?" I'll say "No, Father, she's not." He
won't say that in those words and neither will I. He'll say "Don't
be a schnook. Only go out with girls who are rich and Jewish."
He'll say that. He's said that. I've brought girls here before. He'll
say "Beautiful girls also come rich and Jewish." He'll say "I know
lots of beautiful rich Jewish girls who'd love to meet you. Their
mothers tell me. Their fathers too. What do you think I've so many
photos on my waitingroom walls for, all showing my girl and boys
at their very best. You're a good catch. Handsome, tall, nicely
built, college educated, bright, you got brains—you should begin
realizing all that. And you wear clothes well, so you ought to dress
better. I'll buy you a two-pants suit. It'll be a good investment for
me. How much you need? Actually you should work for it yourself
just like I always did and you used to even when you were a kid.

But I'll find you a nice beautiful rich girl who's Jewish. What's the difference if she's rich? Somebody's got to marry them and you can't imagine the idiots who do. Follow my advice and you'll never have to work another day in your life, or at least not hard." Tool still in his hand.

"Doctor." Masculine voice from the treatment room. "Will you come on? I'm in a rush."

"Just a second," he says. Later he'll say "Open . . . open . . . open . . . little wider . . . wider. That's good, stay." Has hair now. Once bald and gray. Must have been all that massaging my mother said she started doing to his head on their honeymoon night to save what little hair was left. He closes the bag. "Thanks very much but I had my snack," and hands me the bag.

"I don't want it." I give it to Mary.

"Don't want it either," and she gives it to him.

"Now if you'll please excuse me," he says, "but I'm kind of tied up today."

"See you later, Dad," I say and we go. Mary waves. Door shuts. Locks. "Who was those two?" woman in the waitingroom says.

"Think I know, Ma? Crazy. Crazies."

"I don't know," I say to Mary. "He never kicked me out like that before. He always enjoyed having me around no matter how many kibitzers and waiting patients were there. Only with prostitutes. He drew the line. With others he'd say 'Sit, Newt, stick around, stay.' And when I worked in the garment center at various belt firms and dress houses, all jobs he got for me throughout high school, he always had me stopping by after I finished work, hanging around for him to finish up and close. It wasn't a good waitingroom to read and do homework. Lots of dust. Peeling paint. Bad light. He loved company though. About to go—lights off—I'm starving—in would come some guy and say 'Take out this tooth, Doc, right now, it's bothering me, but don't freeze me up as I got to chew food tonight.' Tooth out without Novocaine, he'd recommend a teabag on the root holes for the tannic acid in it if the lesion starts bleeding, and if it continues, ring him at home. And in'd walk another patient, crony, his passerbying sister with stuffed cabbage gifts and asking financial advice, fidgety bereft junkie nephew wanting to be fitted for plates then and there on the cuff. And I'd be waiting, waiting, wanting to get home, hungry, but knowing dinner never began without him. And then the subway ride home with him with his stacks of ratty rubberband-wrapped filled Manila envelopes with their mixed medley inside. Newspapers and clippings pulled out of trash baskets along both ways. Individual toilet tissues for his saliva and nose removed in clumps from mensroom dispensers and which only he also used for his behind at home. Samples, dental tools, upper and lower molds, prosthodontic parts—"

"Hey? C'est enough now, nu? And what about your meeting my folks? We're right by the bus terminal. They live an hour and a half away upstate. Express bus. Seven bucks. One stop. We can be there in at the most five minutes after two and a half hours from now, as the bus leaves once an hour on the same minute after the hour sixteen straight times a day and their home's only a five-minute trot from their bus terminal."

We go to Port Authority down the block. Bus tickets. Get on it. Goes, arrives. Her father admiring the hundred different kinds of daffodils and jonquils he'd planted last year for his wife when he sees us jogging by and says "My, what a surprise." Her mother sitting behind the porch window waving at Mary, face thinner than in her pictures, afghan covering her lap. Dinner that night à l'americaine: measured out shot of whiskey and soda and corn bread baked in iron molds and mutton gumbo and napkin rings and real whipped cream and jello. White-haired couple. Loquacious gentleman, sedate lady. Father invents. Mother composes. He dominates the conversations and has to be quieted by his wife. She dexterously steers the talk to great authors and books and the family silver Mary and then Linetta will inherit and cupboard of Limoges. Charades later. Then mother plays the piano for us while we have postprandial cheese and cognacs. Delicate soft-pedally pieces of hers on the high keys reminding me of Ravel and fields of breezy flowers and Mary cycling to the store for powdered doughnuts Sunday mornings and clouds and Debussy. I applaud and say bravo and her husband Nicholas says "That was very very lovely, my dear." Later some discreet whispering from the cleanup kitchen and Mary confesses her father thinks I'm intelligent though partial to the wrong party and not born to the right religion for his darling girl and her mother thinks I'm whimsical and adores looking at my smile and strong neck and back. I love them immediately and they seem to like me. Love them partially because Mary looks and except for her breasts is built like her and acts with the alacrity and peppiness of her father and just because they are her parents and they because Mary tells them she loves me.

Her mother's sick with a killing illness, has to retire early but first breathe on her nightly breathing machine. Just before she's walked upstairs she takes my hand, brings me close to her ear as if to say goodnight but only to whisper "I want you to leave here convinced of at least one thing. I love my husband and grandchildren but Mary means more to me than my own life. Take good care of her" and I hug her and kiss her cheek and say "Me too, Louise, me too, and I'll take as good a care of her for as long as she needs and wants me to, I swear."

Mary and I walk through her hometown. Ancient history all around. Rebuilt fort. Colonial church. Huguenot patentees. Apple tree Nicholas proposed to Louise under. Their original stone home the town dispossessed them from to include in a historical street to draw tourists. Cellar where Mary's ancestors escaped from the Indians. "One didn't and that's why I've this thick black braid and raven eyes and no hair on the soles of my feet."

When we get back the downstairs bed is ready to be slept in: coverlet turned down, pillows plumped up, kerosene lamp wick ready to be lit. "Think they mind my sleeping here much?"

"They mind. I asked. But since the last bus back to the city has already left and they don't see how anyone can afford the local motels and they want me to stay put another day with or without my kiddies and couldn't give up one of their own beds upstairs, it's okay."

We undress, wash, light the lamp, Mary unbraids and brushes and gets in bed.

"In this bed my father and I were conceived. Not everyone's so sure about my grandmother, though my father says she was, but she told me her father and grandfather definitely started here too."

"I feel ghosts in the room. Some presence or force."

"You do? This place used to be their storehouse. Could be they've come in from the old stone house down the street to be with their relatives and bed and quilt. Blow out the lamp. Maybe they'll really come alive. I've questions to ask them, patches of family history that could be cleared up. And maybe, if they're privy to it or know anyone there who is, if they see any extensive future for us."

Lamp out. We're quiet. And hear nothing. I touch her. "I've never done it in this house," she says. "Even with Myles all those times we were here legal or not."

"Will it be all right?"

"It'll be different."

"Still, let's try."

"Though no noise."

"I won't."

We don't.

Outside: crickets and cicadas or katydids.

Early morning: birds, birds, birds.

Man of Letters

Em—

I don't want to see you anymore. There's a lot else that can be said about this decision of mine, but I don't want to go into it. So that's it then. Don't come by. And I won't be coming up there again. Much love, Newt

Em—

I think we need a nice long rest from each other. You're aware yourself that things haven't been going well with us for a while. Thing that most elicited my decision was that I just didn't like the way you set the relationship for us. The "week" together this summer. On a "beach." Perhaps you have to act like this. What you are, want to become, your history. But it's now too much for me. I won't be coming up. I don't want you coming by. I want no communication between us of any kind. I can't say "Maybe some other time perhaps." I just don't feel like that. I'm sorry. Love, Newt

Dear Em:

I won't be coming to Stonehill anymore. I don't want you to come to my flat again. I just don't want to go on with our relationship anymore. It's not going to change: the relationship or my decision. At least it doesn't seem so to me. Most of all, I'm tired of you setting our pace. That "week" in the summer. On a "beach." It's usually your way. It's a shame you can't just let things happen between us without always analyzing it, trying to control it, putting me to tests, being worried that everything will pass you by and too many things will never be tried out by you if you stay only with one mate.

I do think about you sweetly. Fooling around. Holding you close. Talking. All that. But the other disturbing things that have happened between us, if they're not already embedded in my head, just don't creep in anymore, they rush.

I don't feel responsible for this break. For a little, all right. But it does seem it has to go the way you want it, without any give and take, and I find I can't exist in an atmosphere like that. Especially when it's coupled with your repeatedly turning me on and off and I think your serious remarks about how you look forward to the day when you'll be able to manage two and maybe three successful love affairs at one time, so I just don't want to see you anymore.

I don't say that what you're proposing for yourself is impossible or wrong. Maybe I am "rigid," "superannuated," as you said—whatever, but it just isn't my way. And I do love you very much, but for the first time in my life that doesn't seem to be enough to make me want to stay. So, cheers then—En

Dear Mary—

I won't be coming to Stonehill anymore. I don't want you to come by my place. I just don't want to go on with our relationship anymore. I'm tired of you always setting the pace. The "week" this summer. On a "beach." And I don't think it's because I'm "indecisive" or don't like to make "any decision" that this is the case. You take over because you want to, have to, whatever's the force. If you tell me once more it's partly astrological, I'll have to yell at you again "That's asinine."

I went along like a "dud" because I don't like to direct a relationship based on love. It's a pity you can't let it happen without dashing it to dust everytime it goes well. We've gone on for hours about the reasons for all that: the history. But to me there really aren't any explanations.

I also can't get the bad things out of my head. I think about you sweetly. Fooling around. Joking. Holding you close. Talking. Walking. Working. All that. But the other disturbing things just don't creep in, they rush. And a lot else about what's happened between us just hasn't been etched out of my head yet. Your turning me on and off. Blowing me up. Indifferently letting me go. Separating "for the time being" because you thought it was the "wrong time for us" or it was just "bad timing when we met" and soon after that your returning and for a while staying and being open and loving and then re-going when you thought it was the wrong time for us again or just thought that for yourself it was best. I always felt when you returned "Well that's the last time for that, folks," but it never was. Now I think "How in hell could I have thought any of those times after the first few times could have been the last time?" And after the last last time I suppose I was just holding on." Like a kite. No, a kite doesn't hold on, it's held, and I was held, though not tight like a kite. Oh, I was held tight like a kite sometimes, but we're talking about my holding, not being held. Maybe the kite holds on to a tree. But you're no tree, though you do have roots. But so do turnips, teeth and attributes that lead to actions and decisions, but as you can see I'm the worst at analogues, metaphors and similes. Yes, you can so be a tree. But no, I wasn't a kite that way except maybe in my becoming entangled in you and not being able to fly freely or sail away or something because of the string. But a kite becomes entangled around something, not in it, except if it maybe got blown into a window or cave. But even there it would probably only get entangled around a table or chair or rock in the window or cave, and not entangled around the window or cave it got blown in. Anyway, now I'm letting go.

I don't feel responsible for causing this break. Or, maybe a little. But I'm not going to rationalize it away by saying, as you hinted the last time we drove in, that what we both probably have wanted for the last few weeks is for the relationship to quietly and unemotionally end. Maybe that's the way you want it, but I really don't care. I don't care anymore what you want or what you'll do. Honestly. I'm saying that what we had eventually went the way you wanted it, without any compromising on your part or give and take, and I couldn't tolerate it, so I just don't want to see you anymore.

I still love you, but for the first time in my life the existence or reality or whatever it could be called concerning this love for you just doesn't seem to be enough to make me want to stay. I'm sorry. I hate writing letters like this, like less to get them, but there's no other way I see to express what I must say short of calling you, and I don't have a phone, it's a trudge through slush and snowdrifts to reach a booth, and you know I'm even more uncommunicative, befuddling and in the end agonizingly battological when I try speaking on one. So, best ever then—Newt

Dear Em—

I won't be coming to Stonehill anymore. I don't want you coming by my place. Simple as I can say it: I don't want to go on with our relationship anymore. It's not going to change. The relationship won't. You talked a lot about "growth," both as individuals and as a couple. But we didn't grow together after the first few months, only repeated the same mistakes and agonies endlessly rather than understanding and correcting them and moving on.

I'm also tired of you always setting the pace, the distance, how high we could climb. That "week" in the summer. On a "beach." Why didn't you also suggest what color bathing suit I could bring along and how many hours in the sun I'd be allowed a day? It's usually been your way, do you agree? I went along like that because I don't like to direct a relationship of any kind—love, business, professional, familial, matrimonial, you name it: none. It's a pity you couldn't have let things sail freely without always dashing and mashing them against rocks everytime it went well.

You said you were afraid of getting trapped. Well maybe the reverse is the trap. The trap could be what you think it's not. Maybe. In other words, the trap might not be the one you think you'll get in with me, but the one you go to to avoid getting in a trap with me, which then wouldn't make it a trap. Wouldn't make the anticipated trap with me a trap. The trap would be the trap you divert to to avoid that anticipated trap. No, the trap is trying to establish here what is and isn't a trap.

We've gone on for hours and ruined too many weekends discussing and discovering the reasons for our inability to sustain a preponderatingly smooth relationship—our histories and also the irreconcilabilities built into any more than casual comings together of two people: professional, familial, amorous, etc. (see above). But to me, either a couple make it or they don't. Deep endearing feelings and mutual respect keep them together, and the theories and therapies and the rest of it regarding love are at the most temporarily satisfying but usually stultifying and ultimately desolating and worthless. Even here, the more I think of it, the more I'm giving some theory about it, and the more doltish I am but bombastic I sound and perplexed I get. The hell with it.

I also can't get the bad things out of my head. I think about you sweetly most times. Fooling around. Holding you close. Working. Walking. Talking. Laughing. Jogging. Hogging. Joking. Just dancing to some dumb radio tune together or silently reading different books on the same couch or challenging those boys to a two-on-two basketball game or chasing away those oafs that day who didn't know there were two of us who could bite and bodychop with the best of them to protect old winos and not one. All that. But the other disturbing things just don't creep in, they rush. A lot else about what's happened between us just hasn't been carved out of my head yet. Turning me on and off. Blowing me up. Flying me like a kite or balloon. Popping me when need be or letting me hang or cutting the string whenever you wanted to and letting me go. I always thought "Em won't do that again." I was always so hopeful. Optimistic. See the bright flashing lights in his naive eyes. After that last time—your last break—I suppose I was just holding on. What in the world was your need for always wanting to come back to me after you broke us up "for the benefits of us both" and after I'd finally felt "Good, I found I can live without her again. Took me four days which is a day more than the last three times but two days less than the first, so maybe in my twenty years of developed sexuality or so I've actually grown some." Now I'm letting go. Nothing much to hold on to anyway, so it isn't hard, and I don't mean to sound tough.

I also don't feel that responsible for any of this. Not at all responsible. And I'm not going to rationalize my decision to disband by saying, as you suggested, or more accurately, kidded around about as we drove in last time (and to pinpoint the spot: on the big bridge at the bistate halfway marker which you only then discovered and pointed out after having passed it a few hundred times and my having remarked about the marker to you at least twice), that a quiet uncomplicated indestructible separation is what we've both probably been wanting for the last month. I'm saying that what we had eventually went the way you wanted it, not me, and without any give, take or faint nod toward compromise on your part, and I couldn't tolerate it, though for a while deluded myself that I could because one great day your attitude would change to me and us and my acceptance and sufferance would have been worth it. But now when I think about it I can't stand it and can barely tolerate myself for being such a shortsighted simp and slave.

So I just don't want to see you again—it's important that's clear. I love you very much, that's too damn true, and still do, I'm saying that, no matter how foolish or even gain-making that must now sound, but for the first time in my life the existence or fact of my love just doesn't seem to be enough to make me want to stay. Isn't enough—absolutely—so that's it, I'm afraid. Love, Newt

Dear Emmy—

I won't be coming to Stonehill anymore. I don't want you to come by my place again. I just don't want to go on with our relationship anymore. I'm weary of you always setting the pace. How high we should climb, far we can go. Let's sprint, rest, fall back, on our face, scrape our knees, break our ankles, spurt, zip, lunch, get lost, make it a marathon, two marathons, three. That "week" this coming summer. On a "beach." And "always" is an emotional word you said and I said "It's just a much abused one," but you know what I mean. I went along as I did because I don't like directing a relationship of any kind, personal or professional. What a waste you couldn't let whatever it was between us happen without your customary dashing it to dust everytime it went well.

You said you're afraid of getting trapped. But maybe the reverse is the trap. Maybe the trap's what you're moving to now. We've gone on for weekends about this—our histories. That I met you after not being close to a woman for years. That you met me a few months after you left the man you were close to for years. "That the cross-purposes and inconciliabilities of our aims, outlooks and maybe our natures are monumental." I said "What do you mean?" You said "The most ignorant men are those who feign ignorance." I said "What do you mean?" You said "The most ignorant men are those who continue to feign ignorance." I said "What about women?" You said "The most ignorant of the most ignorant men are those who continue to feign the same ignorance that classified them among the most ignorant of men." I said "What do you mean?" You said. I said. You said that being tied down to one man over a period of sixteen years was enough and that instead of pinning into a second you wanted a rest. I said "I won't keep you back or hold you down." You said "Right now just seeing only one man is keeping me back and down." I said. You said "Truthful as the pain must be to you, I want to explore other relationships, life styles and professions." I said "I suppose I really couldn't tolerate seeing you if you were at the same time seriously seeing other men or casually allowing them to slip it in." You said "If that arrangement doesn't suit you, Newt, then maybe after a few years, if either of us is still available, which sounds impossible, we can try as a single couple again." I said "That would probably be impossible." You said "We revolve undolved without resolve." I said "What do you mean, what do you mean?" You said "From paddle to pedal to piddle to podel to puddle again." I said "Don't I know. But why'd you always, unpsychotherapized always, come back to me after all those times you told me to go or you picked up and went, and never after more than five or six days?" "You mean I never came back to you after more than five or six days?" "Yes,"

I said. "Five," you said and I think I said "I think the maximum was six."

Though I do think of you sweetly most times. Holding you close. Joking, jogging, nuding and screwing around. Sleeping, seeping, eyes uttering, nares stuttering, walking, talking, doing ludicrous things. Precious and energetic and hilarious and creative things. Holding you close. Just playing those boys two-on-two basketball that playground day. Fending off that pack of oafs in front of Oscar's with our hoofs, cuffs and butts when our wits didn't work. Quipping, unzipping, being comfortable and rumpled while silently reading side by side on your settee. Holding you close. Nuzzling. Puzzling. All of those. More of these. Unstrapping, while lips lapping— But the other disturbing things that happened just don't flip in, they flush. A lot else just hasn't been excised out of my head yet. Those four to five times you dropped the relationship cold. Wanted to go back to Myles. "Go if you got to go I sometimes say another way about something else," I said, but when he wouldn't do the bee's dance for you you devised some other plan. "Cancel your plane reservation overseas with me as I want to go alone. Timing, poor rhyming, but we're just never going to materialize, Newt." Your loving letters, each one better, till the last one when you said "When you come to the airport for me could you only come to return my keys and cars?" Then after an exhilarating night and day at the terminal and home you gave me the boot again and three days later got into my building somehow and through my peephole said would I be dumb and daft enough to have you back? "Of course—I'll open the door." Well enough. I'm tired of being turned on and off. Hot water today?—okay. Tepid? —you bet. What's that: boiling, hyperborean?—no sweat. Of being your straw man, tin man, wrong man, enough. Blowing me up. Letting me fly. Like a balloon or kite: piping goodbye as you cut me loose. You: "Howdy-do again, you undrownable goose." Each time my feeling that time's the last. Emotional always so hopeful I was—my eternally gyring eyes, or what you twice called "The naively cherished long overromantic view." Well now I'm letting go. Hip, hip, and nothing much to hold on to anyway, so it's not that hard. And I don't mean to be mean with these remarks, and why couldn't I ever resist your returns long enough till I had become fully unglued?

I don't feel responsible for any of this. Maybe a little. And I'm not going to rationalize my decision away by saying as you hinted when we drove in last time that if we both had the courage to say it, a complete break is what we've been wanting for the past two months. You did, I didn't, and now I don't care what you want or do. I'm saying that what we had eventually went the way you wanted it, with little give or take, and I couldn't tolerate it, though for a while blinded myself that I could—deluded myself was what I was thinking of now and wrote in the previous letter to you that I'm typing this from—and now when I think about it I can't stand it. Can't stand the thought of it all. I don't want to see you again. Don't want you ever to come by here again. If you do—so much as ring my vestibule bell or let yourself in some way and come up and rattle your baby tap on my door—I'll drag you downstairs by the hair and throw you into the street. I will. So don't!

I love you very much, which has to sound ridiculous and suspicious and quite peculiar after all I said above, but for the first time in my life the existence or whatever it is of this love for someone just doesn't seem to be enough to make me want to stay. Isn't enough. So that's it then: never again, and there'll be no other word more. Newt

Dear Em:

I've tried writing you about something that's sitting very heavy on my mind. A series of letters so far. They're all in front of me, one on top of the other, till the last long one I just finished and am looking at now. Nothing useful, sensible or insightful came out of any of them, and at their very best they were a lot of drivel, bad gags and rhythmic rot. Even this one, I can see, still trying to rhyme and alliterate to impress instead of saying simply what I want to express, though no matter how wretched it is I'm going to send it off. What I intended saying in each of the previous letters today was that I don't want to see you anymore. I still feel that way. It just isn't going to work. We aren't. So please don't come by, I won't be busing up, and there'll be no further communication between us of any kind from now on. Very best and my love, Newt

Dear Em—

There's only one thing I want to say here. I won't be busing up, I don't want you coming by, and we won't be seeing each other again. So that's it. There'll be no other communications, explanations, letters, calls, nothing else between us from now on. Thanks for understanding that and much love, Newt

Dear Em—

I've decided we shouldn't see one another anymore and that there'll also be no explanations or communications about it either. Love, Newt

Dear Mary—

No more, and no explanations either. Thanks. Newt

Dear Em—

No more and no explanations. Newt

Dear Em—

No more and no explanations. En

Dear Em—

No more.

Em: No more. En

Em: no more

Dear Mary—

This weekend, instead of my busing up, why don't you drive in and stay here? I think we've some things to discuss, and just for a change let's spend an entire weekend in the city. The snow's supposed to be gone and the sky clear and weather relatively mild.

I wanted to write you about what's been on my mind lately concerning our relationship, but decided against even trying to put it down in words, as I thought it best to just talk things out. We always did that pretty well and I'm sure that this problem too will be resolved. If you can't come in, could you call Harriet? I'll be dropping by her place Thursday night and will get your message and then take the bus up Friday afternoon—probably the 4:55, as that one skips several towns and takes the upper route rather than the river and is less crowded, and as long as I have the choice I prefer shorter more comfortable trips and climbing down to crawling up. If you do come in I've already selected the perfect restaurant for our undutch dinner Friday night and "beeg talk." We haven't had dinner alone together in a quiet good place for a long time and that was always a nice experience for us and lots of fun. As a dining celebration excuse we'll make it your teaching snow day this week, all right by you?

So, if I don't hear from you I'll know you'll be driving in. If for any reason you want to phone me, tell Harriet. Otherwise: my love, drive carefully, have a pleasant end of week and no matter what I'll be seeing you Friday night. Newt

The Meeting

It was not an unusual meeting. Unusual in the sense that we continued and still continue to see each other after nearly two years. No, that makes little to no sense. Why'd I say it then? Write it, I mean. If I don't know, somebody else might. That's infrequently been the case. Let me just start again, though keeping my confusion in. I don't know why, but right now that seems important to me. To involve the reader in the actual writing act. Oh, I don't like that.

It was not an unusual meeting. All right, so it was not an unusual meeting. Why do I think I must stick with that? Confusion hasn't become substance here but compounded confusion, now not only in the narratively limitative sentence about it not being an unusual meeting but also why I insist on keeping that sentence in. When at an inspirational loss and digression doesn't work, try starting with the locational facts.

We met in an old Manhattan apartment building on a flight of stairs. She was walking up, I was walking down. The staircase was narrow and we tried passing one another without touching, but I bumped into her and knocked a package out of her hand. It bounced down the long flight of stairs. We were at the top. As the package bounced I said "Sorry, but what's in there, a blown-up soccer ball?" She said—Mary did—"No, a bottle of perfume—a carafe. I mean a flagon. Not a flagon. Now nothing. Finger-slitting glass." The container the perfume was in broke at the bottom of the next flight of stairs. It was an old loft building we were in. Those kind of stairs. Where the flights rise like any side of a ziggurat and the street door can be seen, if the lights are on or it's daylight, from the top step of even the fifth or sixth flight of stairs. The smell of the perfume shot up the two flights like a sprayed skunk's scent when the skunk's in a state of alarm. When the skunk's alarmed. And not a sprayed skunk, which among other things makes it sound like a spray painting of a skunk or when one skunk's sprayed by another skunk, but when an alarmed or endangered skunk sprays. A smell like that. Though not a smell like a skunk's smell, and by that I don't mean his everyday body smell or his sense of smell but that foul secretion ejected from his perineal glands, but as fast as a skunk's smell would shoot up the stairs. No, this won't do either. Not only the writing in it, which could be improved through subsequent rewritings to what I at least would think would be momentary near perfection, but the story itself. For where do they go now? Downstairs, more small talk, an appointment for tonight or tomorrow or some outside refreshment or perfume purchase now? Then why was he going downstairs, she up? No, the other way, but I mean with specific directions and maybe intentions in mind. I could have them both going in the same direction: down. But then they wouldn't pass one another on the stairs and he wouldn't bump into her, unless he was racing past her in a hurry to get someplace or because that was the way he usually walked or ran down stairs, and then knocked the perfume out of her hand. Or he could be holding the perfume and she could accidentally knock it out of his hand. Even so, would they then talk long enough after one or the other's apology and regrets about the broken phial or vial of perfume to feel they'd want to make some future appointment together or continue their conversation on the street or in a perfume store or drugstore or café or restaurant somewhere downstairs? I'm sure I could work it out some way through additions and deletions and again plenty of rewriting and thought, but it might be simpler and more enjoyable trying something else.

We're in an apartment building elevator. I am, not Mary. I press the button for the eleventh floor. The elevator doors start to close. "Wait," I hear. I see her running to the elevator at the same time

I throw myself on the L for Lobby button to reverse the direction of the doors. Too late. Doors close. Elevator ascends and opens on the thirty-first floor. It's an office building. I find the right office, go inside and ask the receptionist if I may see Mrs. Leogremay. "Tell her Newt Leeb."

"She expects you?" and I say "No, but I was in the neighborhood and thought she'd see me if she's not too tied up. I'm a client of hers."

"That's different." She dials Lynn's cubicle. "Who should I say again?"

I repeat my name. Just then the same woman from the lobby before gets off one of the elevators. It's a new Sixth Avenue office building and this company rents the entire floor. The reception desk is about twenty feet from the opposing bank of elevators. There's a private guard sitting in a corner reading. Several people sit on couches and easy chairs, waiting to be called inside. When the woman reaches the desk I say "I'm sorry, but I jumped on the elevator button downstairs too late to keep the doors open for you."

"So you were the seamy exclusionist who refused to ride duo," she says in mock disapproval, which I wasn't sure then was mock. Days later she would say about other things "What's the good of our relationship if I can't make fun of you sometimes and anytime kid you along?"

"Mr. Leeb?" I turn around. "She says her schedule's pretty tight today and that if you'd like to, you could drop by tomorrow or the next day around three."

"Tell her I'll only take one minute."

"Let me see to this woman first?"

"Lynn Leogremay, please," the woman says. "Appointment. Tell her Mary leBroom."

The receptionist dials. "Mary leBroom at the desk to see Mrs. Leogremay. Thank you." To Mary: "Right through that door."

Mary turns the doorknob to the huge rectangle of offices inside, but it's locked. Readily hangdogged and overwrought, she pounds on the door with both fists and says "Let me out, let me out, I can't stand it in here, no air and the gas." The guard drops his book and looks alarmed but the receptionist laughs and says "Always with you, Miss leBroom, I forget," and presses the buzzer on her desk to let Mary in.

"I really did try downstairs, by the way," I say to Mary as the door clicks open and she goes through.

"You get a gold star when I leave here, McNee," just before the door snaps closed.

The receptionist dials Lynn's secretary. "Mr. Leeb again. Says to tell Double L he only wants a minute."

"Thirty seconds," I yell. No, this will never do. I don't want to meet or be introduced to Mary in or outside of Lynn's office or passing through the reception area again on her way to the elevators while I'm still waiting for Lynn to let me in or when Mary's leaving the lavatory or sick, we could both suddenly be struck sick with gastroenteritis during the elevator ride down, faces blanched and sweating excessively and gasping incoherently for help from the floor by the time the car reaches the lobby—crowded office building commotion, ambulance ride to the hospital in side by side cots, doctor taking our pulses simultaneously with his watch on his lap. And Mary has nothing to do with being an agency's client. She's a high school teacher, if that happens to come up. She could also have something to sell—that original people book she's writing and drawing, though it's really a personal journal. Because teaching, right now, is more than a fulltime sideline for her and what she does best and loves most and all other work and creative activities for her are solely avocational. Try once more, this time closer to what took place.

We're to meet. She's late. Vestibule mailbox bell is rung. "That must be her," my cousin Harriet says. Only moments before I said I was getting edgy waiting here for her and got up to go and Harriet said "Not on your monotonous life, Newt. Years before they crashed I vowed to your parents about getting you mated and generated, in case they'd be away or wouldn't have time to elicit promises like that from a single or double deathbed," and shoved me back into the butterfly chair. Where I am now—in the livingroom, haphazard furniture and scattered clothes and sissing kittens and cats and a kitchenette away from the apartment's front door and intercom, which I can't see from where I wine and sit.

Harriet says into the intercom "Ms. Mary?" A voice mumbles back. "Who or what?" Harriet says. Voice mumbles back. "Skip it, whoever you are, 'cause I can't understand a word you say," and rings the bell to the vestibule to let whoever it is in. Rung back is the opening bar of Beethoven's most famous Fifth. "At least we know it's human," Harriet says.

If it's Mary, she's on her way up. What does she look like? Is like? All Harriet would say was that "If you got her out of a mail order catalogue, even without your asking for it she'd come to you by air special delivery and with too much insurance and overprotectively wrapped." But it's okay. You don't like her, she you, aren't attracted, you're both not especially suited for one another, you say hello, maybe shake hands, talk, have a drink, two, three, crackers, wurst and cheese, and then there's always plenty to interest me in in anyone new for at least a half hour or two, and Harriet will be there, her jokes and twists of daily events and long theatrical and comical accounts of her ex-husbands and a hundred week- to day-old professions she was going to work into lifelong careers and all her barhoppings and amorous jugglings and eventual clobberings and the series of dour A.A. or chanting Buddhists or back to Christ or God church and synagogue meetings she's turned into beery laughfests, and in time one or the other of us will set our glass or half a cracker down and say something like nice as the company is we have to leave, previous appointment too long postponed, and disbuttock ourself from the bridling butterfly chair, or perhaps we'll leave Harriet's together, in front of the building or at the corner, going separate ways. But then it might work out. Harriet had said "Even if she only sleeps on you in your apartment tonight, that'll satisfy me." I objected, saying jointing or any kind of loining or oinking's not what I had in mind. She said "If it's placed by your face and you reject it, promised parents or not, you lose a pander for life." And Harriet's daughter Juniper is here also —now in the next room bickering back and forth with some educational TV panelists about the growing nuclear world arsenal and holocaust capability and end-of-the-earth scare. "You're all suicidal shits," she screams, throwing something breakable against the wall. "You all know how bad it is and can do something, but you're all lying because you all want to see us all get killed, that's all."

"Juniper," Harriet shouts. "Will you tone both it and you down."

Footsteps on the third flight of stairs. Doorbell rings. "There's Mary," Harriet says. How does she know? She knows. Ask Harriet and Harriet will say "Harriet knows, take it from me, Harriet knows." And five minutes ago she phoned Mary's husband and Myles said Mary left fifteen minutes ago and he figured Harriet's place was about twenty minutes away by car. Mary had dropped off their daughter with him for a weekend with her brother, bicycle and dad. Door opens. Synchronous squeals and what sound like pats on the back and hugs. "Howdy, l'étranger," a low extremely cheery voice says.

"You bastard," Harriet says. "After all the crap you've recently gone through, you look too damn good. Turn around."

I look toward the uttermost right of the kitchenette, closest my vision can get to the door. It picks up last summer's Thalia film festival calendar and unwashed dishes and pots. Then a burnoosed figure appears, booted, hooded, black or brown hair, whirling a few times for Harriet without looking at me and then vanishing in the direction of the front door. She seemed big. Bulky. Hulky. At least her shoulders and behind. Maybe she's fat. Though Harriet had said Mary would come wrapped to me in a small package because she was thin and untall. But last time she saw her was months ago in Tunisia where they all lived on the same street like pashas and khedives for a year. Maybe that's it: marriage separation, family disintegration, back in the States on her own for a change with new job and lodgings and used car and little money and for most of the time no son, had produced many hardships and frustrations and as a result cravings for fatty foods and superfluous sleep and sweets. I also never got a good look at her face, so fast had she twirled in and out of the room. A nose. Mouth. Possibly earless or ears concealed by shoulder- or neck-length hair. Big black eyes are only what I think I saw. She could have been wearing dark sunglasses.

They're in Juniper's room. Kisses, hugs. Mary admiring Juniper's new height and resourceful sloppiness, for a girl with so few possessions and for furniture only a mattress and lamp on a bare floor, and saying how glad she was Juniper hadn't been cowed, bulled and buffaloed into tidiness and taintlessness by all the neurotic neatos and launderers who haunt our lives here. "Linetta's become much too orderly and clean since we got back, and I worry for her. She picks up after me, voluntarily scours the inside of the toilet bowl. But the doctor says she'll change. Now show me my big surprise."

"He's in there," Harriet says.

"Horse trader. Sheep's clothing. Well I'm getting while the going's still to be gotten and I can remember the combination to this door," and she tries unbolting and unchaining and unlocking the layer of locks.

"And also to see me and Juniper pill and our great domestic comedown since those days of leaky fountains in our courtyard and weeks of dysentery. Stay."

Juniper and Harriet drag Mary into the room by her hands.

"Hello," I say, trying to extricate myself from the chair to stand and shake her hand.

"Don't get up," Mary says.

"I can't get up."

"My Uncle Fig Newton," Juniper says.

"Don't call him Fig Newton and he's not your uncle," Harriet says. "You may call him Newton, Newt, N, Cousin, Cuz, Cousin or Couscous Newton or Newt, but nothing to do with cookies."

"He's too old to be my cousin. Besides, he's already yours."

"Your cousin, no less," Mary says to Harriet. "I have none. I'm an only child."

"I never one—I mean was one before, but that's what I've become of late," I say.

"Give me time to figure that one out," Mary says.

"Good," Harriet says. "You two already have something in common and to figure out. I'll get drinks and snacks. Don't bother getting up, Newt."

"I can't get up."

"He's always helping me out in the kitchen, the most persistent and obstructive non-chauv I know. But stay, since it's obvious you both have a lot to say and maybe you'll even do it to each other. Talk, I mean. Juniper, don't listen to my foul mouth. Help me slice the cheese and snap the crackers in half."

"No, I want to watch and listen to them make fools of themselves."

"Just go to your room without crackers and watch TV." Juniper does. Harriet slices cheese. Mary and I talk. Been here long? Like it back? Where do you live? What do you do? Sounds very nice. And what do you do? Where do you live? Been here long? Haven't been away? Never left this block? Lived on it all your life? Nice. Sounds very nice. Silence. She watches the cats, is distracted by my shoes. They're space shoes, department store bought and modeled after molded orthopedic shoes, and I suppose they make me look crippled, though I only wear them for comfort. Moreover, the laces are frayed and the leather is black, badly scuffed, and the once thick soles have become low and the heels nonexistent and the sides need to be scraped of Central Park mud.

"Battle injury during the last great war," I say. "Lost both my Achilles tendons and most of my foretoes."

"Oh? God, it's hot. Naturally. My burnoose," and she gets up to remove it.

I say "That's a very nice burnoose" and she says "Thanks, I bought it for a song in Tunis," and I say "A real song?" and she says "Yes, keeps me very warm" and I say "No, I said did you buy it for a real song—one you sang or wrote or did both?" and she says "Actually, for several real songs, couple of arias but not an entire opera. For that I could have gotten—oh, forget it. I was going to say—forget it. An Arabian saddle and doddering old nag, but that's stupid," and she stares at the empty ceiling and then my shoes again and near my heels she spots a magazine, picks it up, flips through it and settles on a lipstick ad. She wears none. No makeup that I can tell. I'm interested in her looks, voice, personality, sense of humor and intelligence, but talking and listening to me she seems ready to fall asleep. Her eyes are big. She wasn't wearing sunglasses. Wide mouth, very white slightly crooked front teeth, plenty of silver fillings in back, likes to smile. I still don't know if she has ears. Black hair, maybe waist length when it fully unwinds. She's thin, hairy arms, below average height, large feet it seems, though sitting up she looks tall. Legs covered by Arab cloth that touches her ankles.

Harriet returns with drinks and a platter of snacks. "You getting to know one another very well? Great, for Newt is my favorite cousin. My only cousin. We grew up together like brother and brother. And this new camaraderie of yours will make it easier for Juniper and me to leave."

"I thought you and I were eating here tonight," Mary says.

"We were. Or you must be mistaken. I forget which, though thanks for bringing the salad, wine and bread. But Juniper and I are eating out with someone else tonight. And you were late, Emmy, and now I'm about to be late also unless I rush. If you'd come when you said you would or only an hour late, then we could have had more time to thrash this sudden going of mine out. Juniper—your coat."

Juniper turns off the television and stands by the door.

"I said to get your coat."

Juniper gets her sweater.

"At least put it on."

Juniper ties the sweater sleeves around her waist and blows Mary and me a kiss. Harriet says "Help yourselves to everything except the salad, wine and bread, and if you can, could you feed the cats before you leave?" and they go.

Mary throws open the door and yells "Harriet, you come right back. You can't leave me with a strange man like this. Not strange, but just a man I don't right now want to know. I don't like being forced upon anyone—that's more my point. And I'm sure your cousin Nelson or Nathan here doesn't like being part of any sneaky prearrangement too."

"The name's Naomi," I yell.

"Harriet, I insist. I see you now, arch dissembler, laughing down the stairs. Tugging on Juniper's braids as you say 'Oh boy, did I ever pull a fast one on them. Do you think they'll get along? Won't it be great if they do? Then we'd see more of Mary and Cousin Nathan or Naomi and you'd see more of Mary's Linetta and her second baseman, Timon. We'd be one big yappy travesty. My matchwork zilch. A meretricious electric moog syllogizing magoo. I don't know what I'm saying, Ju. It's the booze, making me unable to consecrate—that's my treacherous excuse. But is it too chilly for you, sweet? Well, tough titty, kiddy, cause I didn't tell you to get your sweater but your coat. You're lucky enough I persisted with your coat a second time, or you wouldn't even have a sweater on, and where's your socks and shoes?' " She slams the door and brings the wine bottle over and sits. "But I'm sure Juniper, much more reasonable and mature than her mother, will say 'I think you were not only overunderhanded and unfair with them, but that we ought to go right back upstairs.' But Harriet will say—what do you think she'll say? 'Up yours and the horse you rode out on, kid—let's find a dive to dine at tonight in place of the only other dump we can afford, our own home I so slyly gave up.' "

"She did mean for us to meet. But I didn't think it would be this way. She said she had somebody perfect for me. I said no thanks, as I never again want a blind date. She said 'Blind meet, not date, and you just be here and I'll get her over here and we'll all have a friendly drink and pleasant talk. Then if neither of you much like, either of you can be the first to go. But you will like, Newtie, so I'm planning on departing for an hour or so with Juniper and in that time I want you to ask her out for dinner, and after dinner, in for some smooching at your hole. And in three months I want you to be established as a family of three or four, depending on how many of her kids she has with her then, and in a year married and Mary pregnant to have child by you, and no ifs, tiffs or diffs, ya hear?' "

"Harriet's way off the mark." She puts on her burnoose. "I'll give you my phone number, all right, though I won't ever be there. You can then easily get my real number from Harriet. But if you do dial and I answer in a glaring falsetto that I'm my own best girlfriend and the Mary you want's moseyed off for a cross-country spelling bee for a year, it'll mean to hang up and dial the first seven digits that come to mind that you know aren't mine and you'll have much better luck. I just don't want to be seeing anyone except casually or accidentally or professionally or if they're not one of my children or students, so that's clear now, okay?"

"How about dinner tonight?"

"I don't think so. Let's talk some more."

"Like some more wine?"

"Why not? I still have a quarter inch left at the top of my glass."

She holds out her glass and I pour wine in it till it spills over the lip to the floor.

"Would you like some more wine too?" she says.

"No, thanks. I've plenty."

She pours wine into my empty glass on the table till she fills the glass and the wine spills down the side.

I begin licking the wine off the table. She says "Didn't your folks ever teach you how to use a fork? Furthermore, you look rabious and ravenous doing that—like the two whiz kids of Rome—though not attractive like them at all." She gets a couple of sponges from the sink and cleans up the mess on the table and floor.

"I don't know why I did that."

"Let's talk and not pour so much anymore," she says, finished sponging.

"The licking, I mean." We look at one another. We drink. Look
at one another. Drink. Look, drink, look, drink. Drink drink drink.
"What else do you want to talk about?" I say.

"If chitchat's a problem now, what prospects can we possibly
have?"

"You want to talk about that? Fine. If chitchat's— No. And I
finally stopped myself."

"Let me feed the sponges and clean the cats. Then I have to go.
Not have to, but want."

"Sponges." She's cleaned them and is now breaking up bread,
because there's no cat food, for the cats. "That's right—sponges
can also be pets. In erasing or blotting out messy practical jokes
that often result from two unacquainted people not having much
to say at the time or being anxious about one another in some way.
Sponges, in other words, can often go to great reserves for you. No,
that's not syntactically or morphologically correct, not that I know
the difference between those two, or even especially true. There
is some joke there though about going deep down into the deep
deep for sponges and coming up with one that saves me and you.
In other words—fishing. A laughing trip. In other words, it must
be obvious by now I can be a fool lots, or with you, in the short time
I've known you, most of the time. And that sponges will never
foreseeably be one of my favorite conversation pieces or intend-
edly humorous circumlocutions or discursions, not that I'm sure
there's much difference between those two, and that instead of
dinner tonight what about just a dinner and show and post-
cinematic drink and snack?"

"I don't know. I don't like the roles. You asking. Why couldn't
I have asked you? Because again, I don't want to. Why not whatever we might do only when and if we feel like it? Let's start by
leaving here. Do you want to?"

"Yes I do."

"Me too. Then if out front we still want to walk together, okay.
And if not, or even going downstairs we want to part, then we do.
If we don't part on the stairs or in front of the building, and a block

away, let's say, we still want to be together, then we will. And on and on like that till either of us doesn't want to be with the other person or both of us don't want to stop. Well, sometimes in the future one of us will want to stop, but not until that person says so, okay?"

I get my coat and we leave. On the stairs neither of us says anything about not wanting to continue downstairs together. On the sidewalk in front I say "If we still want to walk together, which way do we want to go, uptown or down?"

"I'm for down."

"Me too."

"I hope it's not just because I said so."

"No, downtown seems more interesting to me now. Though possibly what you said had some subliminal influence, though how would I know?"

"We have to go left or right first—towards Columbus Avenue or Central Park West. I'm for Columbus."

"I'm for the park."

"Okay. Some compromises in an arrangement of this sort have to be made, and since I brought up the subject of compromises, I'll make the first."

"That doesn't necessarily follow."

"Then make your compromise that this time it does."

We walk toward the park and downtown a block along Central Park West. I stop at a bus stop.

"You thinking of splitting up now and going some other way, or the same way as me though alone?" she says.

"Neither. Like to take a bus with me further downtown?"

"And if I don't?"

"We could still walk. Either's all right."

"Good idea, the bus. Not that I'm tired, but long time no ride, and then maybe we can go to Radio City Music Hall."

I have the exact change for both of us. She only has the exact change for herself. When the bus comes I get my two fares in the coinbox before she can get her change in, as I'm the first one up the steps and my back intentionally blocks her extended fare-holding hand. She says "If we take another bus ride tonight and I have the exact change at the time, then even if you're in the bus first and I have several packages or cramps in my hands that make it hard reaching the coinbox or releasing the coins, I still want to pay for us both, so you must be patient and not so eager, and if I only have enough coins for myself, then for myself alone."

"I'll remember."

"You might remember but do you agree?"

"I do, I do."

The bus is empty other than another couple in the rear window seat. They kiss. Hold hands. She smiles, he laughs. A big squeeze and hug to end all this smiling and laughing business and her fresh bouquet of stems and a couple of flowers is crushed. They're almost formally dressed. Suit, gown. Boutonniere. Shoes patent leather or shined to that consummate degree: he. She with six inch silver heels that reflect the grimy floor. I say "They look so prim, like they're going to a prom."

"No no. They've come from her girlfriend's wedding and are suddenly thinking of getting hitched themselves."

"They could have been posing for engagement photos at a tographer's."

"Not at nine."

"Is that the time?"

The girl puts her shoulder on his. No, her head, but on his shoulder. It's what I'd like Mary to do to me once I sit. Knees bent, I make my move.

"Do we really want to sit together, stand holding the same or different poles together, or to stand and sit together or apart?" Mary says.

"Sit—clothing juxtaposing and maybe touching."

They do. But too early for our shoulder and head. Maybe later tonight—that other bus ride she'll pay for if she has the change—she will, though voluntarily. I won't force. I won't say "Here, your head, let me introduce it to my shoulder, so they might whisper to one another or snirtle or snuffle or hold hands or just kiss." I want to put my arm around her shoulder, like that much younger man. A squeeze and hug: our chests to crush. Always something to look forward to. Some guys have all the luck. Mary looking out the window and pointing to a same-numbered jam-packed bus that's passing us. "Look look," she says. "We're being overtaken and I don't see the sense."

"By the way, my name is Newton, you know."

"No. I was just beginning to wonder and be embarrassed that I didn't, and then decided on Nathan. I think I like Nats to Newts, but nonnegotiable point as they don't say."

A man, in two coats, inner one longer than the outer, both salvaged, venerable hat, new shoes, gets on the bus and sits opposite us and asks me for a match. "Hey, buddy."

"You're not allowed to smoke in the bus," I say.

"I know the law—I see the sign—but this is for later on."

"I'm sorry. Excuse me for butting in. Do you smoke?" I ask Mary.

"No."

"You're telling me you didn't know?" the man says.

"We just met. And sorry again, but neither of us smoke."

"That's not what I asked you for. Do either of you carry matches?"

"You?" I ask her.

"Sometimes, but not now."

"When do you carry them?"

"When we go camping. Or did. In Europe last summer. After Tunisia, on the way home. Also in a bus. With my husband and children. And in Tunisia when all we had for heating and cooking were kerosene stoves. Times like that. To light my father's pipe."

"Both of us have carried matches," I tell the man, "but we don't have any on us now."

"You smoke?" Mary asks me.

"No. For camping in California once. Years ago, with someone else's son. I had a little bug. He was a likable tyke. It was a big box.

For a single-burner stove. Now it'd be an encumbrance though, as I don't think my pockets are wide enough. But I don't want to remainder everything at once, as then I'll have nothing to chop away later on."

The man asks the couple in the back for matches. The young man gives him a green pack with gold lettering and says "Keep it, I've lots more."

"It says 'Penelope and Elliot' on it," the man says, lighting up a filtered stub. "What's that? New restaurant? Been in this burg all my life and thought I heard of them all."

"Put out the fire," the driver says.

"His sister and my brother got married last night," the girl says, the man taking a last deep drag and stamping out the filter, "and we've just come from the tail end of their party and dance. Read what it says inside the matches."

" 'Thanksgiving 72 till doomsday and evermore.' "

We get off at Seventh Avenue or Broadway. Across the avenue, large crowds are being kept behind police barriers at a theater presenting a Shakespearean musical. Horsemen. Blue helmets. Parked police motorcycles. More lights than usual. Up above it seems the sounds of several helicopters. "Little late for an opening," I say.

"The President and his first family," a woman says. "In New York for the night. And just got in, I overheard a police car radio say, so the show's being delayed an hour."

A fleet of gleaming limousines with little American flags on the aerials and ringed by equispaced police motorcycles and jogging security men pulls up in front of the marquee. The crowd cheers, applauds. Few boos. Picket signs appear. Some comparing him to Hitler. Some to Churchill. One to Disraeli. I see him. Steps out first. Cheers, applause. Flashbulbs and television camera lights. Not in any rush. Shakes two tuxedoed men's hands. Raises his arm, turns. Peers over his car roof, smiles, waves. Cheers, applause. More boos. Picket signs have disappeared. The women he's with are all blond and dressed in white and one wears a tiara and fluffy boa. "I've a feeling the crowd, pro and con, is going to break through the barriers and mob him and his family and cars. You think the cops will be able to contain them?"

"I hope not," Mary says.

"Even if I were a member of the audience and paying exorbitant babysitting fees, I'd still hate to see any kind of violence here."

"Violence? You don't call that other thing violence?" pointing to Asia. "Some things simply can't be clowned about, Newt."

"I guess I've always been a bit late or laggard about politics and presidentships and nations and wars of liberations," but she says, mostly to the theater, "I hope he's bored stiff and his wife loses one shoe and her necklace and that the performers sing and dance slow and break most of their violin strings" and storms east without me.

I shout "Mary, wait up—I'm lost," but she still goes. The President's safe in the theater after signing several autographs and shirt cuffs. I catch up with her on Sixth Avenue and say "Isolationist as I might be, I'm still not that fond of quick vanishing acts" and she says "That's the way I can be so that's the way it goes. You don't like. Well, you know—anytime you want you can say goodnight, pal" and I say "No, I like it here, I'll stay."

The cashier at Radio City Music Hall says the last stage show is almost over but we can still see the trailers and feature film.

"Will you give us half off the ticket prices?" Mary says. "Or to make it fairer, three-eighths off, since you say the stage show's still got a quarter ways to go."

"If one of the Rockettes suddenly died on stage," an usher standing nearby says, "would that mean we'd have to give you a proportionately reductive cut on your ticket as well, and maybe even commensurate with how many minutes and seconds she actually performed before she collapsed?"

"Ah, yuh smart collitch kids," I say. "But why yuh wanna be riding the young lady for, when all she was doing here was injecting a little humor into the air? And if she was being serious, then who's to say what she said wasn't sound and fair?"

Mary motions me to the side of the lobby and says "Thanks,

Newt, but I can handle my own wrangling and accept the responsibility of every scrap I initiate. Anyway, if we can't see the girls as wooden soldiers all falling in a row from a single cannonball, what about the skate show?"

We watch the skaters at Rockefeller Center rink. Mary points to a woman skating with an elderly guard and says "I've seen them dancing together on and off here since I was a girl and always wanted to know who she was and where she got her pretty costume and if she was married and if they knew each other as children, and lately, if any hanky-panky ever went on between them once they left the ice." I ask and she says "Jackson Heights. Red-brick six-story department buildings and public schools all the way. Though used to spend every summer with my family in our genealogical shack in Hudson Valley, where my greatest grand ones were Indians and my parents live now, but last year on the ship to Tunisia was the first period for more than a week for me spent out of New York State. But other than my folks, no kin now except for distant cousins in far-off cleuchs, tofts and swamps. And you?" I give a brief runthrough of my immediate family—four down, all missed and one to go.

Gets cold and we go to three bars in the neighborhood, all of them we have to squeeze into and Mary finds too snooty or snotty or overcrowded and priced and we only get glasses of seltzer in one of them and in the other two use the mensroom and then the ladiesroom. "I know of an interesting, that word interesting, bar on Sixth here—one Myles and I used to watch the World Series at when he worked in the Time-Life and I backpacked one child and carried the other in a front sling. There's an historic story to the bar," she says as we enter an empty gravely lit to me unattractive ramshackle tobacco-frowzy place. "Let him tell you about it though, as I want to see you approach someone and say hello and ask a question direct."

I ask, say I'd heard. The bartender says "How do you do?" and I say "Hi" and he says "Well, for the ten thousandth and first time since I started ministering here—"

"You're doing charity work," the other bartender says. "For the church. For religious people. Last rites and immersions and let's not forget the host of confessions."

"What the frock is he talking about?" he asks me.

"This is no way to begin a good story," Mary says.

"Turns out the original owner wouldn't sell this building to the people putting up Rockefeller Center, or else asked a fabulously outrageous price. Which is it?" he says to the other bartender and to the two waiters playing cards.

"High price," one says.

"Ethics. Down and out ethics."

"He didn't want to lose his old customers and cronies," the other bartender says, "and then there's the apartment and still and vats in back. He didn't want to lose those too."

"One or the others, but the building stayed on this corner like a small sorethumb to all those fat Rockefeller dolmens. And now even more so with so many of these new translucent tombstones being—Ah, but why should I care? I live across the river and my folks are buried with me there and dead. But that's the end of my sad tale and now what'll it be?"

"The decline of the el and downfall of Penn Station and demise of the nickel and dime and quarter and now dime and quarter IND," Mary says.

Ale. Later another, Mary for her second having hot tea. Old to not too recent photos and stills on the walls of much gayer chummier days. Gang behind the bar. Guys and gals sitting crosslegged and standing dapper dan-ish around the stools along with the jaunty sweep-up crew. Annual bar picnics. Rugby and softball games for laughs. Babe Ruth. Jimmy Durante. Johnny busting through an American store window. Saint Patrick's night and green draught and party-hatted New Year's Eves. World War Two pictures: an employee's destroyer in the Kamikaze Sea. P-38. Flying Fortresses. Individual soldier and sailor and WAC snaps, almost everybody looking a seasoned nineteen. F.D.R. DEAD Parking spaces allowed out front then: the owner proudly pointing out to a policeman his new coupe or sedan. Bill Bojangles. Billy

Conn. Big steins. Liquor bottles left on the counter and fewer framed photos on the walls and free lunch. V-J DAY PROHIBI-TION REPEALED   Harry Hershfield and the Harmonica Rascals and J. Fred Muggs the chimpanzee I think and the panel of *Can You Top This?* Caesar and Coca. Fatso Marco. Declaration of Independence. Dennis Day and a capsized *Normandie* and both Irish flags. La Guardia reading the comics and the owner shaking Bill O'Dwyer's hand. Citation. Yankee Stadium groundbreaking. Dixie Walker. King Kong Keller. Kennedy clutching a fisted wrist for his official photo. Sunday *Daily News* color centerfold of the leather-helmeted Brooklyn Dodgers and New York Giants football teams. Harry Hershfield. A signed Milton Berle. Mary pointing out Mary, Myles and Timon to me watching the World Series at this bar. Now a decrepit hodgepodge of torn up linoleum tiles and broken chairs upsidedown on jukeboxes and cigarette machines, most of them obsolete castoffs too heavy to cart away. I say to Mary "No knock on your marriage and slung ones, but this place would make me glad to be outside. If you want to stay a while longer, then I'm having another hundred year old egg and ale."

"When or if you drink too much, do you slur your words and speak through your nose and only make some sense but think you're an even mix of wit and fun and get sloppily sentimental and offensively intentional and forget whatever promises you've kept or money you've borrowed, loaned or thrown away like your cousin Harriet?"

"My first direct and I think truthful statement to you tonight, toots, might be that I don't know, though people have told me on occasion or maybe it's occasions they've said I have."

"Could be my brain cells are finally depleting faster than they're repeating or it's just the evening's old age. But what do you say we make a deal to not being so elliptic or cryptic anymore and to just letting the words emerge straight and clear?"

"I'm not agin."

"I'm not asking for all time, you know, but just till we say good-night."

In the street a man in a fur wrap and printed organdy dress and snood coasts by the window on roller skates a few times and then with the same self-possession and long hairless legs and grace revolves inside the revolving revolving door several times before he steps into the bar, skates to the counter, asks for two Cuba Libres, pays from a ratty changepurse and with the drinks skates on one foot to the phonebooth and shuts the door. He also has a closed parasol, I see, the tip of which gets in the way of the folding door, so he has to open and close the door again. Then tink-tinking of change and the man saying "Dad, it's Marge. Marge. Marge!" Mary, jotting words down in a memobook she's produced from somewhere, says "I think the one thing of interest I haven't said about myself yet is this book I'm writing and doing the sketches for about the oddest and most original city and suburban people I've met. I've bumped into the skater before and once when he was being pulled along on his skates by a big sled dog. For some odd reason, which may make me the most original writer of original people books, I never felt like writing him up."

The skater makes another call—"Piesie, it's lover. Lover. Lover!"—and Mary and I go to a playland on Broadway. We beat each other three out of three at different manual soccer games, sit in an automatic photobooth for two strips of four for a quarter photos, Mary squashed in behind me and turning out invisible in all but one shot. At the magic shop there Mary buys for her children a set of rattling teeth and birthday cake candles that can't be blown out and for her school desk a turned over ink bottle and spilled ink and for my coat a flower that squirts water. She suggests dancing at Roseland. The doorman at Roseland suggests I return with a tie. Mary suggests I make a string tie out of one of my shoelaces and the doorman suggests I won't be able to dance very well with one loose shoe and that we move on. Mary suggests hunger by clutching her stomach and grimacing with her fluttering tongue out and that we eat Lebanese. She knows of a good cheap restaurant on Eighth Avenue near where she and Myles and their children used to live.

In an alley along the way I want to put my arm around her waist.
No, before we reach this sidestreet alley where we see something
very unusual, I think of slipping my arm around Mary's waist. But
I don't. Can't. Not yet. Soon perhaps. Who knows? Can tell? Mary,
Mary, quite contrary, how does your garden grow? With the fleet
in the meadow—no. The first part at least is from a song we used
to sing as schoolboys to all the Mary schoolgirls we knew, the
garden being their pubic hair. I think that's it, and silly, I know,
but the song came to me as I walked with her, and in the alley right
after that we see three derelicts sprawled out on the ground in an
equilateral triangle, none of them knowing they were being observed. One man is kissing or biting another man's toes and the
man with his toes being bitten or kissed has his head and an arm
on another man's ankles and his other hand in the man's fly, and
the man with the second man's hand in his fly seems asleep with
his head stuck between the first man's feet, and so on, little suffering sounds and twitching movements from each of them and
mostly in succession, the triangle beginning to spin till it becomes
a hexagram.

"Let's get out of here," I say and Mary says "Maybe he needs
help" and I say "Which one?" and she says "Um—the drugged,
drunk or unconscious one who's being felt up or abused and
maybe his wallet copped and feet and head held down" and I say
"I don't think so" and she says "But how do we know?" and I say
"We don't, but it seems to me to be ancient Chinese precept of
he who plops too far into the great drop must clop clop out himself" and she says "I don't know, but that seems too hardboiled for
me" and I say "Or maybe poached or just cooked up and what you
say a bit scrambled, though call the police if you want, but I'm not
staying here" and I leave and she follows me and at the corner
does a quick sketch of the men from memory, saying "The book's
last chapter is about people who aren't very original or odd as
individuals or necessarily sit with me well, but can still be considered interesting or odd as a group. Couple to crowd scenes, in
other words—the hardest to describe and draw."

The restaurant's a porno moviehouse for films about men for men. The nextdoor third floor apartment where Mary lived is now a massage parlor, the second floor where men or liberated women can come in to speak to "good female listeners without interruptions, depending if you're not seeking advice," and the top floor where four generations of Salamaggios lived together in one kitchen and toilet and six bedrooms is now a school for creative bellydancing, mystical chanting and martial arts. The ground floor of her building is a padlocked grocery store, a sign on the window reading "Don't run! Fight back!! Gouging new landlords rents trying to force me to leave as they will the rest of you clean decent Hells Kitchen oldtimers & residents!!! Diverse as we are we got to unite!!!!" and it gives the time, place and church address of a meeting last week.

"I know that church," Mary says. "The minister was Mister Goodguy and murdered by a burglar. They got a new one and she started performing far-out musical extravaganzas and homosexual marriages. Timon was once a flowergirl at one of them. And that grocery store owner always gave us credit and wouldn't carry cigarettes and cashed all our checks. Everytime I come back to this neighborhood I feel how good it was for us and I get sorry I left."

We go to a restaurant-bar opposite Lincoln Center and sit at the counter and order blue cheeseburgers and beers and watch thousands of opera, music and dance fans, or whatever they were playing at those places tonight, pour out of the three houses at once. Hundreds wait for the light to change and then cross the street and seem to be heading straight for here. "Oh my god," Mary shouts, spitting out most of her first bite. She jumps off the stool and rushes with the cheeseburger to the door, catching two very dignified smartly dressed men as they're about to leave. Howls all around. Incredible surprise. What's new? Where have you been? You look great. So do you. So do you. One could be her lover. Or ex-lover she still loves. The way they look at one another: the tall bearded man. Or someone she knows and would like to have as her lover. Or maybe he's her husband with a beard now and the other is one of the aforementioned men. She hugs and kisses the taller man and shakes the other man's hand. The taller man points to the shorter man and she hugs and kisses him and shakes the taller man's hand. Then the two men shake hands and hug and kiss each other's cheek and Mary claps their backs with both hands. It's a big joke. Another lively round of kissing, hugging, shaking of hands. The headwaiter and tons of incoming people join in and grin and chortle and shake hands and clap backs. But her cheeseburger. I don't see it. She couldn't have eaten it. Maybe it's on the floor getting trampled by all that flurry and joy. I turn away and watch the Lincoln Center fountain erupt and retract. The Met's lights flicked off. The Philharmonic Hall's. Lastly the State Theater's and the promenade's practically clear. A bicyclist. Two fountainphiles. An old man in a motorized wheelchair being helped and joggled downstairs.

"This seat taken?" someone says and I say "Sorry, yes it is" or was that "'tis"? and then "Taken . . . Taken . . ." to several other people who pull out or put their hand on Mary's longlegged seat. Finally to one I add "By a talking dog."

"That so?" she says, resentfully, and I realize the mistake I might have made in that unintentional vulgar usage of the word dog and I say "By a real Kerry blue terrier, I mean, not l'femme. Or rather, some breed of retriever who's out talking and walking itself now. His name is Fleur-de-lis."

"Fleur de-lis, no less," she says, a skep, and I say "Yes, how did you know? And for a five spot I can get him to say 'Howdy-do, ma'am' and 'How's tricks?' to you and shake your hand and for ten he'll tell you your horoscope or read your feces or the hand it shakes, depending on what's your divining inclinations, preferences or delights."

"I saw the movie," she says. "Myrna Loy, am I right? Though I suppose the talking dog bit will always be good for a few yucks at bars," and she finds a seat somewhere else.

Mary returns, perhaps to pick up the check and her burnoose and leave with one or both of the men. Has happened. Not unanticipated. I'm ready. I'd have another beer, wonder about her somewhat wistfully and go home alone. But the men hail a cab and get in it, the taller one with Mary's cheeseburger sticking out of his mouth. Mary sits and says "Bert, the bearded of the two, was my favorite literature professor at Hunter. He changed my life with what he taught me and also saw in my critical and creative work and became one of my closest friends."

"You were an English major?"

"Then? An American minor. But you know what Bert said to me just now? He said—"

"Let me guess. Bert said 'Munch minch monch mmm mm' right after he bit into but before he engorged part of your blue burger."

"He's lean but gluttonous. Never approach him with any of your edibles hanging out. But he said 'Where'd you pick up that stunning-looking young stud, Emmy, or is that Myles transfiguratively unhirsuted for you?' "

"He called you Emmy? Why I ought to knock that block's prof off I oughta."

"And I liked what he said. Hear that? He has good taste and it pleased me. He was the only one except my mom who said Myles was all wrong for me and I shouldn't marry him, which took guts, though she said it because we were too young. P.S. His friend Sidney only said ho-hum to your good looks and thought you too tattered, sallowed, older than you looked from too much tippling and being prematurely bald. Sidney's a doctor and maybe was upset by Bert's attention to you, but he said he likes hair. You know, I've a great idea."

"You do? About my hair? Let's hear it. But hold on." We're getting along. I order another blue cheeseburger and French fries and beers. If we were loving lovers, now'd be the time to touch.

"In Tunis, Harriet was always playing practical jokes. Without letup to all the English-speaking people on the lane. And then first time I see her back here she pulls another one on me, so I'd like to play one back on her. What do you say? One that won't end her practical joking days forever but will let her know what a good one feels like. We'll collaborate. Think."

We think. Beers arrive. Burger. So quick. "You sure this was cooked especially for us?" I ask the bartender. "And well-done rare?" To Mary "Truthfully, I find I kind of like the joke Harriet played on you tonight."

"Point is she's been getting off way too easily all these years. Just one. It's never been done successfully to her, she's said, and I feel now's the time. Come on. Think."

Think. Think. "Let's write a note and slip it under her door tonight that says I tried to rape you."

"Great."

"Or something like that."

"No, it's great. What else, and how?"

"You came up to my apartment for what you truly believed would be coffee or tea. I made a pass. You politely resisted. I wouldn't hear of it and tried to force you onto my bed. You said 'Come on, Newt, joke's over. I have to go.' I went crazy and ripped off a lot of your clothing and ruined your best Tunisian smock and you actually had to tear a gash in my cheek and pull my hair back to get me off you and then kick me in the groin a few times before I let you go. Then, when I was on one knee hurting like hell from your kicks down there—"

"No knee."

"—I said I was sorry and that I'd never done anything coming even close to this before and I got out of your way and you left."

"Paper? Pen?" I produce them. She writes the note. "Don't correct any of my spelling, as Harriet knows I can't spell a damn." The note approximates what I said: Apartment. For coffee. Pass. "I said no thanks and that I wanted to go. He grabbed me. I said 'Hey, baby, lay off.' He said he couldn't hear me and pushed. I pushed him back." Ripped off her burnoose. "It's the only good piece of clothing I own." Most of her clothing underneath. Gash on my cheek. Bruises on my shoulders and arms and a bump on her head. "That idiot even tried bending my ears back to a convex shape." I ought to be locked up. She could press charges and still might. "He definitely needs to see a psychiatrist or head specialist of some kind. Skinner and slideshows of naked ladies and lassies in erotic positions coinciding with electric cattle prods on his balls and thighs comes to mind." Christ, she still can't get over it. Will probably always be shaken by the image of it. She was trying to joke it away before but she's really never experienced anything as ugly and frightening in her life. And she almost gave in to me because she thought I might beat her unconscious and then, when I was trying to get in her, accidentally tear her crotch. "I'm sure you didn't plan any of this (of course you didn't, though you know what I mean). But after knowing him for so long you should have been able to see something was very strange or wrong about him with women and so you never should have arranged this *date*. Because your Newt or Newton or whatever the fuck you want to call Cousin Creep is dangerous and insane."

"Done." Signs it Em. "But if I slip it under her door, then I can't sleep there tonight. I was supposed to stay over and go movieing with Harriet tomorrow afternoon."

"Stay at my place. I live right around the block from her."

"All right."

"Only thing is, I just have one big bed."

"I'll find room."

"It's a highriser. Really like a queensize double bed with an uncomfortable crack down the middle separating the single marriages. Mattresses."

"If you have a sleeping bag for the floor, I can always take that. Did you go over the note?"

"Read it. Very juicy. Not at all unlike me. Ruddy complexion and repelling profile—you caught it all. And ample amount of misspellings and grammatical errors. She'll never think I had a hand in writing it. And she'll believe what it says because it's from you and written well and what's said about me is so improbable that it's almost got to be believed. I don't know what I'm saying. But I think Harriet will fall."

We pay up, walk the ten blocks to Harriet's building. Mary doesn't say "I think I'll tear up the note." Or "Do you think we should tear up the note?" Or "It's too dirty a trick on her. I'm going to forget the note and sleep over at Harriet's after all." I'd feelings she'd say those. She doesn't. We talk about museums and music, deafness and decibels, erasers and chalk and pounding the chalky erasers against schoolyard walls to get rid of the chalk, and the paucity of stores carrying real live fountain pen ink. On Columbus, down the block from Harriet's, I take her hand with the idea of pulling her to me and kissing her and she looks at me as if she wouldn't mind if I pulled her to me and kissed her if that's what I'm thinking and I pull her to me and kiss her and she kisses me back and we kiss.

"Hey, brother," a man in front of the corner bodega, "don't get your tongues tied too tight in knots too much or you're going to have to walk home that way." Someone with him slaps his hand, laughs. I wave to them from a kissing position.

"Ooo ooo ooo," the other man says. "Give it to him, mama. Harder. Hard."

"What time is it?" I ask her. We're still in the hug.

"Why do you want to know?"

"One day in the far future I just might have installed a steel plaque on the sidewalk where we're standing or on that building there if they won't let me install it here, saying that 'On this spot' or 'On the sidewalk over there,' depending where the plaque's installed, and I'll give the exact time and date and axial and terrestrial directions and polar coordinates of the place, 'Mary and Newt first smooched.'"

In Harriet's vestibule we ring someone else's bell to let ourselves in. As we climb the stairs a third floor tenant says from her dark apartment past two doorchains "Yes?"

"Harriet Leebers?"

"One flight up. Next time you lose her key or want to get in without her knowing, ring the top floor bells, not mine," and she slams the door.

Mary sticks the note under Harriet's door and we leave. In front of my building she says "My sewing machine. It's in my car. You think it'll get stolen?"

"I can never answer questions like that. It might, it mightn't. If it's old and unhidden or new and hidden or new and unhidden, the chances of my answering the question get better all the time."

Her car's blocks away. We get the sewing machine. Old heavy portable, difficult to carry without banging a welt into your leg, and I carry it to my apartment. "This is a dreadful place," Mary says. "Paint peeling from the ceiling to the point of perilousness. Barely any furniture but without the benefit of polished floors and orderliness to make it seem like a spare monk's spare flat. Bookless bookcase. Dingy windows with no view. Chair, table and bed. Two spoons—one for your table and another for tea. Refrigerator filled with moldy rolls and butter and wines and beer. No plants. Radioless no less. Urine in the toilet that's gone too long unflushed. Lights to go blind by. Though plenty of cold and closet space. You live like Cousin Creep. Maybe you will beat me senseless, try to take me overpoweringly if I for a moment get shy. I don't know if I'd give in if you tried. Take off your shirt and pants." I do. "As long as I'm here with my machine I might as well sew up your torn shirt sleeves and the hole beneath your fly."

She sews. I give her two more shirts and a pair of bluejeans and she sews up these holes too. I get some wine. We sit on the bed. I'm in a bathrobe, she takes off her burnoose. She says "You've a lot of gray hairs on your chest—more in proportion to the brown ones on your head or under your arm. Maybe you are older than you act and not premature as the doctor said."

We lie back on the bed. Our glasses of wine, resting on the mattress, spill. I put the empty glasses on the floor and spread out a towel on the wine stains. We lie back on the bed. I feel her through her clothes. She says "Pay attention to the little knolls, the pebbles on top. Some men like something more to hold on to and a fuller mouthful, but since I like to run, jump and dance around a lot I'm glad they're not."

I start to undress her. She says "I've a long crooked slit down my stomach that was made when I was too young to think of punishing myself like that. I usually only let a man look at it if he's both my husband and still nice to me after three years or in the pitch dark. Feel it first. It might bring you good luck. If you don't want to be with me after you feel, I'll accept it and either leave or shut off the lights or shut off the lights and say goodnight."

She says "Both our bodies are considerably hairy all over, so I'm not that initially embarrassed by my mass black patches with you as I have been with other men."

She says "Do you like women with large buttocks? Well I have them—that's obvious. They're in fact fat buttocks, but that's maybe more a matter of interpretation. If you don't like them or can't tolerate them then all I can say again is I'll shut off the lights and say goodnight, but it hardly seems worth leaving the apartment for."

"You know," she says as she's putting me inside her, "you don't have to make love with me tonight if you don't want. We can just talk. Or read to each other or to ourselves or just shut off the lights and go to sleep."

"No, I want to make love now."

She says "That was pretty good for an opening, don't you think? Now I'm tired. Could you shut off the light if you don't want to read? I wouldn't ask for any other reason but that it's on your side."

She gets up several times during the night to go to the bathroom and scrape the mold from my butter and bread to make a sandwich and to prepare powdered milk so it could be cold in the morning. When it's still dark out a storm starts. Lightning, thunder, a sharp rain. "What is it?" she shouts, jumping out of bed, running to the hallway, then to the bathroom. I say "Come in here, it's okay, get in bed." She curls up with me, says "I was having one of those knifemares you said you get every other week. Two young women. They looked like druggies. They cornered me in Harriet's lobby and pulled knives out and said they were going to cut me up. Then it started flashing and cracking outside the lobby and they turned to look at it and I grabbed one of their knives and the other one stuck me in the belly with hers and I woke up thinking my knifemare was real and I had this wound to close."

We watch the storm from the bed for a while. I pat her body, kiss her hands and face. She falls asleep. I fall asleep. Next day we have breakfast out, go to a few art museums across the park, later walk through the park, have lunch, ride the merry-go-round, watch the chess players, the ice skaters, she persuades me to get on the ice with her where she tries to teach me how to skate. Then around five, planning to spend the night at Mary's house upstate, we go to Harriet's to pick up Mary's overnight bag. We'd long given up that our note was ever taken seriously.

Harriet opens the door and says "You guys. Where the hell you been? Look at you, happy as larks. I was frantic with worry about Mary. I thought it was true. I was even crying. Juniper was convinced. I just called my mother about it and she said to hide the note in case this Mary does press charges. I've also called Myles, Mary's father, Myles' parents and a few of both your friends if they'd seen either of you, though I never told any of them what it was about. I thought Newt had temporarily skipped town out of remorse and guilt and I was too scared to think how hurt Mary might be. You're the older one, Newt, so you should have had more sense. I'm never fixing either of you up with anyone again."

Mary's daughter is giving a slumber party tonight so we have to pick her up. We drive to Myles' apartment on the East Side. Mary speaks into his building's intercom and Linetta comes down with Myles and Timon. Myles nods hello to Mary, then begins arguing with her about something. She looks down at the ground, doesn't say anything to him. He throws up his hands in disgust at her and stares at me in the car and kisses Linetta and says he'll see her next weekend and also this Wednesday for dinner and goes off by himself toward Fifth. Mary starts for the car, then runs after him and they begin speaking calmly this time.

Timon and Linetta walk to the doubleparked car. I say hello to them and seeing me at the wheel, Linetta says to Timon "Oh no, not another one—who's he? Anyway," to me, "I'm Linetta, not that you'll be around long enough to remember the name or at least get to use it much—Mary's daughter, but I guess you know who's she. And this is my brother Timon."

Myles leaves again for Fifth. Timon puts out his hand to me through the window and we shake and I say "I'm Newton" and Linetta says "Newton?" and Timon says to her "Don't be rude" and to his mother he says "See ya again, stranger," and he kisses the two of them goodbye. Linetta gets in back and Mary gets in the seat beside me and we drive off, Timon waving to us as we go, Mary wiping away tears as she looks back at him. I say "What happened?" and she says "Nothing, nothing, forget it" and Linetta cups her hands and says to the ceiling "Please, whoever thou art, get my family back together again so they can be together again because this is getting to be too hard on us and for her too sad."

Conclusions

Okay. We're finished, done. My head careens, heart flops. She clenches her teeth, whirls her back to me, says "Just go. Please? Will you leave?" I think of my brother's grave. Looking at her back: I don't know why the grave's what popped to mind. Where is it again? Oh yes. On Long Isle. Been a long time. Long time no see we used to say about other things, among other things. What it must look like now. Overgrown like my own head hair. "Then I'll go then," she says. Though go from her own house? Her small bright once rented recently bought old stucco house. Her child's inside. Her thirteen year old girl and two year old cat. Her furniture and diverse work appurtenants. Her dog, car and garden in back. All I got inside is half a dresser drawer I share with her sheeting and on the washstand my razor and tooth- and shaving brush. Though the garden's mine in the sense that I rended it from rubble and trash. And have been watering, weeding and singly though not exclusively tending it. Turnips. That's only one of some twenty roots and legumes I've planted there. White radishes another. Two rows of each plant and all ripe for picking now. In fact I've picked plenty. Pickled plenty also, since nobody here but me likes them cooked in any of the many ways I've learned to prepare them or even sliced thin into salads or cut in half and concaved with a cheese dip in them on a plate of mayonnaised kohlrabi and parsnip sticks and other hors d'oeuvres. "Boo, turnips and radishes," Linetta usually says. "You and your roots picturesquely heaped up to us in a thousand detestable ways," Mary's said. Mary's left. Her house, but temporarily she must have meant. But she's nowhere in sight and I want her to hug me as I hug her and

92

apologize. I think I know what I'll say. I'll blame my infantile egotistical outburst and attack on her on the book I've been reading which blames just about all of man's infantile egotistical outbursts and attacks, genocide or any otherwise, on his almost constant repressive fear of death. "Em?" I call into the house.

Linetta, looking like an old photo of her mother looking out of a similar livingroom window, looks out the window overlooking the screened-in porch. "Mom went through the house and out the back way in a tough."

"You mean a huff."

"No, she looked tough. I don't know what that is, your huff."

"Come on, you remember—to huff and to puff. And I think to huff is to puff, though to puff tougher than your ordinary puff. Huff. H-u-double-f. Something to do with loud empty threats or being vexed. Consult my new Third New International you use as a piano stool boost."

"I wouldn't use it for anything if you'd remove as you promised to the piano casters and their trays."

"For you I'll gouge out four holes in the floor or saw off a small part of each piano leg."

"You think you're funny but you're not. Just take off the casters and trays."

"You're right. I'm not. Or I wasn't. And I will." I blow her a kiss and go through the house and out the back way though not in a puff, huff or tough. Mary's not there. Her car and my garden are. This morning I manured it all. After that I tarred the entire roof because Mary, who's said she only fears death when she fears for her life from open heights, complained last night of leaks all over the top floor and not enough pots and jars to catch the interior drizzles and insomniac drop by drop drips. Early afternoon we took down the basement's false ceiling and denailed the now exposed beams so the room could ultimately become Linetta's TV and slumber party area and with a divider Mary's potting studio. Then I snapped the long wood slats in half with my shoes and the halves in threes and twos and made a couple dozen bundles of firewood from them which I stored under the front stairs. "A winter's supply of kindling, not firewood," Mary said when she saw it. "That, you and I still have to find and chop for the next national energy bind," affectionately compressing my cheeks between her thumbs and kissing my distended lips. I said "Sounds so much like children—kindling—but small-kinded children, kinda kind kindergartners kindling sounds like, wouldn't you kinda say? But wouldn't you kindly consent to our kinda kindling one another in your single kindred beds?" "Right now? We're both too grubby and bushed." We looked like bandits. Blue bandannas over our noses and mouths and knotted in back, her hats protecting our hair and foreheads, coal miner grime round our eyes. I said "That's good. It'll be like making love in the mud." We didn't. She wanted to shower and shave, then draw me drawing her in her new studio as she sat on her kiln in front of her old just hung self-portraits and with her feet on the potter's wheel. She went upstairs. I thinned out the rutabaga sprouts, went to the bathroom to wash. All steam. She was in the shower and she said sudsing her underarm hair "You know I like total privacy in here." "I only came in to wash." "You could have done that at the kitchen sink." "I don't want to dry myself off with a rancid dishcloth or paper towels and I also wanted to brush the basement muck from my mouth." Argument. It led to. My hostility. My scorn. My ego arrogance disguised by the humble role. Our arguments. Getting more numerous and humorless and much worse she also said. Her ex-husband. "You dislike Myles mainly because I was so committed to him and can't be that way with anyone again including you." "Kootchy kootchy koo with his Gucci Gucci shoes." "Dumbo." "You got me pegged." "At least he didn't bait and suffocate and pester me to death as you do. Now will you get out?" "Oh. The discussion's finished when you say it is. But I still think your attitude about having total privacy in here is unreasonably selfish considering the circumstances. After all, I busted my ass for you today." "Okay. You want to have it out, we will. But somewhere else after I finish my shower, as I don't want to slip and break my neck in the tub. And

I'll be swallowing none of your martyring. I don't want anyone fulfilling their life and focusing their needs and working out their inner conflicts and contradictions through me." I left. Out front I fumed. I kicked the wall. I threw over a lawn chair. She came downstairs and said she sensed tremendous tensions from me and was a little afraid of what I might do to her. I said don't be because I was all right and whatever tensions she sensed were all in her head. She said "But I can still feel and see it, so how could I be so wrong?" "You're not." "So why'd you say your tensions weren't there and try to make me seem like the crazy?" I said "Stuff it." She said "Well you're the one who forced this talk." I grabbed her upper arms. She screamed for me to let go. I would have but it seemed she'd swing at me first chance after I released her and I tightened my hold. She yelled "You know I can't stand being physically held down or back" and kicked and scratched at my chest and arms till she got free. I yelled "Selfishness, phoniness, woman of a hundred faces, fifty different voices, sometimes I hate your guts." "Good." Slap. "That's it. That is it," she said. "The windup for all time. Don't you ever touch me again. Never come near me. We're finito forever, brother. Tongue-tied and mad as Myles got he never hit me and in my whole life my folks never once even threatened me with their hands. We're finished, done."

I think of my brother's grave. Now it seems more logical why. Finito. Forever. Way out on the Island a hundred or so miles from here. Only routes over superhighways or a sluggish bus to the big city and from there a tedious train trip and long cab ride to the grave. I'd need a car. I don't have a car. She does. There it lies. Convertible, plucky VW, I'd wear the stylish shades she bought to modernize me, it's a sunny open-top day. But she'll never loan the car now. Earlier today she might have said "You betcha, lover, and if you want I'll come too. We'll make it a day. Late lunch, dusky swim, Linetta loves both those two shores." But that was then. Keys in the car: today she'd send the police after me. But I'd like to see the grave. Clean it up. Weed it. Its bills haven't been paid. If that goes on too long, do they remove the casket and monument and then fill in and re-use the grave? To leave several pebbles on the headstone as is our custom for all the times I've never been there. But no casket. He's not even down there. Binny went down in some ship never sighted again or found. Just a lifesaver with the name of the ship *Aerie* washed up on a Norwegian fjord beach. But my folks had the yews and stone planted with what words or word's on it again in parentheses under his name? *Inter Vivos* or *Nolle Prosequi* perhaps. *Causa Sui* comes to mind. But the exact birthdate and just the month and year of his death and at the foot of the grave a granite bench bearing the family name. Gravesite with enough plots to accommodate a soccer team and its water boy, my dad used to say. Though the folks, now dead, never made it there as was their express wish. No mystery. Died in a European car crash and soon after a bulldozer pushed the charred car off the narrow mountain pass into the unreachable ravine below. Thought the ashes had been removed. Mistakes are made. Many. Repeatedly. Mine with Mary before for example. Shouldn't have said what I said. Tongue-tie yourself, dumbo, I should have advised myself. She's still in mourning. Her mother dying. Saddest period in her life. Lots of ups and downs and backs and forths between us recently, but that's nothing new. Why the slap though? Trying out catharsis for size? Now it's done. Finito forever, brother. This time I don't think she'll come back as the five or six other times I'll remember and could relate. No hugs of renewal, teary regrets, subsequent sex to seal our bond. End to all our ends. But why twelve? I asked. My dad said "For your two brothers and sister and folks and anyone else in the clan like uncles and aunts or wives or your sister's husband if she can ever catch one and even old hobos if you meet them and I'm dead then who haven't a final rest home of their own."

"Em?" I shout. "You in there, Em?" Behind the garden and parking road is a state forest and a few feet inside it is a hikers' trail that continues for a thousand miles each way north and south. I choose right, her favorite direction for short walks, and hike along it for a while. If I see her I'll throw my arms out and apologize. I

don't want to leave. I'll even get down on my knees and rout out
a good cry. Real tears. I'll feel them too. I feel them now. She was
always moved by my tears and maybe the one thing I've held back
from her these two years is how easy it is for me to draw them up.
I smell wild onions. I see the sassafras tree I once hunted down and
made a medicinal tea for her out of its dried roots. Those are
trilliums. That's a scarlet tanager. Above it cumulonimbi. So why
can't I revive those words or that word again that describes my
brother's absence from his grave? *Dominus Litis* or something.
In Situ? I know it's not *In Absentia* and Benjamin was his real
given name. Our sis never made it to the site either. We donated
her to science, just as she'd instructed us, but were later told she
had no useful organs they could then use. Last time I saw her she
weighed fifty-five to sixty pounds the doctors said, though her
condition was too delicate to have that guess confirmed. "Why me,
Newt?" were her antepenultimate words to me and I said "We all
have bodies." Maureen. She was twenty-three. Died on her birthdate. "Full cycle," she said. We both broke down, she because of
her pain. "Order them to give me more morphine," and I left the
room. Nurse said she'd see what she could do. She went in. Doctors
and more nurses summoned on the double to Maureen's room.
Same thing to me: "Please do not go in there for the time being."
Then nurse came out and said "Your wife is dead." I said "My
sister." "Your sister?" "My baby sister." "Then I'm sorry, but your
sister is dead." "Did you kill her?" "Please, how can you say that?"
"I'm not blaming you. I only wish you would've let me be there
to hold her hand." That moment my folks stepped out of the
visitors' lounge and walked toward me in the hall.

I've walked and run about a quarter mile on this trail. A hiker
approaches. "Hi," she says.

"Hi, hiker," I say. "You perchance pass a young dark-haired
woman wearing a pair of white short shorts?"

"Five minutes ago, going the opposite way. She didn't look like
a hiker though."

"Her clothes?"

"Also no equipment and that face. So agitated and depressed. And walking too fast for a hiker and looking as if she wasn't going to stop unless she was tackled or till she dropped or fell. I asked her 'Anything the matter, honey?' and she said yes. 'Then anything I can do?' when she just kept on walking and she said 'No thanks but no.' Her exact words. Just now I was still trying to figure out what she might've meant. Something drastic must have happened to her. But now I've got to get moving again if I'm going to reach the Nyack hostel by dark."

"You'll make it. It's only four miles from here and you really seem to keep a brisk pace."

"I'm tired though." She goes. The sun is half past its downward phase. Looks like I'll never be able to catch up with Mary at the speed this woman said she was going, and the cemetery will be closed even if I did steal her car for the day. I could look at the grave from the road right outside the cemetery gates, but it isn't the same thing. I want to sit on the bench. Hold my head in my hands and maybe say some words. But why look or go? I don't pray and what words would I say? Oh father whose art is heaven?—no way. And there's nobody down there—not even a box. Be more sensible going to the ocean or even down to the wide river running past Mary's town. There's more where Binny might be than any gravesite. I return to the house. "Find Mom?" Linetta says.

"No. And I'm going now, sweetheart," I say.

"Does that mean I'll never see you again?"

"We'll see each other again. After the summer. Of course we will. Even if it's got to be just you and me." She's watching TV. An educational children's news and special events program where the kids who moderate and host the show speak mostly in a language where every vowel has before it the letter P. A child on the screen is talking in that language now. I don't understand much of it after overhearing it for about a year. Mary and Linetta have held long dinner conversations in it and wouldn't pass me the wine or bread till I asked for it in P. I kiss Linetta's head. She says "Gpopodbpype, Npewtpipe."

"Gpopodbpype, Lpinpettpa, and spee ypopu spoon. A little wrong, I know, but you know what I mean."

I leave the house and walk down to the river. I look at the river. I take my shoes and socks off and wade in the river. I take my shirt and pants off and jump in the river. I swim in the river. A man comes to the riverside and says "You can't swim in that river. One thing you're nude, other it's polluted."

"No it's not."

"But everybody knows it is. Scientific reports and studies both federal and state have declared it polluted. You can get sick with all sorts of microbic diseases from swimming there besides getting picked up by the police. You should come out right now."

"And you should come in here right now."

He walks away. I continue to dunk, splash and swim. I don't feel free of her yet but I at least feel refreshed.

Newt Likes the House Neat

Newt's coming today. I'm looking forward to it in a way. He likes the house neat. I don't like the house neat. Newt does, gets excited if it's not. Not excited but what? Bit nervous and agitated and even mean. He's peculiar like that. Sees dust, he sees death, but okay Newt my man, house neat? neat house you'll get.

I start cleaning the house. Not a job I like to do in any room after so much schooling work. Where's Linetta? "Hey you little daughter of a bitch, where the hell are you? Come on down here if you're here and help me clean the place because Newt's coming today and I just got home and I'm beat and he likes the house peepot clean."

Probably in her room, door closed, consumed in a book. I go upstairs. She's not there. On a blackboard in the kitchen downstairs is a message which says "Daddy came early. You'll probably search for me before you find this. Till Sunday. L."

I finish cleaning the house. Rub here, scrub there, mop the floors, get rid of all the dust balls, find things, put away things, that's the way he likes things, though I don't touch Linetta's room. I'm being too kind to him but have to if for anything then for what I'm going to tell him which is going to make him sad or mad. Which do I predict? Both and more.

I hear him coming up the porch steps. He's always got packages. "Hello," he says, "anyone home?" He likes to be greeted generously so I go to the door with my arms wide and big smile, though it's not how I feel now, and long kiss on his lips which he likes to be greeted with best. His arms still hold his packages and weekend valise, so they can't get around me though they seem to want to. He gets an erection on contact. Sometimes he says "Linetta here?" and if I say her father's picked her up or she's over a friend's house for the night, he says "Can we go upstairs then? I'm really feeling like it, are you?" Most times I don't feel that way so soon after I see him and lately not even the first night I'm with him. But today when he asks I suddenly do and can't explain it after all my planning, but I don't want to as what I have to say to him has to come first.

"Too bad. I'm really feeling like it. I've missed you all week."

"And I've missed you. Not all week but one of those days and a few minutes this afternoon."

"Then let's go upstairs."

"I can't right now."

"Period? Just starting, or that yeast infection?"

"No. I'm all right down there. Everything's healthy and perfect."

"Or you might just not want to. I can understand that and won't go into it. I don't like trying to encourage you and you don't too. Though I read, just in the newspaper coming up, which I dumped at the bus stop so I can't quote it exactly, an interview with a new Broadway star who said every woman likes to be taken occasionally if you do it gently. I don't believe it and don't want to force you into anything either. I'll settle for another one of these," and sticks out his lips.

We kiss. He still holds the packages and valise. "I wonder," he says, "no disparagement or underestimation intended to any group, if he also meant every lesbian occasionally likes to be taken by a second lesbian but gently, or just the more feminine of the two wants to, if they still take those roles."

"I think the interviewer twisted what he said or the actor's actually very stupid. Put the packages down so you can hold me or let's go inside. I'm getting cold."

"By the way, this one's for you," handing me a bag. "It's running shoes."

"You already gave me a pair."

"Not running shoes then. Open it."

It's a book. Roget's Thesaurus.

"It's a new edition. Just came out and I thought you could use it and in hardcover. I bought one for me too."

"Thanks. It's very nice."

"Very romantic also. All the words for love and sex and endearment and relationship and so forth. I wanted a new one for relationship that the previous thesauruses didn't have and thought it'd be in here. They had plenty but not anything I want. Assemblage, affinity, rapport, proximity, connection, concernment, liaison, union. I think union's the best of the bunch though it still seems there isn't a right word. One's all I'm asking for, so I won't have to sound silly to myself saying it, because relationship as a loving or longtime union between two people who aren't married but go through most of the same enjoyments and troubles of such just doesn't work."

"And the other bag?"

"For Linetta and you." Dozen or so bagels smelling of every kind.

"Thanks. She'll appreciate them, even if you again mixed the garlic and onion ones with the cinnamon-raisins. I'll freeze half."

"They're still warm as my dad used to say when he brought them home but only from the Lower East Side where they made them then, but warm solely from being under my coat, not a half hour out of their special stoves. I love you, Mary."

"And me too for you, Newt, so?"

"So is there a reason why you won't tell me why we can't go upstairs?"

"There's no reason and I'm going to tell you."

"You want to tell me after?"

"I have to tell you before because there might not be an after."

"I don't like the tone or coloration of that. May I see your tongue?"

"Why?"

"To see what color it is."

"I'm well and if I show it to you here it'll just be the color of night."

"Maybe it glows. Show it."

I stick out my tongue.

"I can't see it too well." Puts his eyes nearer to my tongue. Sticks his tongue on it. "My tongue has multisensory reception. Your tongue," he says in a way that I can barely understand him because he's saying all this with his tongue sticking out, "is the color of love."

"And yours of manure. I've never seen you," I say, same way, barely understandable, because my tongue's touching his, "so loving as you are tonight."

"What?"

I take my tongue away. "I've—"

"Don't do that. Put it back. Bad luck. Nobody's broken our wish yet."

I keep my tongue in my mouth. "Usually you're just sexy or grumpy when you first get here, probably from the bumpy or fumy busride. But tonight—what is it with you?"

His is still out. "Miss you. Kiss you. Wish you. Thought about you. Every day this week. Twice, thrice, per. Fumy ride up too."

"Sorry again but I haven't you except for those few minutes today which was about some money I forgot to repay you, and that one night."

"Nice thoughts? Tongue thoughts?"

"Please put your tongue in. You're making yourself unnecessarily feeble and gross. You're in fact making fun of an afflicted group or two talking that way."

I push his tongue into his mouth. He licks my fingers but mostly the top of the bagel bag they hold, puts down the valise, holds me while I can't him because I've got the heavy bags now and says "Nice thoughts? Tongue thoughts?"

"That night nice thoughts. Thought of you and those same fingers you licked masturbated me with you in mind."

"What night?"

"It was actually the other hand. The bagel bag hand is the left."

"Maybe it was the same night I masturbated to you and same exact time too. That would say something about our synonym."

"I don't remember which night."

"Mine was Wednesday. Flute and harpsichord music on the one radio station I listen to later at night, so during their chamber hour, eleven to twelve. I know it wasn't yesterday, and Tuesday was a late movie, as I don't like to the night before I see you."

"Mine was earlier in the week, long before eleven, and we don't pick up your radio station here."

"I did it to a photo of you. I wish I had a nude picture of you to masturbate to rather than that photomachine one with you collared up to your ears and most of your head capped. But it still had your mouth and I masturbated to that."

"Let's stop this. It's not exciting or interesting me and we have to talk."

"Sounds serious."

"Is."

"It's going to queer our whole evening, I can tell."

"Might. And also the weekend. Depends how you take it and then how I take the way you take it and so on. Come inside."

We sit on the couch. He takes off his coat and says "I've a feeling this is like so many of the domestic movies I used to see when I was ten or so where the wife— They were always married, happy and childless and a few years younger than us. And it came at the best or worst possible of times in their life. But she tells him, usually over the dinner table, whispers into his ear so we won't hear, often when he's carving a turkey and wearing a tie—"

"It's true. I am. I wish you hadn't guessed or led up to it that way."

"I didn't know, honestly. Just was going along with the seriousness of it, experiencing it, no, that's not it. Though you know what the hero also then said? 'Pickles, ice cream, do you want some?'

No, that was later when they were in bed, kitchen all cleaned, she'd wake him and he'd say—"

Tears are in his eyes.

"I mean she'd say 'Darling.' 'Yes?' he'd say. 'This might sound odd to you in the middle of the night—' "

He looks so seriously sad, his eyes, face, color, tears dropping off his cheeks, voice about to choke.

" 'Darling,' she'd say and in these movies I'd wish it was me. This darling, turkey carver, tie wearer, though I was only ten then or the most thirteen. But looking forward to when it'd be me, that's what has to be it. 'This might sound funny and odd or whatever,' she'd say. 'Yes?' he'd say— Oh my darling Mary, what do you want to do? Because I know what I want from you."

"Finish off what she wants in bed, then we'll talk seriously."

"I'm not talking seriously?"

"You are but what does she say? Just to get it out of your system."

" 'Pickles and ice cream.' 'Together?' he says and she says 'Separately but at the same time. And we have none in the icebox so could you ask a neighbor or drive to the store?' 'At half past four?' So many of the movies did that. She never said she was pregnant till *The Moon Is Blue.* She only whispered in his ear. We in the audience knew. He'd smile so happily. What I'd do if my situation was his. Because I want to tell you something, Mary. I want it."

"I don't."

"Well I do and I'm going to fight for it."

"Tell me articulately—why would you?"

"Because I want a child. I've wanted one since I was ten."

"Then adopt one."

"Don't be malicious."

"But single men can adopt children these days. You'd have to make a better living and probably have to accept a male child of another race and probably one with problems too."

"I want your child—ours. I want it. I'm not going to take a no." He starts crying. Shakes his head almost violently. I don't know if to get the tears off his face because they're itching him, but they spatter me. I wipe them off. He's crying violently. I have to take him in my arms while he sobs. I don't have to but I do. It's what he'd do to me, for me, has done, most times, and what I want to do.

"There there," I say. "Poor little lovey. I know how you must feel. I once wanted a third child when Myles didn't want one too. Now I'm glad I didn't have it. You won't be glad I didn't want this one, but I can't just now. I have too many things to do. You don't have enough money. Babies cost thousands to produce. Where would we get it? Probably from my hospital insurance, but how would we take care of it and Linetta when I'm on leave? I have a job though I want to do other things besides teach. I'm repeating myself. I already raised two infants. They're not too many years from being totally on their own though in need of college money and two is enough for any woman. We met too late. We always come back to 'bad timing.' Maybe someday but you can't count on that with me. Come on, Newt, try to listen to this and understand me. I love you but I can't just now and no doubt never will."

"Think it over."

"I have. I'm just not committed completely to you. I don't live with you nor do I want to. We see each other weekends. We go away with each other for a couple weeks in the summer if we're lucky. I've never spent more than a month straight with you and you yourself said that time was hell."

"It was good."

"It was mostly hell."

"One thing I want to ask." He sits up straight, wipes his eyes. "Don't get mad. I'm not asking it to antagonize you. But it's important I know so I don't have to feel I'm making an ass of myself again. Please don't take it the wrong way."

"I do take it your wrong way and the fetus comes from you."

"It's big enough to be a fetus?"

"And have a heartbeat, though we can't hear it, about two months. I wanted to tell you when I was going for the first test, but we had an argument just before, so I didn't, then forgot to call you, then had another test to make sure. If it wasn't yours would you still want it?"

"No."

"And if I wanted it?"

"I'd ask you to abort it and then conceive just with me. I've always wanted to but never had the chance to make love just to conceive. I think that would be the most exciting freest kind. Or I'd tell you if you wanted to have it, this other fellow's baby—and I'm being honest now, seriously—then have it just with him."

"And if he didn't want to but I still wanted to have it?"

"Still, I want a baby only with you. I'd still want you to abort it and if you didn't want to, then I'd see you and take care of you best as I could but I'd be disappointed the whole time the baby wasn't mine."

"How would you treat it?"

"Is it mine or not?"

"It is. I have seen other men besides you, you know that, but haven't slept with anyone else for a long time. I've been too busy. Don't ask me how long but long enough. Where were we?"

"You were giving me reasons why you don't want to keep my fetus or have my baby. You never lived with me more than one hellish month and wouldn't want to bring up a baby without living with me and right now you don't want to live with me and besides that you don't want to have a baby now, feel you've had enough babies, have a lot more things and maybe even better to do than having babies, like changing professions, etcetera, and so on. It all makes sense."

"And I also couldn't afford to depend on you financially when I had the baby. You understand that also, no?"

"I do."

"Really?"

"I do, I do, I swear to you."

"So those are the main reasons. Besides being not psychologically prepared for it. I want to plan having my next child, if I ever do have another one, and if I do then as of this minute I'd want to have it strictly with you. You'd make a great parent and my children love you."

"I so much wanted to be that Joe in the picture."

"I know but don't go into it again."

"I won't. Okay. We'll do what you say. You don't want to have it, can't, all that, don't, and I'll be right beside you all the way."

"That's nice. That's sweet. That's more than those. I love you." I kiss him. "Do you mind the house is still a mess, much as I cleaned?"

"No."

"I wanted to really spiff it up for you like you've never seen it, maybe so to make nothing else upset you and because I know you hate it even a little dirty and disarranged, but I'm just not much of a cleaner."

"I think I'm a bit crazy my wanting things so clean and neat. But it's all right. Place looks nice."

"You're not crazy."

"I said 'a bit.' Maybe eccentric about it then. I always feel I can't get work done or feel comfortable in even a little formless disorder. Well I want to get rid of that trait and idea too." He takes his sweater off and throws it to the floor. He takes his shoes and socks off and his pants and throws them across the room. His pants land on the rocking chair and rock it. One shoe ends up standing against the wall. A sock lands on a lampshade and falls through it to the table. The cat at first jumped at these flying objects but ran out of the room when the shoes hit the wall. He empties the bagels on the couch. "Bagels don't have crumbs," he says, "so it's okay."

"But the couch has cat hair."

"True. Forgot. Disorderliness should only go so far. Eccentricness too or else I'll begin calling myself a bit crazy again." He puts the bagels back in the bag. "Like a bite?"

Gives me a bite, takes one himself. We sit there and chew our bites. We both swallow. He holds my hands. Kisses me. We kiss. Sticks his tongue in my mouth. We tongue, lick lips. He feels my breast. I feel his penis. As usual he's hard. As usual

I'm wet. We feel each other. "Sure Linetta's not around?"

"Sure."

I pull off his underpants. He's only recently taken to wearing them because I've told him without them his long pants begin to stink of piss. I take off my panties and leave on my shirt. "I didn't think I'd want to," I say.

"The couch is too narrow and full of cat hair."

I turn over the couch cushions but there's just as much cat hair there. He spreads out his sweater beneath him and we start doing it on the floor. Cat comes in and runs out again. Newt picks me up with him in me and bounces me up and down on him as he walks across the room and then leans me against the wall so he can rest.

"Put me down. You'll get a heart attack."

"No, I want to do it this way, it feels great."

"You're scaring me. We're going to fall."

"We won't and I'll hold you tight."

He bounces me up and down on him again. I feel like I'm floating in air. Bouncing in air then but as if I'm not even being held. I'm not holding on anymore. He is to me but so lightly I can barely feel his grip. He staggers, still in me, while he's grunting, looks around for a place to fall, falls on the couch as we're both coming and hits his head against its wood armrest and laughs though he hurts, while I'm still coming and safe on him and making my noise. Blood dribbles down from his forehead as he dribbles and then drops out of me.

"Let me take care of your head."

"No, it's okay. I want the scar."

"Don't be a fool and you're bleeding on my couch."

He presses into the cut with his underpants and the bleeding seems to stop. We sit on the couch kissing one another and me holding his penis and he the pants to his head. I hardly ever feel sexy after I come but this time I do. I take his free hand and rub it into my nipple. He kisses the other nipple but still holds the pants to his head. He often stays hard after we make love but usually not for very long and if he tries to have sex soon after the hardness always goes away. This time it doesn't. I get on top of him on the couch and stick him in me. I bounce up and down on him. Maybe I'll abort this way. That'd be a discharge he wouldn't expect and a mess he'd hate. No, it won't come out like that. And thinking about it I no longer feel like sex and get off him and lie on the floor and curl up with my body and cry. I do want to have your baby, I think. I want it more than I want anything except the health and love of my children and my not wanting to have another baby right now not even through you. I look up to tell him this but he's out of the room.

"Newt?"

"I'm upstairs washing my head."

"Need iodine?"

"Found it. It's stopped bleeding. I'm okay."

"Then you won't need stitches."

"It was crazy of us to start making it again when I was still holding the pants to my head."

"I didn't even think of it."

"Neither did I. That's good I guess. That we didn't think about anything else after all we spoke about just before. I love it that way when all we want to do is screw."

"Love and screw. That's us. Love and screw."

"Which one's me?"

"You know what I mean. We don't take things too seriously."

Newt has a dream the eve of the abortion. I don't dream about anything that night and am not frightened. It's around 3 A.M. when he sees or hears me come back to bed and he says "I had an interesting dream and don't want you to get upset if I tell it, so I'll just say I think it directly relates to the abortion."

"What is it?"

"We both go to a party on West End Avenue. An apartment house, number four-seventy, which is where my uncle and aunt and a couple of cousins lived years ago. We go to the front elevator, again where they lived. The operator takes us up. Several people ride up with us, all party dressed. It seems to be around Christmas, that type of holiday spirit and mood. Maybe even a tree in the lobby—I don't remember seeing one but I did smell pine. I ring the doorbell. We're both dressed up too. The hostess opens the door. She's excited to see us and is wearing flowing satin or silk to the floor. Very elegant, around my age, and I don't recognize her. But behind her, glass in hand and deep in a conversation, I see my brother Binny and yell to him 'Hey Bin.' We slap backs and shake hands and act as if he'd never gone down and hadn't been found, and he introduces us to his woman friend. I don't think this is important but the people who were in the elevator with us also came to the party. She's very heavy and doesn't pay any attention to us when we all sit on a marble bench in this room. I tell Binny you're pregnant and that like your first two, which I explain came from another man, you probably won't start showing till your sixth or seventh month. He says that's great, I should be very happy to have your child and that we seem like a compatible couple, and leans across me to pat your belly."

"I dislike it when men do that—pat a pregnant woman's belly."

"It's only a dream. His friend didn't show any reaction to my news. Want me to go on?"

"Go on."

"I sit and talk light stuff with Binny, his friend excluding herself from us, more fascinated with her shoes and the new people coming in. Then there's a commotion in the next room. I first sense it physically—a rumbling under my feet, a painting shaking—and next hear it, a loud group yell and lots of chatter. I ask Binny what's happening. He says 'Go see, I'll stay.' I go into the next room but am worried you'll become attracted to him while I'm away."

"I've other things to think about."

"In the next room are about twenty people looking out of what looks like the solarium windows of the hospital you're going to. My mother was once very sick in that hospital, so I know it has solariums on every floor, or did then, and I was born there too. Anyway, this room, a lot further down than that long elevator ride would indicate, overlooks the East River, which of course is the wrong one for West End Avenue, but it's only a dream."

"Only a dream."

"The early morning sun's on a spot out in the river some hundred feet from the building. The spot's very bright and glittery and about thirty feet around. In the dream I think this very spiritual-seeming spot is what's awing all of us watching it, when I see something in the middle of it struggling to get out. It's gray, almost like an octopus, but scaly and tentacleless, so no octopus, but it's a large sea creature of some sort and seems to be drowning, flapping its fins to keep its top part above water. Several frogmen are swimming out to it. They dive down and come up holding it under each fin and swim with it to the building right below where we're watching this from."

"Excuse me, but mind if I drop some crumbs on your bed?"

"You don't want me to go on?"

"Yes. I only want to know if you mind my dropping crumbs around. Unintentionally. I raided your icebox. Forget it. What happens next?"

"A trapdoor's pushed open in the middle of the floor. Then, when we're all standing around waiting for what will come out other than the frogman who opened the door and walked out first, several women in white dresses and white hairnets rush past us and say 'Make way, move aside,' things like that, pushing us away if we don't move quick enough."

"Nurses."

"A couple doctors in white smocks and masks too. They help the frogmen with this creature step out of whatever's below the door —I think I saw a flight of stairs and water. The creature's bigger than anyone in the room by about a head and is part sea animal, part human being. No legs—a long fish tail there, so it has to be held up as it can't stand—and fins instead of arms and it's oily and slopping wet. I get a glimpse of its face as the nurses usher it through the crowd. At first it's a scaly fixed fish face, like a Japanese painted kite of one, and then it's Binny's face and he turns his head to give me a big wink as he's dragged away. I run to the next room to tell you what I saw. You're not there. Nor are Binny and his friend. Party's still going on as if nothing had just happened and I leave. I didn't take the elevator or don't remember because next thing I know I'm on the street. It's on top of a steep hill, apartment buildings on both sides, no moving cars or people around, when I hear a noise near me. It's Linetta, looking around eight or nine and inching towards me on a skateboard. She says 'Want me to show you a few wheely tricks?' and does a number of skateboard stunts, jumping on and off the sidewalk on it, three hundred sixty degree turns. I say 'Real nice but isn't it a bit late for you to be out?' She says 'Yeah, I better get home, see ya,' and skates off. I say 'Need me to walk you?' but she just skates down the hill, looking lonely, stopping here and there to do her tricks. I start walking the other way to someplace, turning around every few seconds to watch Linetta gradually disappear from my view. Then the dream ends or my remembrance of it does."

"All very significant and not difficult to interpret if someone wanted to."

"Does it bother you, this dream?"

"Yes, but I'm glad you told it, more for you than me. Now I want to get some more sleep."

It's still dark in his room. I find his hand to hold, the pillow for my head, when he says "I said I'd never ask this again but I have to take that chance."

"The answer is I don't want to."

"Let me ask it, Mary. We can still have the baby. I'll be a beautiful father. You said so yourself. We'll support each other in every way. Emotionally, lovingly, financially, whatever. Half and half. Much more than half on my part if it comes to that. It'll be unlike most adults with their child. In everything with it including its first two years. We can get married."

"I don't want to."

"I want to marry you, Mary. I'll live where you like. Up there where you are, fine. Of course that's nothing new. I've told you and you don't want to, any of those. Baby, house, marriage, my living with you, at least not now you've said. Maybe not ever you've said. But I had to ask one more time. I want it. Please."

"I only want to have the abortion at noon."

"Then I won't mention it again."

We go to the hospital at nine. I check in, pay the bill, am taken to my room. It overlooks the East River and is a few stories up. With me are three other women, only one with a man. A second woman talks a lot on the phone to a man. She keeps saying "Why can't you—I have to have you here. I need you, you bastard. Go eat shit then. I never want to see you again." Then she warms to him: "I love you, sure . . . Always . . . Sweetheart, remember that time when you said . . . That's right, in bed, in Cannes . . . I'm sorry and you're right. I said I could do it myself and I can."

The third woman, more a child, sixteen at the most, is with her mother, who's brought along chocolates, sandwiches and fruit. They talk in whispers and never look at the rest of us. They seem poor. She's the first one to be put on a stretcher and rolled out of the room.

The woman and man have matching wedding rings. He's very matter-of-fact, so's she, as if they've done this a couple of times before. We smile at each other but don't say much. He tells her he called home, the children had a good breakfast and got off to school on their own and want him to later phone them after she's had the abortion so they'll know how she is. Then he looks at his watch, says he'll be back at three or four to pick her up, says "Want this?" she says "No, I have my book," he puts the newspaper in his attaché case, kisses her and goes to the door. She blows him a kiss, says "It'll be all right, don't worry."

"I'm not. Do I look worried? I'm not," and leaves.

I'm the last to go, maybe because I was the last to check in. Though we were all scheduled to arrive at nine, the rest of them got to the hospital an hour or more before. Newt holds my wrists and hands. The nurses come and go, ask questions, close the cur-

tains, give me the urinal, tell me I should have an enema, I lie and
say I made at home. Then I'm put on a stretcher and rolled out
of the room and Newt walks alongside me to the elevator.

"I'll be here when you come back," he says.

"Don't hang around. Go out for lunch."

"I will."

We wave goodbye to each other. He's very sad and I'm not. He
never puts up much of a front and neither do I. The elevator goes
up. I'm rolled into a room, put on a table and meet my doctor for
the first time. He says "Hi, I'm Dr. Jacobs, your doctor today.
You're going to be fine. I've done this a thousand and one times
before and my patients never even got anything so bad as a hem-
orrhage from it. Now breathe easy." He takes my pulse, someone
else sticks a needle in my arm and I wake up in the recovery room.

"You're terrific," the nurse says there. "All your friends downstairs were wheeled back to the room unconscious. Feel good?
Then let's start the short trip home."

That night when Newt drives me back upstate I tell him he was
wonderful and if there ever was a reason I'd want to have a baby
with him someday, it was the way he handled the whole situation
and especially today.

"I'm still sad over it but that's natural and I'll be okay."

"I'm sorry," I say.

It begins to snow when we get a little past the city line. A couple
inches have fallen by the time we get home. The house is cold. A
friend's put some food on the stove. Linetta's written a message
on the blackboard saying "Dad's picked me up. Thank you Newt
for phoning me before. I love you loads mom and glad you're OK."

I tell Newt I'm tired and want to go right to bed. He says "Want
me to sleep somewhere else tonight? Another room?"

"No. Come to bed when you feel like it. I think we should talk
about this some more but not tonight."

"We'll talk about it when you like."

I drop my clothes on the bedroom floor. He picks them up,

smells them, puts the smelly ones, I suppose, in the hamper, folds the skirt and puts it on the dresser. I get in bed.

"I'm too tired to even cover myself," I say. "Still too weak maybe. Goodnight." He covers me, puts an extra blanket over me and massages my neck.

"Too tired for even that, lovey," I say.

He smooths my hair back, bends over behind me and kisses my head. I take his hand. He stays bent over me and I put his hand to my lips and kiss it and keep holding it. The light's still on and he's stroking my cheek with his other hand as I fall asleep.

The
Franklin Stove

My story's burning. As I write this. Just a short manuscript. I looked at the first page of this first draft of a story and thought no, this will only be another one I'll keep in a box by my typewriter for about a year and look at from time to time but never rewrite and later stick in my file cabinet with about a hundred more. I always thought I'd take one out of the box or cabinet one day and get an idea for it and rewrite it or just sit down without any idea of even rereading it and finish it and it would turn out to be a story I like and maybe as good as any I've written. This one might have. It's still burning. I threw it in the stove only a few seconds before I started writing this.

A certain amount of time's elapsed. About two minutes since I threw the story in the stove and fifteen minutes since I came into this studio after breakfast, did fifty pushups to immediately get warm and started the stove to stay warm while I wrote. But about a minute ago I opened the door on the Franklin stove to retrieve my story, with the idea of blowing or stamping out the fire, rewriting the burnt parts from memory if I could and putting the story in the box with the other first drafts I might one day rewrite. But too late. Already burnt. Too far back in the stove to poke up front and save even a page of. Mostly ashes. Now while I watch it burn it becomes all ashes. Black clouds. Lit city. Burning city. Burnt unlit city on a starlit night. Stars gone. Sky demooned. Black alligators crawling out of swamp mud on an eclipsed starlightless night.

And now I'm miffed at myself for burning it. I always wanted to destroy at least one story. I've spoken to writers who've burnt the only draft of a novel or sheaf of poems and they said it freed them somehow. This one didn't me. My file cabinet's in the city. So I should have, for lack of a much older story, combed through the box for the story I liked least instead of grabbing the last story I put on top. And now I forget what page one and the rest of it's about if I'm to rewrite it and possibly get a better story than the one I burnt—a finished story, one to send around. A story that would dash my dumps and lift my spirits a bit and maybe even make me ecstatic as some of my finished stories have and in fact could only have been written because I burnt the previous piece.

So what happened in that burnt story? I don't write from notes. I go right into a story once I begin it, finishing the first draft in a single stint. But I can't think of anything but the first word of the story: The. But so many of them have started off with that. The what? The boy? Man? The lit city burns? The black ashes disintegrate? The story's gone? The Franklin story burnt my stove? The quick Franklin stove jumped over the foxless story? I slam the stove door shut. I throw my typewriter through the window in a crazed state of dejectedness. Of course I don't. Too cold to break windows and I'm still typing on this. And what would I say to the director of this colony? "I tripped rearwards through the window while excitedly typing the final line of a new draft"? "Were you hurt?" he'd ask, scanning me worriedly, "or any damage to your work?" Always so much forgiveness and bigness and forbearance to the artist here, which I think is overgenerous humaneness to the humanities and possibly even pity for its practitioners and can't take. "Stand on your own twos," I like to urge myself. "Tell the truth." So I'd explain "It was really a chipmunk who jumped through the window to get at the sandwich on my desk. I'd opened my lunchpail three hours before noon. Most mornings I finish off my two sandwiches by the time I get to the studio. And he didn't see the pane. Chipmunks are notoriously jumpy and strabismic and walleyed. To make amends I'll take care of his medical bills if he isn't covered and see that his winter granaries are filled if he has to be hospitalized for a long time." But start the story. Forgot the line and plot, show you're a pro and think up new ones. A story, to really make up for the destroyed one, that would have in it the burning and writer's reasons why and subsequent regret and dejection and then that he couldn't recall any of the story line. I can title it "The Burning Story" or just "The" for the only word I can remember in its right place in the destroyed story and also as a sort of testimonial to that article or adverb that's begun so many of my stories and titles. I'll even put in the chipmunk jumping through the window and possibly getting hospitalized. The ashes, images of singed cities, dawdling alligators, starlit eclipsed nights. But start it before you get too tired typing what you plan to put in. There was a story. (This is the story.) Rather: My story's burning. And the title before you forget it.

The

The story's burning. It's in the Franklin stove. It was in a box. The box is on my desk. I'm sitting at the desk next to the stove. I'm at an artists' colony. In a studio in the woods. Woods on the colony's grounds. Grounds in upper New York State, etcetera: America, Earth, Universe, and I came to this studio from the main building they call the Mansion where I had breakfast at eight. Time now is nine. It's actually ten after, but nine rhymes with time. So I must have sat at the desk a few minutes after I lit the stove, read the first pages of the top story in the box and remembered it was about a man who returns to his native city and rings the doorbell of his parents' flat whom he hasn't seen in ten years —his parents, their flat too. Maybe even their dog. No dog. Too many dogs in the city as it is.

But the story's coming back. In the original he rings the downstairs bell to their apartment. A voice says "Yes?" and he says his name over the intercom to his mother whom he hasn't seen, spoken or written to in twenty years.

"Hank who? I don't know any Hank." He says "Maybe you won't

know me, and sorry for the surprise. I'm your boy from way back. Hank B. Stritin, or Stritinitinvitivitivitch before it was changed." She says "Henry? Oh my god" and there's this mad scramble—no, mad scramble came when she ran downstairs—a noise, like a lamp crashing, something breakable breaking—and he says "Mom, you okay?"

Footsteps. Hers? Or his dad's. One of them scrambling downstairs. Then through the vestibule door he sees her rounding the second flight—girdle, open housedress flowing, slippers slipping loose and preceding her downstairs. She trips on the last step, jumps up and opens the door and hugs him and bawls, head wedged under his chin, body growing limp, arms sliding off. He drops his knapsack and holds her, afraid she'll fall.

"Dad's dead, you know," she says. "We couldn't reach you. How could we? We started thinking you were maybe dead ten years ago and five years ago gave you up either way for hopelessly lost. What you put us through. If you ever came back, your father said to tell you to go hang."

"I'm sorry." Walking up with her he sees himself thirty or so years ago bounding up and down these stairs. Walloping the walls. Stick, bat or pencilcase slapping the balustrades. Singing. Whistling. Such a happy kid with his Indian whoops and war cries. "Hey shorty," a neighbor would shout, "you got a real sweet voice but someone in here can't stand canaries and also works the night shift."

Resting on the next landing because she's breathing uneasily, he asks after his sis. "Doing great. Two adorable babies, both twins. Fine intelligent provider of a husband, and resourceful to boot. Flushometer breaks, he climbs right in the toilet bowl. Car falls apart, he ends up a greaseface. Kids that bright and filthy too. Three year old one's my sweetheart. Naturally they're both three, but the second's not so keen on me and in fact beats a retreat each time she sees me and prefers her other grandma. She's Peony, my lovey's Penny. I'm always getting their names and looks mixed up, which can lead to loud screamfests when you rush up and try cuddling a girl who hates your guts. I've tried to get Ida to have one of the twins grow a mustache so I won't make those mistakes, but your sister can blow stacks too. But how are you? You look like I feel. Bald also, but you were fast losing that straw when we last saw you, which was how long ago? Seems like 1919. Remember? 'Folks, I'm driving my honey across country and will be back in a month.' You dropped us a card from Wyoming. 'Having a ball,' you said. Then another from Wyoming, sent the next day but arrived the same. First card a closeup of a monkey on a bronco horse. Second of the same rodeo scene taken from faroff so we could also see the crowded bleachers, and the message 'Still having a ball.' I remember your father saying 'Got a good memory, your son. Remembers what message he wrote the day before and also his address.' I still have them. Magnets hold those cards to the inside of the kitchen cabinet above the phone. Same black and white Scotties you used to get mesmerized with endlessly as a boy. They made them toys well then. In a Fabulous Forties antique store down the street they sell that pair for twelve dollars, so when things really get sticky for me economically those'll be the first of my holdings to go."

They go in the apartment. No new furniture and all in the same spots. Bedroom, livingroom, bathroom and that's it except for a walk-in closet and pullman kitchenette. Folks slept on the convertible for twenty years behind a Chinese screen. View through caged windows now of caged rear windows of other brownstones and ailanthus trees covered by tent caterpillar canopies. He sits.

"Sleepy? I'll make you coffee. . . . Then soothing spiked tea." Can't drink. Too tired. She makes up a bed for him in the bedroom. Ida and he slept in these twin beds. Then Ida got too woolly and bumpy to undress in front of him, so he had to cover his eyes and turn over or sleep in the walk-in closet. When he still couldn't stop peeking, she moved in with an aunt. His mother comes in.

"Just give me a brief rundown on what's gone on with you for the past two centuries and I'll never busybody you about it again."

"Married, assaulted and battered, jailed and unmarried,

drafted, wounded and deserted in war, worked on a number of assembly lines and produced two more marriages and boys. Then started writing at night to pay alimonies and child supports, and so impressive were the number of stories and novels I sold that I got loads of selling jobs in department stores, working myself up to phone orders and 'Hello, Little Kids Shop, Nom de Magasin speaking.' But seems I lost my memory somewhere along there. Because of reading books, I always wanted to grow up a siblingless orphan. Or to be a foundling left on a rector's step or a tot gobbled up by the woods and raised by wolves. Childhood fantasy finally fulfilled in middle age when I walked into the woods, stuck a rattle in my mouth and went waa waa till wolves devoured me. No I did. Cannot tell a fib. After you and Pop it was skunks who brung me up, Ma. I don't know why I never contacted you. Thought I had. Once from Wyoming. Then another from Wyoming. Both picture posts but I thought better than no photos at all. Plain unvarnished truth is that the first day I reached the West Coast I fell asleep for twenty years. Woke up last week and asked who I am and how come I have such a long beard? So I shaved and bathed, mooched enough loot to bus and subway to the address on my old draft card and here I am, wit as a riddle and right as a slum. Forgiven?"

She tucked him in. He had a bad dream. Something about a beard strangling him to death. What happened next? Forget. Should have read the story through before chucking it in the stove. But something about a Henry, a Hank. Goes home. Long time no see mom. Girdled and housedressed, she falls down the stairs and lets him in. Plate-glass door breaks. Nah. She's stoned. Nope. He's. Nuh. Holds and hugs her as she cries "Dad died. We tried to reach you. I had to take care of him alone the last five years. Bet you had lots of fun though."

Walk upstairs. She mumbles. He says "You've addled since I last saw you." She says "And you look younger. Living the soft life I guess. Off women and their brats I bet. You were always no good. That's what Dad used to say and at first I objected, saying 'Hank's okay. Not the refined English frog by any means, but don't make him worse with your blames and insults.' Later I had to agree. Bike thieving. Car stealing. Pickpocketing relief people and batting old hags to the ground for their handbags. And no grades in school and relieving yourself in church hallways and Jewish shuls and all the teachers and shopkeepers and girls' parents phoning us about how you tried pinning their Mary Ellens and Sues to jump and hump on and force to screw. Lucky for them they combed your eyeballs with their fingernails and kicked in your nuts. One didn't. Couldn't reach. Tinier than I am, that's why. Overpowered her, ya bastard, though without your father's good looks and charm. One time. Boom. More harm than an A-bomb. Marion Broombie, remember her? Son old as you were when you left."

"What's he called?"

"Henry. Big slap at you. Only other breathing creature named your name by people who knew or heard of you since you were three are their pet spiders and Venus's-flytraps. I can't stand the boy. Comes over here only to sponge off or torment me. Inherited your mean sneers and grubby ears. Told me if he ever sees you he'll kick the shit out of you for what you done to his mother and for the raw deal you did with him with your genes. Which reminds me. Know what your father's last words about you were? 'That stinking kid. You ever see him again, Kay, spit in both his eyes for me for all the crosses he caused us, you swear?' I told him 'You know I never swear, Hal,' and he said 'Then vow,' which I did."

Spits in his eye. "Thought it'd be bad luck and irreverent if I didn't. Now I got the other to do."

"Let me snooze first. I'm pooped."

Goes in his old room. Twin beds. One his sister slept in, other his. Used to watch her undress when she didn't know it, powder her puff and check her own breast rise. Knockout, his sis. Tried jumping her in her dreams once when her covers were off and sleepshirt wasn't working, but she screamed for the folks and his father beat his back bloody with a strap while his mother held him down. "That'll teach you," his father said, "or at least with her." Didn't. She got married soon after anyway and was in a plane crash coming home from her honeymoon. End of Ida. Now he's the only child. His mother comes in. Hot tea for both of them reeking of rum.

"How'd Dad die?"

"Young age. Everything functioning past perfection. Blood vessels so clear you could send salt shakers through. He died. What do you want to hear? That you weren't around to help out those last years? Even your rotten son came to the funeral. He, me, your Uncle Ted and two of your father's business cronies, Crazy Louie and Manny the Bum. At the cemetery it was only Henry the Second and I. Other three the limousine had to drop off for the eighth race at the Big A or they'd die. Your son. For one week he was a dreamboat, can't deny. Did all my shopping and talked to me till way late. Then my week's grace was up and he said 'Mourning period's over, Grandma,' and emptied my changepurse and fruitbowl and left. Last time I saw him was a month ago. Stopped by with his new young chippie. Cheap. Bleached. Bracelets up to her armpits and cheeks working on six gumsticks at once. You would've loved her. No better than his mom. Ah, Marion wasn't that bad. Goodlooker at least when you took her but now pussed out like a hag. Got married, you know. To a light heavyweight who beat the bags out of her morning and night. So she hit him with a hammer. Claw end square in the nog. He went down for the count of a million. Came home a cripple for nine years when he died. She took care of him good during that. Cleaning up his piss and shit. Spoonfeeding him baby food she made and mashed herself. It changed her life. Now she's working in a hospital as a nurse's aide. Night shift. Tough job. Very nice girl. Taking care of him wore her out. But she was guilty over it. She phoned once. I said 'You're killing yourself physically for that pig. If he deserved it, be another thing. Park him in an army nursing home for the duration of his war.' She hung up. Maybe I was wrong. But I felt pity for her. What's been with your last twenty-two years?"

Doorbell rings. She says "Don't tell me anything till I get back" and leaves the room. Loud voices, then someone rushing in. Young man. Looks just like Hank so who else could he be? Lamp in his hand. Raises it high and says "Crapper. I've been waiting for this. I knew you'd be back one day no matter what this old fart said."

But he talks too much. Still jawing on about how he's going to make mincemeat of Hank's head. Hank rolls out of bed and socks him in the nose. Splat. Everything goes. Kid drops to the floor cold. She's screaming. Hank wraps him in a blanket, drags him down the three flights of stairs and lays him out on the sidewalk next to the garbage cans. Police car's coming. Fast service. She must have called them. Policeman steps out. "Hey buddy, what you got there?"

"My son. Yapped back to his papa, so I gave him the ole heave-ho."

Policeman questions Hank and seems he knew him in school thirty years ago. "I thought you'd never come to any good."

"That's what my dad said and he's dead. But you're a cop now. Got your own car even. Big deal."

"Don't wise on me. I got the badge."

"Oh, the badge now, the badge. Stick that tip on another patsy. I was right in busting the kid's beak. Just as I'd be in breaking anyone's face who threatened me including the police."

Hank's handcuffed, sat in the car's rear seat. His mother's taking care of his son.

"Put him away for life," she says.

"Thanks, Mom," Hank says, "though you can be sure to your flophouse I'll never come back."

"Bastard," his son says.

"Oh, I'm the bastard?"

Ambulance comes. "I don't need no ambulance," his son tells the attendant.

"Any ambulance, you moron," Hank says, middle finger up to them as the car drives off. Then something happened. I forget. Car crash. His car crashing another police car going the wrong way. No, I'm only making that up now. And his son never came to the apartment either. Hank was lying in bed. And not such a tough guy either, nor his mom. She was asking him where he'd been the last twenty-two years, when the phone rang. "Excuse me," she said, went for it, returned. "You won't believe it but it's for you."

He picks up the receiver. "Hello?"

"Hankie?" It's a woman who says she knew him twenty-two years ago and a half hour before saw him walking up the block. She's taking care of her folks as she does once a week. Stays the entire day. Cleans, shops, sews, launders, cooks enough dishes for them for the week. "They're practically helpless now so I do about everything you can think of including bathing them and paying their bills. And after I wash a week's dishes and sit them in front of their favorite eight o'clock TV show, I kiss them goodbye and go home to my husband and son. But there I was. Staring out the window. Truthfully to distract myself from one of the hundred chores here today, when lo and behold. It's him. Spitting image of himself. Still the same tall handsome dark rangy rascal you were when I last saw you, though built even stronger and with longer curlier hair."

"Who is this?"

"Still don't know? You were my first lover, lover. Same place you're in now. Your folks were out. You conned me up. Though I knew what I was doing. And we shared a couple beers and then you stuck it in, you devil. Broke me good. I couldn't walk right for a week. We were thick lovers for a year after. You even gave me a heart for my neck. No initials or loving inscription, but inside was a set pearl. And every time one of our apartments was free, we'd make it like hogs. Bags we used then. What laughs when I'd help you put them on, though they stunk. You bought them by the gross and I don't know how many times you must've bought a gross. Three? Four? How many hundreds in a gross? You devil. Know my name by now?"

"No."

"Lie. You even once said you loved me. I finally tore that confession out of you soon before you left. Never saw you again. For years I asked your folks about you and they said for all they know, you died. Then five years ago your dad died. I loved that man. So smart, sweet and kind. I still see him sitting out in the sun. Bundled up. Fedora down. I used to wheel my dad over to him. We could've done that together if you'd've stuck around. Both of us wheeling our dads. Maybe on our dads' laps our kids—twins, one for each of theirs. But they'd talk. Politics. Economics. The old days and fulltime jobs after school till late when they were eight or nine and how they'd walk the five miles home from work to save the nickel trolley ride. But you devil. Come on now. Who am I? Could it be Marilyn?"

"Marilyn, Marilyn. No, no bell. We were once together though, right?"

"What about three hundred sixty-six times times once? And then double and triple that for all the nights, noons and afternights and very early in the days when you or I or both together couldn't wait. You broke me, you bastard. My gorgeous virginhood. Deflowered a prize flower—one that could've won best of entry awards worldwide. Tons of blood. We brought the sheets to a laundromat. Then you said 'Screw that' and trashed them and bought a new pair and we went back to put them on your bed. But instead went at it again and there was more blood and you said 'Now we've really done it, as I have no money for new sheets or even to clean these.' "

"I said that? Doesn't sound like me."

"Almost the exact words. I know. Diaries don't lie. I came across that scene a week ago when I was poring over my entire fifteenth year. Icy freezing February day it said. 'Deflowered when there are no flowers out by an amateur gardener name of H. Taken by a big boob with a small tube.' "

"Now I know you don't know me."

"Aha, got you in the heart then, right? Still the same egotistical heel you were at sixteen. But you know what we did with those sheets?"

"Oh yeah, the sheets. What?"

"We stole some newsstand coins, washed the sheets in the laundromat and put them back on the bed and then you started getting hot again. I said I was sorry but I hurt too much. All from my diary. You said 'But it's bad luck the first time not to do it at least three times in the same room on the same bed with the same guy on the same day. If you don't, your sex and reproductive life will be ruined for all time.' I didn't believe a word of it but said 'Okay, let's have another try at it. Maybe this time I'll feel a little something in there but a scrawny itch.' "

"Bull. I can tell by the way you're speaking of it, with whoever you first did it with, that it was great for you all those times too. But tell me more about those twenty-two years ago. It's interesting."

"So we did it again. Kissed. You showed me tricks. Then I showed you some I developed on my own on just that first day. We became lovers. Gross after gross. But we should've gotten warranties, because I had two abortions through you. Both up in the Bronx and butcher jobs. Phone calls from the corner booth nearby. 'You can come up now, babies,' telephone voice said. El train screeching by as she D and C'd. 'We gotta hold it, wait'll it passes,' she said, spoon between her teeth. Big butch. Room clean like a latrine. You squeezed my hand, more scared than me. Second time she sliced me like meat, but by then you'd disappeared. Okay okay. Long time ago. Since then I've married three times, got that one kid. According to your prognosis that first day, I should have by now nine and at least three thousand great comes. And I hate my third husband as much as I did my second and first. Even when he catches too few fish on a picnic day, he takes it out on me. And I thought, just for sentimental time's sake—hell, because I'm horny and want to get laid—if you knew of a spare bed with clean or bloody or just no sheets where we could have one more whirl around before I say goodbye or you do or whatever for forever for good. Right now, H. Your mother's there, send her away. Or ask her. She's cool and we're of age. So how about it—chicken or game?"

"Sure. Your talk's got me climbing the wall." Hangs up, tells his mother "A woman's stopping by who might be spending time in my room, okay?"

"That idiot from across the street? She could use it. And I like her. Takes care of her folks. And that sonofabitch husband of hers beats her silly I heard. Bet she still loves you. Play dumb and they always do. Well good for her, fine for you, okay by me, so I'll leave. I never cared for that huffing and puffing fanfare of two people renewed after twenty-two years."

Vestibule bell. He ticks back and lets her in. They shake hands. His mother says "It'd be nice to see you two settled already" and leaves.

They go in the bedroom. Marilyn says "Haven't much changed in the body, have I? Except about twenty poorly placed extra pounds and this wig."

"Look, I've had blackouts before. But far as I know I've never seen you nude or with your natural hair."

"You've seen me, darling. Think I'd get in bed with a perfect stranger? Oh, if he was perfect, maybe, but let's begin. Mind if I put my hair on the chair?"

Doorbell rings. Front door opens. Loud voices. "My husband," she says. "Lock the bedroom door. Long as he caught us we might as well try and get one good bang in."

No, doorbell doesn't ring. And I already had his mother leave the flat. She could've come back. Be sitting knitting in the living-room when bell rang. Husband, barges in. Kicks open the bedroom door when Marilyn's atop. "Hi dear," she says. "Home so soon from work?" Husband pulls a gun. Points it at her. She jumps out the window. Or Hank jumps, so it'll have to be the second or third floor, landing on an awning below. Naked and knocking on a garden apartment door. "Excuse me. You won't believe this." But Hank didn't go up that street. His mother's been dead for five years, father for thirty. Hank remembered him putting a shotgun in his mouth. Pow. Nothing left but the lips. No gun. They were in a car. Hank screamed. Father tried dodging a truck. No luck. No crash. They were on this same sidestreet. Hank's hand in his.

He was eight. Walking to his grade school his father also taught at. Telling Hank about the sun. Will eventually die as many stars have and all suns must. When wham. Car jumped the curb and came straight toward them. His father shoved him. That was the wham. Hank bouncing off an ash can. Too late for Dad. Saved Hank's life. But no curb or car smash. Father didn't save but did die. They were in a boat. Sunny beach day. Hank languidly steering with a twig in back while his father rowed. Motorboat coming too close with two skiers in tow. Father shouting for the boat to get away. Big splash and crump and his father flying through the air in a crash dive. Hank woke up ashore. Uncle pumping water from his lungs while his mother blew air in. He vomited back. Wiping it away she said "He couldn't've done that if he wasn't alive." "Dad?" he said. "He the shouting man with you in the boat?" "Yeah." "Then they think he died." "No." "Yes. They don't see how he could've survived." "Yes." "No. You got to start facing it, son: your dad done died when your boat capsized."

No, not in the boat either but a plane. Of course. That's where it took place. Father and Hank flying back to California where they'd gone to see his grandfolks. Sudden fluttering of cabin lights. "Captain to passenger area: got a small touch of turbulence up ahead for the next hundred miles." Bam. Minute later. Plane nose and mountaintop meeting face to face. Hank sole survivor. Also a girl and her doll for a while, dragging them from the flames and later burying them in a double grave. "Doll's name is Delilah," wrote in the snow. "Girl's about six and never said what was hers." Found his father up in a tree like a bat. "Hey Dad." No reply. Shook it. Came down on his head but seemed already dead. Buried him upsidedown where he fell. Nobody came to rescue him. And no more shoes, belts and briefcases to eat, he started consuming himself. Starvation is a loss of about one third normal body weight. Death when he's down to his last sixty pounds. Legs better, started crawling down from the wreckage site. Days later, sheepman found him. "Where's your kin, boy? They don't feed you so you run away? Don't you know you also need shelter and clothes?"

Rode him home on his horse. Sad tale: wife died at childbirth with their only son. So he raised Hank as his own. Hank was an orphan now anyway and always wanted to live and work on a ranch out West with his dad top ranch hand. Later went to college. Ran for Congress. Served in the Senate. Married a blueblood Blackfoot who gave him many moons and suns. Never happened. Hank walked up that street. Into his building. Mother answers. Slaps his face and slams the door. That's all. Goes downstairs and there's a man standing out front who says "Stritin?"

"I know you?"

"Sure: Tulie Moore. Geez if you haven't changed one bit. Still the spitting image of spit." Tells Hank what's happened around here the last twenty-two years. "Your dad died. Next your sis. Then your teenage sweetie Marilyn in a car crash with your bastard kid. And war, death, famine, etcet, though the ole block survived, now filled with litter and dog shit." No, there wasn't a Tulie or story or Franklin stove. I had nothing to burn. I've this manuscript now, but no stove to stick it in. I could throw it out the window. Because it's not exactly a piece of words that will help me change careers. Story starting off with a man who's written enough stories to file away about a hundred of them and burn one? A man, if I can recall, who's been writing them for twenty years, compared to the real life me who's only written this uncompleted one? If I had a Franklin stove I'd burn it. Not the stove, the story. Probably the studio also, because I don't know about working those stoves. In other words, if I'd been writing for twenty years or so, then I too would probably have by now produced a body of work that would make me eligible to get in that free artist colony upstate that a writer friend of mine was recently at and where among the many things they give you, besides elegant living and dining and a swimming pool, is a studio in the woods. But really in the woods. With foxy red foxes sometimes limping past the window his writing desk overlooked and plenty of morning rabbits and cute chipmunks always going chick chick and cack cack as they zigzagged around the colony grounds.

"Actually it's an artists' paradise, not a colony," my friend said. "Because you should have seen my studio. Cot. Old fashioned oak desk. Even clean blankets and a pillow and a Franklin stove." I asked what's that, "besides obviously being a stove, if it really is one." "Oh, it is one. Stove devised by our own Big Ben. And you run out of wood for it, just sign your name at the Mansion message table and lickety-split a pickup truck whips you up a woodbox more. Paradise, right? So I just spent my working day tending fire and fiction. Story I didn't like or inoperative page I'd typed both sides of, I'd throw in the stove." My friend running on about arting and this artistic paradise. He's where I mean who I got the idea to begin my story from. Maybe that's how it's sometimes done. See someone intriguing on the street or sadly trudging through a subway car dragging a dozen stuffed shopping bags: you write a story about them. Person you know well and talk to: better. Yourself: well I'm not so sure that's a good idea unless in the most objective and impersonal aspect possible. But then I met him. After Paradise. Subbing in the school where I teach science at. I was on hallway patrol and passing the room he was supposed to be teaching language arts in when I see him through the door window wrestling a girl to the floor. I ran in, pulled him off, her blouse torn and one of her clogs being hot-potatoed around the room and the class shouting "Rape! Rape!" Then as the girl's crying and this guy who I'd seen around and knew his name was Newt is explaining to me why he wrestled her to the floor—something about trying to disarm her when she instead of answering a grammar question pulled out a saber-toothed comb to scratch his eyeballs—a boy rushed him from behind with a wastepaper basket filled with books and smashed it on the back of his head. Bang. He went down. Class went wild. Jumping on desks and overturning chairs and flowerpots and running out of the room and down the hall, pounding on other class doors. I yelled "Everybody! Shut up and sit down!" and got on one knee. "Can you hear me, sir?" He wasn't dead but unconscious. The class was still uncontrollable. Other teachers came in and I grabbed the boy and girl and marched them to the dean of boys. As I was marching her to the dean of girls, the comb neatly back in her hair, she slammed her foot down on my toes and kneed me in the groin and ran past the uniformed guard to the street. "Hey you, girl," he said. She didn't belong in the school anyway we later learned. Came to sit with her lover, the boy who assaulted Newt. The guard finally got off the stool to help me but I said "Let me just rest here till the pain stops."

When I got back to the classroom the assistant principal already had an icepack on Newt's head and salts under his nose, which he kept pushing away because the smell was making him nauseous. Then an ambulance came. The hospital people thought he'd been stabbed and seemed a little put out that he hadn't been. An attendant said that Newt should at least get on the stretcher so they can take him in for x-rays for a possible fracture. "If you want to get accident leave or compensation, just going in for x-rays helps."

"It's okay," Newt said. "Just a little fracture. Probably just linear. That's me all over. No bother."

"Take him for tea at least," the AP said to me.

"I said it's okay," standing up, whole body buckling, what looked like sweat but I guess was the icepack seepage trickling down his neck.

"Hey," I said, "I get to get out of hall duty and you your class, so let's go."

We went to the teachers' cafeteria. I'd say that day we became not acquaintances but friends. I liked him right away. A funny guy and not much bushwa. Similar background. Same age about. Never married but said he now wants to be. Biggest difference between us was our life styles and work. He'd gone everywhere and done just about everything it seemed and not just on chartered teacher flights for Easter week in Crete, and at the time and now again was deadlocked in a love-hate relationship with this superenergetic and to me very beautiful divorcee who he calls La Mare that will surely in the end sink them both I think, but that's another story.

Because he was a sub, Tuesday through Thursday so the rest of the week he could just write, he had a rough time in school, while I at least knew how to handle a class and was the only teacher there who admitted I was in it as a career. Newt's students ran him ragged in figure eights. Never shut up or came to attention and threw things at him throughout the day. Once, for instance, he entered my class and his clothes were dripping red and blue and his hair covered with yellow and behind him a trail like a rainbow I was sure all the way to his art room and he said "What do you think of my new suit, Mr. G—bit too flashy?" and I laughed so hard in my chair that I fell backward and bumped my head on the blackboard. Incidents like that make for lasting friendships. I also invited him to our home for dinner a few times, with or without La Mare. Always lots of fun there too. But what happens? In a month he starts making it with my wife on the one weekday he doesn't sub or she nurse and both our kids are in preschool and I teach: Monday. It was also during the time he and La Mare had permanently split up for the third time in a year.

This May my wife even went to see him at that artists' paradise, where he'd gone a second time. Asked would I take care of the chickadees while she drove to the Cape for a much needed solitary rest. "Sure, anything you want, honeybun." Then surprised him in his mansion bedroom at one in the morn and stayed the weekend with him in his studio, which as far as paradisiacal taboos are concerned is comparable to defecating in the pool just before the colony's trustees are about to wade in. Still, my wife and I worked it out. How? First I had to learn of the affair. That took the type of initiative and curiosity I don't have. Newt avoided me when he returned from the colony and immediately started subbing somewhere else. When I told my wife this and how weird it was that he just left like that to an even worse school that he had to go to by subway while to mine he walked three blocks from his house, she told me why. I said "Guilt, huh?" and something like "Well, what is life anyway, dear? A lot of sadness and a lot of boredom and a lot of mistakes and a lot of fun. Also a lot of sleep" and I went to bed for three days. They went camping on Fire Island for two weeks. That was my suggestion. "Better you two see if you got something going besides sex," I told her. "If you do then maybe you belong together and I take or don't take the kids, dog, car, but definitely go my own way." What can I say? I might sound indifferent and cold. But my personal ethic is love but don't push it or try to figure out its mystery and you'll be a lot better off.

Though set for the worst, it worked out as I thought it might. I didn't pick Paris for them, that's for sure. Sun was too hot, tent like a furnace, almost no privacy or shade, flies in their food, dug clams condemned, beer and wine twice the price than on the mainland, they argued, felt like grubby hobos, barely screwed. Perfect. Ice cold showers to get the sand out of their ani and ears. Couldn't be better. She came back to me. Not so much to me, though eventually she did. Couple of months later I said "Is it all right?" and she said "Go ahead, I don't dislike him anymore" and I said "I never did" and she said "Well we all know what a prince you are" and I said "Who knows but you?" and called Newt and said "How's subbing?" and he said "Worse than it ever was anywhere" and I said "Look, don't be a dunce. The appointments secretary's crazy for you and I hold no grudges and my punches I don't even pull, so come on back and sub at my school, I could use some laughs" and he did.

In time I invited him for dinner too. Since then it's been like a ménage à trois without the trois person directly participating and he's also now more of a friend with my wife than not liking her or her him and so between them it kind of worked out too. My wife and I are again pretty close and she says if she ever does take another lover she'll tell me this time or at least soon as she can without aborting the new relationship and Newt's back with La Mare and for the time being they seem tighter than tight too. But all this is getting away from the Franklin stove. As I said, he's who I got the idea from. And this story would also be thrown in the stove if that stove was here or I was in that paradise studio and had the stove to throw the story in. Though if I was there, this wouldn't be my first story, or it could be. I could be a novelist. Three under my belt, up there to write or revise a fourth novel when I get an idea for my first short story. So I write the first draft, don't like it and throw it in the stove. But would a novelist do that with his first story? Doubt it. But enough fantasies. Just finish the draft of this one, put it away and maybe go over it with the idea of making a final version of it another day.

Dear?

That was my wife. Just got home. Mary I'll call her, to save her face. She works Saturdays in a hospital as a registered nurse. Three nights a week also and one other day. She's in the next room. Our kids are outside with the sitter.

"Dear?" Mary again.

"I'll be out in a second, love." That was me.

"What are you doing?"

"Writing a story."

"I can hear it. Never heard you typing so fast. What kind of story?" All this from the next room.

"Short story."

"Short sad story to our creditors or fake short story to pay a million bills?"

"Fiction. First time. I'm really only trying."

"You? Fiction? Let me read it?"

"Let me finish it."

"Then you'll let me read it?"

"How was work?"

"You didn't answer me."

"Yes I'll let you read it if I don't throw it away or burn it in a Franklin stove."

"What kind of stove?"

"The stove that could have been in the studio at that paradisiacal colony you and Newt were at last May."

"Newt who or just who this Newt?"

"Don't try and pull the wool, dear."

"What do you mean?"

That's where my story should end. End: "What do you mean?"

Bringing us right back to the beginning. Or this is where the story should begin. She comes into the room.

She comes in the room.

But she does come in the room. She's standing behind me. Over my shoulders. She gets a chair behind me and tries standing on my shoulders so I can write while she's standing on my shoulders that she's standing on my shoulders, but she can't. She doesn't fall. Just gets down. Slides away the chair. She wants me to stop writing. She's come from a tough day and long week at work she says. She wants a little play too. She's tugging at my erm. Tht's why the tupings all messed up. She's saying #Some on, finish that story, I want to heve a lirrle fun too, im tired. Leta8f go to bed." "What kind of fun can we have in bed if you're tired?" I say. "And how do they correspond: fun and bed? Or tiredness and fun?" "They correspond through love letters," she says. "Très touching. You go to bed and I'll join you. In your dreams. Right now I don't want to finish but begin a story. I have the first line. Your walking in here gave it to me. I suppose that's also how it's sometimes done. 'She comes into the room.' That's the first line. And I'm going to call you Mary in the story." "But my name is Mary," she says. "I'll call you Mary nevertheless." "Mary Never Theless?" tuggink on my arm agaon frying to gew me awry from this typewriter. I'm joined to it though. It's a new experience. My first extramarital affair. I like it. She can't draw us apart. "Don't make me abort," I say. "You had one, I can have one too." I was only able to get Newt and her apart by putting them together in sandland for two straight weeks. She reads that. "What do you mean Newt and I together for two weeks? Who's this Newt? Somebody I'd like? Who'd go for me? You going to fix me up? That'd be a nice change." "You were in love with him." "Was I?" "You admitted making love to him behind my back you she-eviltress." "Did I? Am I?" "When I was teaching and Newt was separated from his La Mare and subbing in school but not on the one weekday you weren't nursing then and the children were at nursery or postnursery or preschool or whatever that kind of school for posttoddlers is called—writers know the words of things, the names of things and how and where to use them and how to fool around with them to make even more use of them and and—and then what?" I'm no longer saying these things to her but just writing what I think I'd say and while she's reading them. "He'd come here and you'd go to bed with him in our bed and make lovely love and noises with him I suppose and fell in love with him you never said but I suspect and he with you too though he never said but because you're lovely and make noises and lovely love so I suppose and then you brought it out when I didn't suspect it and I suggested you two go off together but not Paris, etcetera—I didn't suggest you not go to Paris but didn't suggest it either, but it's all in this piece."

"Show it to me."

"Part of it you're reading. The part you haven't read and the part I haven't written you'll get after I finish."

"Then you won't burn it in your Franklin stove?"

"Oh, you now remember the stove."

"You only spoke or wrote or spoke-wrote about that stove a couple of minutes ago. Don't you remember?"

She takes off her clothes. Nurses don't have much on. Maybe some do. No, some definitely do. Some of Mary's colleagues say for possible rape protection they wear lots of underwear and body-hose or both under their white pants suits. But not my gal. Panties. With holes in them. Sheer where you can see her hair through. Shoes and stockings already off in the next room. Likes to patter around the apartment barefoot. Sits on my lap. She's making it quite tough for me to tupe. Again: misepllings, typogripical eras, wife in my xlap. In my lap I mean. Slip of the slip that one. Her slip also on the floor. Unbuttoning my shirt.

"I am unbuttoning his shirt, folks," she says.

"Hey," she says, "this is like being on radio."

Sticks her tongue in my ear. "Or on TV," she says. "Candid Chimera. Or one of those vinegar verite flicks. This is a cinema cerite story. No, can't be. Your typogryphical eras are making me say things I never said. A verite story. A veritable verite story. A veridical verifiable verisimilous veristic—"

"Why are you looking up those words in the dictionary under veri to put in my mouth?" she says. "You know I don't speak like that. You know nobody does. Maybe some people, but we don't know them. Me, I'm plain-speaking." Mary. My wife. Unbuttoning my life. Shirt unbuttoned: kissing my globes, my lobes. Taking off my tie.

"You don't even own a tie," I say.

"I said it, not he," she says. "Or him," she says.

"Ho ho ho hum," I say.

"I said that too, chief," she says. "You know I said thief," she says.

Nibbling my shoulderblade. Licking my chest. Sucking my nips. Making me want to leave the typewriter to go to bed with her in this room. Or to the floor on her slip. We're carpeted. Gift of the previous tenant who wanted to sell it to us but we told him to pick it up as we wouldn't pay a cent. But I won't go. I've a story to write. "One piece at a time," I actually say. And the first line of the story is "She comes into the room." Or "She comes in the room." "Which do you like?"

"Which one of what?" she says, lips on my eyelid giving me what she calls her butterfly kiss.

"Of opening lines."

"What are they?" Neck, nip and blade. Dezippering me. Feeling me. Playing with me. "Up Johnny up Johnny up Johnny whoops."

"Read the page. The two lines are on this page."

She reads while she continues to hold. "You mean between she comes in or into the room?"

"Those."

Opens her legs. "You want to do it here or there?" she says. "I can take you where I'm sitting right now. I've been thinking about doing it all day. All those patients. The old man. The one from two nights ago? Poor guy. Oh, now I'm turning myself off. Hot off. Well he talked about sex today. Suddenly he starts relating in detail about how great were those days with his wife and only up to a month before she died they used to do it all the time. Almost every day for forty years. And how they had the richest love and sex life creatable and how they first did it four times a night and then week after their honeymoon they broke it up into four times a day and then three and then two and over the years just once a day but that once, oh boy, he said. 'What we learned about sex in forty years couldn't be put in a book, which is why I'm telling you this, miss. So you'll know it can't be told,' he said, the old guy, this Mr. Stritin, a very nice man."

"Stritin? That's the main character's name in my piece."

"Because I spoke of him before. I had to. But I'll read it later. Anyway—is this talk making you less excitable? It's not for me anymore—just the reverse. He told me when they were past seventy they would take an hour or so to do it but they'd do it. If not an orgasm then for sure gobs of fun getting close to one, with all sorts of kissings and fondlings he said, and it made me think of you. Not your face. Your thing. Of this thing. This thing I hold here, folks. Of us. Of our doing it. Loving it. Of my munching and you mine and tonguing our hips and thighs and all the positions we do it in and all that we haven't tried and all the flawless highs I've had through you with it by you with it together. All that. And all day after I left Stritin—no, it was Silbit. Stritin was the old guy who was declared spontaneously remitted today and left the hospital singing and polkaing and carrying an open champagne bottle and attended by a multitude of children and grandchildren and friends, when we just about kissed him off forever two years ago. Well Silbit, not Stritin. He made me think of you and all we do and I've been thinking of it on the crosstown bus and then the number ten here and walking from the bus stop and seeing the kids on the street and not home I was so happy I gave them each and the sitter two bucks and told them to go to the movies and then another two bucks for the three of them to buy candy there, something I hate doing because of their teeth and because I know our kids are too young for the movies and will fall asleep there after they eat their sweets. But I wanted to be with you alone here and here I am with you alone and what are you doing with me alone but holding back from me when I want to do it so much, and all because of this piece you're writing. Well okay," she says, getting off me, "that the way you want it, dandy by me," and she slams the door and I write everything she said since she said "Well Silbit, not Stritin" or as best as I can remember it. And now I hear something behind me and it's she standing there when I didn't know she was there and for all I know she never left the room.

"I didn't."

And so she didn't. She was there all the time watching me write what she said. And now she pulls my chair back from the typewriter a few inches and sits on my lap again and is playing with me there again and she never had to unzip me as I never zipped myself up again and she has me going again and she's kissing me, as she sits on my lap facing me, and I'm leaning around her left side to type with one finger the rest of this and what she's doing to me now to make me stop typing. She is making me stop writing this story which isn't yet a story or whatever it isn't yet but which at least has a first line which is "She comes into the room" or "She comes in the room" or even "Mary comes in the room." "Which do you like best?" I say, all typed with one finger, Mary nude, Mary naked facing me, Mary holding herself up a ways so she can get me inside her, Mary sitting down on me again with me inside her, Mary bouncing up and down, Mary making noises. Mary's eyes closing. Mary's mouth opening. Mary bouncing harder and harder on me. "Mary Mary Mary," I say, her two hands on my shoulders as she goes up and down on me, "which do you like best: 'Mary comes into the room' or 'Mary comes in the room' or 'Mary came into the room' or 'She came in' or 'comes in' or 'comes into the room,' which?"

Em

So it happens again. Does it never end? "Dearest," she says, "I love you but feel I really need to be free and away from you for a while. I think we should part for two months." "Separate" was the word she used. "Maybe through June." That would make three. "Then we'll see." Telling me all this in my single room. She on the only chair, me sitting on the bed. Hands folded in my lap. I remember that. There's no reason I can see that I made those two sentences almost rhyme. The lap and the that. But there we were. Chair: bed. Two pieces of furniture existing opposite one another about four feet apart. Chair with its coat on, bed in its bathrobe. The chair had previously knocked. The bed said "Yes?" The coat said "It's me." He opened with glee. The rhyme there was done intentionally. All this taking place two nights ago. Last night was something else. But she knocked on the door. Waited for him to open it though she had her own set of his keys. They kissed. They pressed up tight. Me: she. He held her face in his hands. He was going to say "He held her face in his." Now he does. There's a long corridor from the front door to his room. Actually his flat has three rooms: small kitchen with a window, large bathroom with a chest of drawers and a window, each off the main room. But they walked through the corridor holding hands. He walked first. No reason except one of them has to as the corridor's too narrow for them to walk two abreast. But could it also be called a hallway? Or does a hallway, when it's in an apartment, only join up two or more rooms, while it's the corridor that connects the apartment building's public hallway to get to the interior of the flat?

But let me get on. They go in the room. He says "It's been too

142

long." They last saw each other the night before. They'd gone to
a party. She lives thirty miles upstate, teaches in a high school,
lives with one of her two children in the community she teaches
English in. They'd met five months ago and have gone together
since. Many times he stayed at her house for an extended weekend
or week. He can stay that long, as his rent and expenses are cheap
and for income he subs when he wants to in a New York City
junior high school. He didn't go back with her the night of the
party as he had a nine o'clock appointment the following morning
with a New York internist. She was coming in the next night
anyhow to see her family therapist. She's presently breaking up
with her husband. No, they're separated, been separated for almost a year, and once a month they meet with the therapist to
discuss such things as how they can make their separation easier
for each other and their children and to resolve problems revolving around money, mutual property and support and custody of
the children. He's not sure if that's why they meet. She's told me
several times, but on the subject of her husband, therapist and
child custody and support I look at her interestedly but don't listen
well. Anyway: she'd pick him up after her session. One or the
other of them would drive her car to her place upstate. Usually he
drove. He was the better driver. That's not why. "A better driver,"
he once told her, "is one who directs almost his entire attention
to his driving, and unless it pertains to his driving performance,
disregards most of what's occurring in the car." So she was there.
They are there. "It's not that I don't love you or love you any less
that I don't look at you when I talk," he thinks he said that same
time in her car, "but because I think it best for both of us if I give
my full vision to the road." They walk through what I'll be a little
perverse about now and settle on as the passageway. But I've done
that move. Done their sitting on the chair and bed, she in her coat,
he the bathrobe. She came earlier than he expected, so though he
had his things packed to leave, he was still reading in his robe on
the bed. The only other furniture in the room is a night table with
a lamp on it by the bed and an end table next to the easy chair (if

it was by the bed it'd be a night table) with a lamp on it and soon a bottle of beer. Neither of them smoke. So there'll be no smoking or sharing of an ashtray or lighting or putting out matches and cigarettes. The coat speaks: There's something I want to tell you.

The bathrobe replies: It's obvious you got something bothering your mind.

The chair: It is?

The bed: I don't want to be sidetracking you, but you seem a little depressed yet anxious—

She: I am.

He: I was going to say "anxious to get it out, to tell me."

Mary: Well I am depressed, though not anxious to tell you what's causing it.

Newt: Just say it. Everything now hurts.

Ms. Em: I can't just come out with it outright.

Mr. TS to his friends: Want me to say what I think it is for you?

My stringbean casserole: No.

The man she once said he'd have to guess or figure out why she semioccasionally likes to refer to him as her prince of priests: I mean say for you what I think it is?

Darling Diana Monkey: Don't worry, I'll shpill. By the way, what the doctor say about your back today?

Dearest Douroucouli: I knew I shouldn't have sidetracked you. And I didn't go to today's doc for my back. That's what I saw yesterday's osteopath for and he went snappery crack with my neck, shoulders and back and fixed me up one through Z. Want a beer?

The coat nods. The bathrobe gets off the bed and goes to the kitchen for a beer. Or the bathrobe got off the bed and went into the kitchen for a beer. Or the bathrobe goes into the kitchen for a beer. Or the bathrobe got off the bed and in the kitchen got a beer. Or the bathrobe gets a beer. Or the bathrobe got a beer in the kitchen. Or in the kitchen the bathrobe gets a beer. Or the bathrobe, in the kitchen, got a beer. Or after the bathrobe got off the bed and went into the kitchen or just got off the bed or just went into the kitchen, it opened the refrigerator for a beer or got a beer out of the refrigerator or got a beer. Or the bathrobe went (goes) into (in) the kitchen (and), got (gets) a beer out of (from) the refrigerator (icebox) and yelled (yells) "I've also some ale ("I've also some ale.")."

The coat says "Beer, dear." That rhyme was unintentional on my part. I mean that out of the many remarks I've written so far that are free renderings or near, or maybe for some of the shorter statements exact quotes (my memory of things said isn't the equiv-alent of photographic of things read), that last one is the only one I'm sure of that was just as the person said it. He said "Beer, dear?" He also said "You're a poet and you don't even know it." "Yes I do," she said. "If you say you do then you do," he said, "but I think I'll have an ale." She said "What?" and he said "Nothing, I was only talking to myself out loud. I said I think I'll have an ale instead of a beer. Actually, I said if you think you're a poet then you are one, but I'm going to have an ale. Actually, I didn't even say that but something pretty close to it." "Oh," she said, another exact photo-graphic equivalent, and unless there's an important reason I see for citing another one, which is not to say that this one was impor-tant, which is not to say it wasn't, the last I'll name. He sticks his head past the kitchen entrance (there's no door to the kitchen, which is why I call it an entrance, though I suppose it could just as accurately be called a doorway since I don't think a doorway has to have a door on it to be considered one) and said "Like some-thing to eat?" "Will you please?" she said, beckoning him back into the room and with the same finger pointing to the bed. "Right," I said.

He opens the bottle of beer and with the other end of the church key, the can of ale, and goes into what I'll from now on call the livingroom. He sits on the bed, leans forward to hand her the beer (I can't be exact about any of these actions, as my memory of movements and especially gestures and expressions made is even less the equivalent of photographic of things read to things said. Though I can say that if he did give her the beer without his standing up again and moving a step or more toward her, he would have had to lean forward if she at the time didn't lean forward to take the beer out of his hand or stand up and move a step or more toward him while he was still sitting on the bed holding the beer, neither of which he thinks she did), sits back on the bed (he also can't recall just coming back into the livingroom and handing her the beer before he sat down), drinks some ale (he's simply assuming he did, since it's what he thinks he'd normally do before he set a can of ale down), sets the can on the floor (he'd have to do that to fold his hands in his lap, which is the one action out of all that went on there then that he almost definitely remembers doing: perhaps it's almost always, when he can get his hands free, part of his listening pose when he's not only preparing to look at someone interestedly but to listen well), folds his hands in his lap (I don't like confusing things even more than maybe they already are in this long sentence with its many parentheses, and which I no doubt did even more so by saying before that I don't want to confuse things even more, and now even more so with that last phrase explaining the first one and then this third one explaining the second, but if the night table had been on the side of the bed he sat on, he probably would have put his ale on it instead of on the floor) and looks at her and waits.

They'd planned to bike around the Benelux countries this summer and he now questioned her about it and she said she still wanted to go but he said "No, I'm sure that's off" and she said "Maybe we should cancel it then if that's how you feel" and he said "Me? How I feel?" but he said he would, since he was the one who put the deposit down for both of them on the flight, as she was going to pay the balance of the fare when the charter company asked for it in June.

It's now April.

She said she knows she's being a big jerk about the whole thing and was thinking today how she could really be blowing a good relationship with him by her actions, but he must see by now how much she needs to have the freedom she doesn't, and not because

of him, have with him or has had with any man since she left Myles
and which she can almost say she almost never had with Myles
either, and he said he understands.

"And I do love you, my toots sweet, and you're the most understanding man I've ever known in this way and the more I talk with
you the more understanding you seem to be to me and so the more
I love you and think of you as my azygous toots sweet however
regrettable or unintelligible or whatever able or ible you said that
endearment sounded like to you. And I do think if we stayed
together we could go on ento uternity as you once said and which
is still to me too construable to fully understand, but I don't like
that feeling about myself that right from Myles I jumped to someone else who I loved and who I can say truly busted my cherry as
we diddled jills used to say before we became janes but who never
really satisfied me no matter how contradictory those two statements might seem to you said successively like that. And then
three days after him I started in with someone else who satisfied
me even less, and this has nothing to do with sex, than the previous
man or Myles did during the last months of our marriage, but who
I also thought I loved and then to you without even a week's
breather from the man after the man after Myles after sixteen
years," and he said "I think I understand."

"There's really nothing about you I don't like" and he satisfied
her in every imaginable way "and it's never been anything with
anyone anywhere anytime as it has been with you in bed or wherever we did it—"

"On the floor one time," he said, "standing up."

"You caught me unawares."

"You mean I caught your unawares."

"You what?"

"Or your unawares unawares when you also weren't aware you
weren't wearing your underwear."

"My what?"

"I'm not quite sure. But it still sounds like a passable depiction
of both the act and place of contact and even our correlative parts

we made contact and then concurrence with, though I'm not quite sure as I said and have said so many times about so many things I've said so many times."

"I'm shtill shtumped."

The fact is she was in his livingroom slipping on her shirt when he caught her unawares unawares, or to be more direct without rebeginning this set, happened upon her with her body bent slightly forward over the bed spreading her shirt out so she could more easily slip it over her head when he etched in behind her, both naked from at least the waist down, and suddenly he was erect and within when all he intended with his caress was to put his arms around her chest and kiss her neck, and it was morning, a Sunday, shortly after they'd shared one of his Instant Dairy Screams as she liked to call his invariable daily breakfast mixture of creamed cottage cheese, wheat flakes and grated fruit and were planning to bike to Prospect Park and had only been done making love some twenty minutes before during some song to God and Earth and Praise the choir of the church a few backyards away had sung. Let me also say, concerning that time, that they both on their individual quake gauges registered their highest readings than with anyone else before, and it was so accidental. A fluke, she said. Whatever wit was, he said. Whatever what weans, she said. When they both thought they were through conjoining for the morning, he thinks she said, or at least neither thought the other wasn't. And let me say they've tried reduplicating those sussulta-tory shocks as she called them, on other mornings and afternoons and evenings, he standing up and she leaning over the bed though without their going through the prelims of planning a bike hike or spreading a shirt out or sharing his IDS or winding up making love shortly before—the initial intercourse as essential foreplay, as one of them put it—the absence of all or some or one of these conceivably accounting for their failure to not only reproduce even once that so far inimitable exquisite physical thrill at the end but of even coming close to matching the memorable intensifica-tion or the dizzying alignment of their respective connective parts during the act, which could also be the single or principal or contributory reason for their repeated failures. But let me finally say that this has all been said, over and over and over again.

But that was that day some two or so months ago, but two days ago the coat sat huddled up in the chair and the bathrobe was taking another swig from its ale. Or at least he's assuming it took a swig. But the coat said. But I forget what the coat said. But the bathrobe said to the coat in response to what I forget the coat said "Well do what you want, as whatever you decide on I'll go along with you and without any big emotional scene or difficulties to you either. If you don't know whether you want to go back to Myles or not, then maybe now, in the time you'll be by yourself—those two months you mentioned, the three months I refigured—the time you'll be away from me I mean but of course with your daughter. But if you asked me what I think about your going back to Myles, I'd say, if you asked me right now that is, as I don't know what I'd say if you asked me a minute from now, although I might say the same thing I'd say right now, word for word even, though I'm sure that would be less apt to happen than my saying the same general thing in different words. Anyway, what was I saying? I was about to say what I'd say to you if you asked me what I think about your going back to Myles, which is close to a minute after I would have answered you if I hadn't gone into that business about what I'd say a minute from now to the same question. Though if you did ask me now the same question that you might have a minute ago about your going back to Myles, and I didn't start speaking about what I'd say to the same question if you asked it a minute from now, then I'd say that I think a lot of things about your going back to Myles and many quite different from some of the other things, so what I really think about it would be unworthy of regard, of little interest and in the end counteractive to any decision you might hope to make with the help of what I'd say. That's what I'd say right now to that question. Now if you asked the same question a minute from now or even right now, which is about a minute from the time you hypothetically asked the question and I answered it, and I didn't start speaking about what I'd say to the same question a minute from now, if you asked that question right now, or two minutes from now if you asked it a minute from now, then I don't think I'd say anything much different from what I just said."

"But he's all wrong for me," she says. "I never got along with him. Well of course sometimes I did, but mostly never. Never is perhaps too expressive and confining a word. And expressive is perhaps too emphatic a word and confining not expressive enough. But maybe you get what I mean. His assessments of things are so different from mine. I don't even think I like him that much."

"Do what you want. But I make myself clear. I say I love you. That's not important. I give unequivocal evidence that I do. Our relationship's been a good one. We haven't fought once, and not because either of us isn't temperamental or holding back what we want to say. We just haven't. And I am temperamental, you are temperamental. We've been good for one another like that. I don't know what that means. Everything's been good. Let me think now. I've never seen another couple like us who kiss in the street and on stairs and in museums and restaurants and even between courses and during courses and between sips of wine or beer. Any drink. And maybe other couples do kiss between and during courses and even with forkfuls of food in their mouths. Or spoonfuls or even handfuls or at least one handful. And even male couples, female couples, and all over the world perhaps. In Vatican City. At the Londonderry barricades I bet. Even in foxholes. Even foxes, in or out of foxholes, theirs or anyone else's, including other foxes'. Even fox terriers and fox sparrows. All birds. Even pigeons. Especially pigeons. I've seen them pecking away at one another in the park. And on sidewalks and streets in New York and Vatican City and Londonderry and probably at or on the barricades there also and also in foxholes there if there aren't any foxes or fox terriers already there or wherever there are foxholes, barricades and pigeons. Not with forkfuls of food in their mouths, unless they're being force-fed, but possibly with some food. What I'm saying is all couples kiss, all sexes, all animals. Maybe even paramveciums too. I don't know. But if they do, then probably with some food in their mouths or with whatever they kiss with, though I'm sure none of it force-fed with a fork. In other words: everything. From fox moths to foxgloves and maybe bathrobes and beds too. Twin beds. Maybe they do kiss. In their own way. Even on the barricades, if that's what the barricades are partly made of and the beds are close enough. And coats and chairs too. Chairs on the barricades also and coats kissing one another in dark closets perhaps. Or maybe their best kissing's done when they're suddenly thrown together on beds. But I was talking about what a great couple we were. Maybe we'll be one again. But now you want to be off on your own for your version of a couple of months and where it might work out with your returning to the man who, one, right now you're quite sure doesn't want you back, and, two, who you don't even think you like that much and you almost never got along with and who you think is all wrong for you besides, which is three and probably four. Well fine. Settled. Now finish your beer and go."

"Don't be mean," the chair says, she does, Mary, Em, the coat.

"I said that last line about the beer and for you to go because I thought it would so melodramatico. But what I was really thinking is that what we both now might be thinking is that we could go to bed now and end it that way for a couple of months. Not to go to bed for a couple of months, as that would hardly allow you the time to be alone for your two months, but just once and until it ends or even before it ends, if that's what either of us wants, or until we want to get up to dress, if we undressed before we got or once we got to bed, or just to get up to straighten out our clothes, if we kept our clothes on in bed, if we even do it in bed, if we even go to bed, if we even do it. And then later you can leave with me accompanying you to your car, if you came by car."

"I didn't come by train."

"Then you're saying you had to have come by car?"

"I don't know about the bed idea, Newt."

"Bad idea my bed idea?"

"Linetta expects me home in an hour."

"You can call her up."

"You don't have a phone."

"We can go to the corner store."

"Once I get outside I'll want to drive straight home."

"Then it probably wasn't a good idea."

"It wasn't a bad idea."

"But not a good idea?"

"Well not a very good idea."

"Then it certainly wasn't a great idea."

"I think we'd have to see how it turned out to be called a great idea."

"I think it would turn out to be at least a good idea."

"It never once turned out to be a bad idea."

"How, in percentages or whatever proportions or comparisons you want to use, would you rate this subject as an idea?"

"You mean in bad, good, very good and great?"

"No inexpressible after the great?"

"I think we've had a couple of inexpressibles and one time after a great."

"That time you were putting your shirt on and I came up to you from behind?"

"I don't think that time could be said to be beyond the inexpressible once I said it was such. But no bads, lots of goods, quite a few very goods, several greats and a couple of inexpressibles."

"Shouldn't we even try now for a good?"

"I've got to go."

"I'll get dressed."

"That'd be a good idea."

"You know what'd be a very good idea?"

"A really great idea?"

"Maybe even inexpressible."

"Please express yourself."

"Right." He quickly dressed. They left the apartment. He thought about asking for his keys back, but decided no, as one of the things they'd just talked about was that she could come by anytime, call him if she knew where to reach him by phone and send letters to him whenever she liked. He'd probably get one soon, mailed or dropped off by her, and like most of her letters it would be a poem. She'd sent him a poem by mail or personal delivery, as she wrote on the envelope whenever she stuck it in his mailbox or shoved it under his door, about once a week since after the first month they met and twice a week before that. One he remembered she wrote went And now years have gone by/ remember that?/ when each hour represented a day/ or was the day a week/ that weekend several months?/ I forget./ I forget that your eyes aren't black but brown I think/ why is that?/ I remember where you live though./ Simple things (such as how I feel about you)/ a name, let's say (I only forgot yours once)/ an address (Newton, Newton, the pleasure of your arms and our embrace)/ I don't forget, though I probably do. I forget.

There's more and she called it "To the night of know things from the lazy who can only give shpace." He remembers it ended — Actually, he only remembers that first part and has been looking for and just located the poem in his desk. So he also has a desk, a lamp and typewriter on the desk, a dictionary of international slang on top of a thesaurus on top of a dictionary on top of the desk, and right beside the desk an old dental cabinet he uses as a file cabinet that belonged to his father the doctor the dentist and which is still filled with the chemical residues and minuscule mineral remains of his forty year practice along with a few blackened cotton alcohol balls his pincers after his fingers must have pinched and several real or false individual teeth in the drawers' corners. The poem, written while she sat against a car fender waiting for her therapist and Myles to show up, was shoved under his door after that session, though he was in and heard the envelope sliding on the floor and ran after her down the stairs and in the street yelled at her doubleparked car pulling away for her to stop while

he stood on one and then the other foot trying to get the backs of
his tennis sneakers over his heels. But the rest of the poem goes

> I think squirrels forget
> (their nuts, I mean)
> where they leave them: that I didn't forget
> even if that little animal life fact might not be true.
> I won't go into elephants, and not because I can't fit.
> I also forget that with my last so-called poem to you
> I was to be finished with them for good.
> Oh I forget. My way to you: will I also forget that?
> I thought of it, but forgot what I thought of course
> and no doubt I should forget this entire piece too.
> I forget the reasons for what I do
> soon after I've contrived them, or through
> serious contemplation: oh, forget it
> as I forgot what I was going to say
> why I was going to say it
> and my long-thought-out conclusion too.
> Perhaps all I don't forget is that I forget
> though I can't be too sure on that point too.

They also agreed in his flat that he would call, write or drop by
her place anytime he liked. But he didn't think he would. This was
her show. She wrote and staged it, so he'd just watch, maybe
applaud to be polite and possibly review. How was that for whatever figure of speech it was? The audience and stage walk downstairs holding hands. The figure of speech falls apart when he
realizes they both helped produce the play. In the street she says
"It's very cold for April. They even expect it to shnow." "Brrr,"
he says, wrapping his arms around her and clasping his hands
against her back while she wraps her arms around his and maybe
clasps hers. "You've got to keep me warm," he or she said. Or
"We've got to keep me more than wee warm," she or he said. Or
"wee-wee warm." No they didn't. Nothing like that was said. Edit
out everything from "You've got to keep" to what I'm saying till

now. But they laughed to whatever one of them said, and kissed.
You see: they were always kissing in the street. Not once in their
five or so months did they walk for a couple of miles or in the time,
if they were driving or standing relatively still, that it approxi-
mately took them to walk a couple of miles, without a kiss. Never
once does he remember them even sitting in a luncheonette or at
a ballet or play or any theater really where they didn't kiss. The
Moorish City Center to see the Bunraku last week, for example.
Which they took her daughter and son to and sat in the last row
of the orchestra after slinking there during intermission from the
last row in the second balcony (her son Timon, out of integrity,
refusing to make the move), and where Mary was viewing the
puppets and to him near invisible manipulators through her husband's grandmother's opera glasses and listening over a rented
headset to the translation of Japan's most famous classical play of
forbidden love and double suicide, when he got his lips in between
the wires and under her arms and opera glasses and kissed. She put
the glasses down and worked one of the earphones around and
kissed him back. Then they placed the glasses and headset on her
lap and embraced, is the only word I can think to use for what they
did and he, inside her blouse from below while she stroked his
chest, got one of her nipples erect—probably the right one as he
was sitting on her right with Linetta on her left—by lifting the
nipple up with the backs of his middle and index fingers and
rubbing and skimming the top of it with his thumb, a habit or
procedure he thinks he picked up by giving his dad insulin shots
twice a day for two years. And where Mary later said "Linetta saw
us and put her program over her lids and insinuatively said ohhh.
If she lets on to Myles he's liable to accuse us of corrupting her and
maybe use it in court to get full custody of both Timon and Lin
if we get divorced. Can a child, like one's spouse, be barred from
testifying against one of her folks, if that is the way the law goes?"
But everywhere. That's what I've been saying. That's the kind of
couple we were. Though what does all this talk about physical
activity mean when she also said in his flat "Are we supposed to

be beyond saying things like 'Lots of times when I'm sleeping with you I make believe you're Myles'? for if we are, I'm not." And "Intellectually and sexually we're very close but emotionally you won't let us go all the way," which he said to some could seem like a contradiction coming so soon after what she said about making love to him through Myles or the other way around. And which he also "out-and-outedly" denied, saying that his remark about what can she really ever do for him? and which likely invited her previous remark that he won't emotionally let her in "didn't mean you could never do anything for me, but what can anyone do for anyone else to stop the deepest and ultimately least problematical realizations from seeping in about the betrayal of time and boundaries of being and self-deceptions that we'll ever find fulfillment and self-knowledge and the well-meaning lies and myths of all our customs, codes and social and emotional tricks. Saying all that while even here, right after I said it, I probably don't believe more than a word of it and just said it as a cop-out of some kind, just as just what I just said to you could be a cop-out, just as just what I just said to you could be a cop-out too," but now they're heading to her car.

"Where's it parked?" he says.

"I always think it's parked where I parked it the last time I was here."

But it's not a hard car to spot if it's not parked too far down the block and she puts the key in the passenger's side door and when he says "But I'm not driving back with you, right?" she says "Belief and doctrine, my head" and goes around and unlocks the door at the driver's seat.

He comes up beside her. Maybe they briefly held hands. They did or didn't quickly kiss. That pick-peck goodbye when he or she's going to the grocery store and the other person's staying home. But he definitely remembers slapping her back a couple of times, patting it really, like a good-time Joe to a good-time Sally, and said "Well so long" and she said "That's it?" and he said "I don't know: what do you expect me to say?" and she said "It really

doesn't take you long to make the end or separation of these things
a total blank in your mind" and he said "Maybe it's like my father
used to say to me when I'd really start bitching" and she said
"What was that?" and he said "No, it's got to be too corny a man
saying what his father used to say to him when he was a kid" and
she said "You mean if he can lose his father and mother he can lose
you too?" and he said "I didn't think I told you that" and she said
"Well now that you've lost your parents can you lose me too?" and
he said "I don't want to speak about losing my parents or anything
related to that yet please" and she said "I'm sorry, I forget. But I
told you I always forget. I even wrote a poem to some man I liked
about forgetting which I now forget not only who it was to but
what it was all about" and he said "To me" and she said "My poem
called 'Forget Me Snot'?" and he said "No and it was about your
remembering those first weeks after we met when we were so
close and felt that each hour represented twenty-four times that
in time" and she said "You see?" and he said "Dumbhead, dumbhead" and tapped her forehead with his knuckles and said "So I'm
shoving off now, okay?" and she said "Godshpeed, matey, and how
does she head?" and he opened the door and removed the keys
from the lock and gave them to her and as she was getting into the
car he walked further down the street, though he didn't know to
where. For a beer? Movie? Someone's house? Something to eat or
to a store to buy food and drink? But what? Whose? Why did he
go that way rather than straight home? Or at least pretend to go
home by walking in that direction, even down the steps to his
building's landing or into the vestibule if she still hadn't driven
away, and then back on the street toward Columbus Avenue once
she was gone. For if he now made a right at Columbus she might
think he was going to see a woman he once went with who lived
a block north off that avenue, and if he made a left at the corner
at Columbus she might think he was going to the bar three blocks
away he so often went alone or with her to and for some reason
he didn't want her to think, if she was watching him, that this
separation or end, as she said, was driving him to a bar where he

just might get crocked or cockeyed drunk and stinko, as his father also used to say.

He ran across the street. This man was a runner let me add. Let me also add he ran four to eight miles a day just about every day and only heavy snow slowed him down and reduced the miles of his run to about one and torrential rains and paths and walks coated with ice meant he ran in place in his apartment or inch by inch through the passageway and rooms for twenty minutes twice a day. I'll add too that he even had his running shoes on. Or running sneakers or whatever real runners like the runners who run in marathons and belong to a certain running club in the city called the Roadrunners Club I think it's called call these sneakers or shoes. But he ran down the north side of West 75th Street to Columbus Avenue. He sprinted across Columbus and then walked in a brisk manner, as some people used to say, farther west along 75th toward Amsterdam, the next avenue. Everytime a car passed he turned to his left to see if it was hers. Because this would be the street she'd logically drive down. For she lives upstate as I said and to get to her house, if she was parked on West 75th anywhere between Central Park West and Amsterdam or even on Central Park West between 73rd and 75th facing north, she always made a right at Amsterdam and 75th, or first a left down 75th if she was parked on Central Park West, drove to 79th and made a left and crossed Broadway and West End Avenue and Riverside Drive and got on the West Side Highway and continued north on it or Henry Hudson Parkway as the highway's also called or only called once a car passes a certain unspecified landmark farther uptown or down, to the George Washington Bridge and then to the Palisades Parkway and then onto another road or highway or parkway to her town that's within sight and earshot of the traffic on the Tappan Zee Bridge and then up a hill to a street and lane to her house which isn't.

So he walked in the manner he said. Three cars passed in a row. None was hers. All were larger. Every car's larger than hers except the tiniest Fiat and Honda and whatever that Fiat's called when it's made in Spain. The small car was perfect for her. She was small. Her voice, mannerisms and aspirations were small. Her body was lean and small. Her buttocks weren't that small and her thighs were kind of large in fact, though not that large as it might sound when someone says "her thighs were kind of large in fact." He adored her small body. Worshiped it he used to say. She used to say "I have a short awful body" and the first night they met and were taking off their own clothes after each had removed the other's shoes and socks and he had untied her blouse bow on top, she pointed to and then covered up a long scar below her navel that furrowed perpendicularly through the middle of the hair to the vagina and said "This is the ugliest part of me you'll see. I had something even uglier inside but the medicine men cut it out" and he remembers thinking Oh my god, she has a long scar on her body. And fairly large thighs and chubby knees and kind of big buttocks. It will affect my relationship with her. It'll never work out. And she's really not that pretty when I get a good look at her full face. With little bumps and a couple of chicken pox pits and a bleached mustache and jaw mole with a hair or two in it and small teeth and conspicuous gums and a wide fleshy nose and nostrils that stayed flared. And I need to have a pretty woman. It's always been a pretty woman. She's got to at least have an almost beautiful face from all three seeable sides if she's small and her body's only halfway attractive to me or marred with a long visible scar, or have a beautiful body if she only has a very pleasant though not exceptionally attractive face. That's what he actually thought that first night and could quite conceivably, though again with subsequent self-reproach and avowals not to think that way again, think the same thing about another woman in the future, though he never again thought that way about Mary. Because he quickly came to love that face and buttocks and thighs and scar and height and all her extrusions and holes and folds and pits and hairs and sounds and drools and rheums and even her smells. Even the intestinal ones. No, not the intestinal ones, though they hardly bothered him anymore. "If you can take mine then I can take yours," he once said in a hurry to get to the bathroom she was coming out of and she said "Why even mention? Who even cares?" though when she was around he still tried to conceal his own smells by opening the bathroom window, if it wasn't too cold out, and lighting a match above the bowl and twirling around the room with it after he flushed: so there was a lighting of a match in this piece. But the cars. They passed. Maybe she made a left at Columbus to avoid seeing him and being seen and got on the highway at 72nd.

He was nearing Amsterdam when he heard another car behind him. He turned and saw Mary in the front seat of her car, crying hysterically. Throwing her head back and forth uncontrollably. The windows were closed. He couldn't hear her. She wasn't looking at him. He knew she must be making loud sobs in there. He thought she'd bump her head on the dashboard or the back of the seat. "Mary," he said. She didn't hear. He didn't say it loud enough. Didn't shout it out. "Emmy, don't cry," he said just as low. The car drove past. She might never have even seen him. The car stopped for the red light. He walked past the car. His hands in his pants pockets. His body hunched up from the cold. His jacket was too thin. He'd lost the fleece lining two winters ago. He should have worn a sweater. He didn't look at her. He stopped at the corner. He thought she'd make a right at Amsterdam when the light changed. He ran across the avenue against the light and was near Broadway when he heard her car coming along. She was driving very slowly. She wasn't looking at him. She was still crying hysterically or had resumed crying that way from the time he last saw her till sometime just before now. "Mary," he yelled. A lady across the street turned around. The car drove by. Mary never looked left or right. The lady was looking at the apartment windows above. "Em, you shouldn't cry," he said. He held out his hands. He wanted to cry. He was smiling. It wasn't a malicious smile. If Mary saw it she might think it was. The smile wouldn't go away. It was out of embarrassment and helplessness. Out of sadness and pity. Out of lots of things. Out of wonder. Concern. Nobody bawling and tossing her head around like that should be driving a car. She stopped for the light. His smile went away. He wanted to run to her car and tap on the window and say something. He walked fast on the sidewalk till he stood parallel to her car. He looked at her. If she looked at him he would wave. He would motion her to pull over so they could speak. Or just to pull over and then she would open the window or door and he could get in or stand in the street by her car and speak. He still never heard her sobs. The car must be solidly built, the convertible top double or triple lined. She was crying for lots of reasons, he supposed. She was probably thinking what am I doing? Why am I doing this? Am I crazy? An idiot? Should I be put away? Do I kill everything I love as Newt said? He'll never want me back. Do I even want to go back? Do I even want to be with a man? What do I want? Will I even know what I want? Is it just that there's nothing I want? Or what I don't want is a man who has too few or too many or just any wants? He must think I'm crazy. Nobody wants a crazy. Or just a woman who's always saying one thing to the man and then when alone changing her mind. She of course could be thinking plenty of other things and then maybe none of that. Though that's what he thought she was crying about.

The car behind her honked. The light had changed. He went right and ran to the gourmet shop a few blocks away and bought lots of goodies to console himself with: rich Jamaican coffee from the high mountains, black Brazilian espresso freshly ground, Brie cheese, Switzerland Swiss cheese, dark bread, German mustard, French mayonnaise, four bock beers from Denmark and an Irish stout, a ripe Colombian plum and ugli fruit, fresh carrots with the stems still on, three Belgian endives, an undamaged artichoke he might steam when he got home and a quarter pound each of health salad and stuffed grapevine leaves. She never passed him on Broadway. She must have crossed the street and gone to West End or Riverside and made her right there.

The next night I dropped by my cousin Harriet's place and while her daughter made a zoetrope out of the canister from the canister of clay and with the sculpting tools I also bought her, Harriet said "Don't worry. Mary will take care of Mary all right." After a couple of condoling drinks and toasts she said "By the way. There's a very nice actress type who works as a temporary at the next desk from mine and who's quite pretty and kind of bright."

"Not so soon."

After I left Harriet's I went to the neighborhood bar Mary and I used to go to. It was around ten o'clock. The bar was crowded. The hockey playoffs, someone said. I don't like hockey or TV. I stood at the back of the bar away from the television set, ordered a draft and thought I'd call the son of a woman I used to live with in California a number of years ago. The boy was eleven now and for a few years had thought of me as his father. I still sent him presents on his birthday and holidays and money when I had it to help pay for his summer vacations with his real father or to buy a special coin. I loved calling him. He always made me cheerful with his high excited voice and what he had to say about what he was presently involved in and had recently done. So I went to the phone booth in front. Someone was in it. I put down my beer, thinking I'd get back to it after the call, and took my jacket off the wall hook to call from one of the booths outside. As I opened the door with my jacket in my hand, a man with an aluminum hard hat on and who I thought had looked at me sort of contemptuously when I came in and who of course stood out among his friends and everyone else in the bar because of that hat, stopped me and said "Oh no, you're not going to steal my friend's jacket."

"Your friend's?" I looked at the jacket. Sure enough it wasn't mine. "There's mine," I said, handing him his friend's jacket and getting mine off a coatrack near the wall hook. I put my jacket on and started for the door. "Sorry. It was an accident."

"Accident your ass," he said.

"It was an accident. Why would I want your friend's jacket?"

"Because it's better and cleaner than yours."

"Better it may be, and cleaner also, but mine has my keys in it," and I patted my jacket's breast pocket which made a jangling sound.

"You thief," he said.

"Now listen. That's ridiculous. I come into this bar a lot. They know me here and they know I'm not a thief. I made a simple mistake. Both jackets are waist-length and dark suede. Mine must have dropped from the hook I almost always hang it on and where your friend's must have been and someone probably picked mine up and put it on the coatrack and that's how the mistake was probably made."

"You Jew," he said.

I don't know why. Because of the gas showers? Crematoriums? Jew-baiting and walled ghettos? Because that's the generation I was brought up in and it was an extremely emotional issue in those days? Whether I'm actually a Jew or not I don't even think matters that much. But I suddenly began strangling him with both hands. His hard hat fell off. It wasn't aluminum but aluminum-colored plastic. His friends dragged me off him. While they held my arms he punched me in the face. His friends let me go. He punched me in the face again before I could get my hands up. Was it because of the rum tonics at Harriet's place that I didn't feel the blows or any pain? Both bartenders rushed up front, one climbing over the bar and the other with the bar's team shirt on and darts in his hand, as he was one of the players in another round of the dart tournament between bars taking place, and they grabbed me and said "Go in back, Newt."

"But I didn't even hit him," I said. "I strangled him for a second, but then he hit me twice and once with my arms tied."

"In back!"

"All right." I grabbed my beer off the bar and went in back. Then I said "But I was only going outside to call someone from a phonebooth. Your booth is filled. Then I was coming back to finish my beer and have a hamburger, so I couldn't have tried to steal his friend's jacket as he said."

"Call from my phone," the bartender behind the bar said.

"It's to California."

"Then you better call from outside."

The dart-playing bartender walked me to the door. I was heading for the phonebooth at the corner when someone shouted "Hey you. My friend here wants to know why you wanted to steal his jacket." It was the hard hat and the man whose jacket I suppose it was, since he was wearing it, and who must have been somewhere else when the scuffle took place. I thought of saying "Take off, will you?" and walking away, forgetting the phonecall or at least from this booth. But I went back to try and explain to the friend in a calm rational way that I had grown very fond of my jacket over the past ten years and that the only set of keys to my apartment other than the ones in my jacket pocket were thirty miles upstate on the key ring of a person I didn't especially want to see now and the reasons why I think I took his jacket off the wall hook by mistake.

I started my explanation to the friend by saying "Now let's talk this out in a completely unemotional way."

"You bet," the hard hat said right beside us.

"Don't listen to him," I said. "Honestly, I never intended to steal your jacket. I go in there a lot, as I told him. My house keys were even in my own jacket. So my jacket must have fallen to the floor from the hook your jacket was also on and someone—"

"You got blood on your nose," the hard hat said. I turned to him as I felt my nose and said "Will you just go away?" Then the friend punched me in the face and they were on me from in front and back and while my head was being pummeled from above I bent down and grabbed one of their legs apiece around the knees and I swear lifted them off the ground and threw them further up in the air. I screamed something like "Yaaach" and ran after both of them and kicked one and slashed my hand down on the other's neck and then kicked that one and slashed the other across the head and was grabbed from behind by two other men from the bar with one of them saying "We're only trying to protect you" and I said "Bullshit, because in the bar while you were protecting me you let that bastard there get one off at my face" and I threw them off me and began kicking and slashing away at them and the friend who had come back to try and tackle me. And then I was free of them all and in the middle of the sidewalk and they were against the parked cars and a tree and the window of a grocery store and I said "Well come on. I'll take on all three of you. All four." And I really felt I could. I felt that powerful and aggressive. But the hard hat said "Fix your nose" and they all went into the bar. The doors closed. Some other people from the bar had been watching. Both bartenders too. The man who had come out of his store to watch said "Crazy."

"That's right," I said.

"I didn't mean it in a harmful way."

"I know. And I didn't mean it to you in a harmful way either."

He went into the store. I started for home, laughing a little as I went. At the way those men, at first so belligerent and brave, could be beaten off by just one not too strong man, though probably strong then. For I don't like to fight. I can't remember when I last had a fight. I really would stand there and let a man hit me in the face without hitting him back and then say something like "Fine. Did it feel good? Are you through?" and walk away. I won't go into that bar again. And I suppose, which is why I brought up the incident, that my maniacal counterattack and sudden surge of unforeseen strength, as we used to say, came not so much from any flashing thoughts about crematoriums and gas showers or weariness of the continuing and probably never-ending contentiousness of men, but from something I had to get rid of concerning Em.

Mary's Piece

He wrote me the other day and said "I've written about us you know" and I dropped him a card back saying "Yes I know you've shown me some but I want you to know also I've written about us too." That wasn't true yet. And actually I haven't sent that card out. I also wrote on this card I've written him and will send "I'm going to send you what I wrote about us and if you don't like what I've written I'm afraid I can't tear all the copies up. I'm in fact going to send them to some of the same places you sent and will probably send more of your work to about us. I know where you send your work out to. Knowing you so close for three years I've picked some immaterial up. They'll begin to think it a bit bizarre and I think think differently about taking your work when they see my work about the same things too. They'll maybe conclude it's a little too much like fiction too closely following fact or vice versa or versa vice vice versa or should I put it fact following fiction following fiction following fact or whatever order it is or they are though you know what I mean. But what can I say except I don't like my life and my children's lives being made light of like that?" That's what I wrote him. My writing's microscopic and minuscule. I've the card right before me, on my residential desk. I send it out. Rather, today's part of one of those two-day Jewish holidays where my school's closed and I'm going to bike to the post office to get stamps and more cards and check the library bulletin board in the P.O. to see what movies it's playing this week and so when I get there I'll send this card out.

But I really don't know where to begin with him and us other than what I've written in what I've begun with about his letter to

166

me and my postcard back. In the park perhaps. Since that was one
of the highlights in our life that he described in one of his pieces and
so an incident that might seem particularly peculiar to those people
in places who read his pieces with my piece so quickly following
fiction following fact. For except in the name of the press or if the
cause increases circulation, no organization dealing with writing
wants a lawsuit, plagiarism or invasion of otherwise, plain as that.
We were there with Timon and Lin. Those aren't their real names
though they are my son and daughter and for obvious reasons I'll
use the same names Newt used though that's not his real name too.
And I really should have said "We were there with Lin and Timon"
so I could end that sentence before the last one with "daughter and
son." Newt would. For the timbre or tone of it he liked to sound.
Though in my rating that's forsaking content for the sake of rhythm
and rhyme. But I'm not Newt so I won't say it the way Newt would.
This piece is Mary's piece and will be done my way no matter how
strong or pervasive his scribbling influence. So we were in the park.
Four of us. On Doggy Hill one Sunday past dusk attending one of
those free experimental Sunday Movies in the Park on the grass on
the hill and bring your own picnic supper and wine and lemonade
and try to find a place away from the doggy dung spots. It got dark.
Movie starts. Began to light rain. Most people braved it and stayed.
Timon and Lin slipped under two shopping bags Newt had crea-
tively torn in a way that made it a snug pup tent for them complete
with sticks and twigs for tent poles. Newt and I were on the back
half of the blanket behind them. I was cuddled up to him head on
his thighs. He cut two other shopping bags and stuck them over me
though without poles. More like a tarp that covered me from head
tip to tucked up toes. So what did I do. I said "You know as long as
I'm down here" and he said "You know I had the same idea" and I
did it under the bags in the park in the dark on the hill behind my
kids among some five thousand staunch hardy moviebuffs the
newspaper the next day said and it was the old bit but don't do it
with noise and he didn't and that was the first time it ever worked
where he jerked into my mouth and which he never did except for
leaking drips because as he said he always wanted to end it in my

hole of holes as he sometimes labeled it where it was the most exploiting or what I would call my young bumptious cunt or just my cunt. Such a think. I mean a thing. What I said. Not my thing. But this isn't true Myles my xed husband if you read this write. Though Myles isn't his true name too. So don't think I'm corrupting our developing dears, dear, where you can then get the law to let you keep them even for odd and even weekends from me so you and your newest highflying loved one can corrupt them in your own ways too. But that happed. In the park. On Doggy Fill. Watching a movie during the moment some dog on the screen screamed like a banshee instead of barked like a narc before it swandived out of a window off Williamsburg Bridge from on top of the Chrysler Building from a distant plane onto an Orchard Street peddler's cart which fell on the peddlers playing cards which most of the people thought hilarious but which most of the dog audience bayed and howled inharmonically at because of what I'm sure was the sight of seeing that live looking stuffed doll dog take its life so many times.

Moments. Another was at my adopted twin sister's burial. Family grabsite. Ungrave grubsite. I don't want to go into the rest. I was running the show. Parents were too upset. I was too. But get on. That's what I thought. At the site. Fall day. Last fall. Leaves falling. Golden red orange scarlet leaves she always pressed between sheets of wax paper and kept till next fall or at least spring on the windowsill to see through. Sisser. Leaves falling. Being lowered. Her fiancé falling. My father fell. On his knees: mother falling to one knee to help him. I felt like falling too. Feel like falling too. But somebody of the family had to keep stood up. No. Those moments I can't say yet except they had something related to rudiments related to Newt or some snuff stuff. Take a guest.

The last day with him and her together with me was the happiest of the lot or one of them anyway till it turned into one of the saddest or I'll say the saddest of my life. That turnaround reminds me too of the time Newt was never more sickest or neediest. Soup coming out of his poop. Pee from his weewee. Vomit, sweat, slaver, eyes and nose running and if I looked I'm sure I would have found some drool seeping out of his ears and unhealed wounds and whatever other apertures and openings there are I haven't mentioned or don't know about yet. He was on the floor. Flued I can say. Had gone there to shave. Was whistling, whistling stopped. Trying to lift him and razor out of his hand without slitting myself he said "Ello me, Em, elp me, I don't want to die" and that moment I don't think I ever loved anyone more, smelly, slimy and unsightly as he was and because just a few minutes before I again thought again well this is the end my friend I don't love you anymore and though I knew it was gastroenteritis and not death. But she wasn't well. The most dreaded disease. We drove up. Linetta was with us. Timon too. Whole family there first time for we considered Newt then family too. We all played that sentence game Scrabble puts out. Newt made funny sentences work. He slaughtered us with his funny sentences and also to cheer my sisser up who came in second with her scientific sentences and Timon a dirty word third and Linetta in last after my mother and me or I but really me, Lin, sisser's fiancé and my father last because he casts spells rather than can't spell. But main point I suppose is Newt's last sentence in this game and which he won with was "I know you will get better now sweet girl and more love from me and goodbuy" which is a tremendous sentence worth all sorts of points if you buy the buy and we bought it and then he got up and kissed the tops of our heads because he's so much taller and we were also all still sitting and left. The house. On top of mine at the time I thought I felt a ceiling drop dropping. But left. Raining but no leaks my father said. I had to drive up to him at the bus depot because he ran. I hadn't thought he could be this serious. Wasn't his style. No emo New. And he still had time. Or little emo but always the walls. Wall after walls. You could never really get in. He let it out when he felt it safe to let it out but I hadn't really seen one real route in. All right. He had other points. He couldn't sleep over they said. All right. No room. They were against that besides he was slated to oddjob in the city next day besides that sisser was so sick and there were kids. But more points. His bus left with both of us blowing soul kisses and few hours later sisser could barely breathe and I freed her lungs from her tongue and blew air into them while someone phoned the doc who said hurry hurry her up to the hosp which she never left. Weeks later she left. Later that night Newt called and said "Sorry for calling so late at night my love but oh my darling tell me I'm mistaken that something's gone very very wrong." Sisser. I miss her. They rhymes. Newt would appreciate those lines. Rhyming in his way. And like the last one for its contentless timbre or tone.

Others. First night I met him I wasn't especially attracted to him or found him very clever or even liked him much but was just you know jest having reckless one to two night adventures with men in between serious affairs. So I did need some pressing to go home with him I think and went and his bed was split down the muddle for highrising and his room was perfect for a one night stand as he had for his possessions and number of rooms just one of everything but he was a good luber and soundless sleeper and had a nice body and still has and has been one since. Week later my new luber Newt asked if there was anything I saw very different about him. I said "Plenty of things and no doubt more I'll know and never know about but I'll enumerate the few I do." I did. Partless hair. No sideburns. Huge lobes. Almost always cheerfully exposed. Jumps out of bed in the morning while I shift and crawl. No. No? He said "I know this might seem dumb and dense of me but I also want to show you what I also sometimes think about inside me so here goes. You're the first person I've slept with who hasn't com-mented about the size of my penis." I said "Do I have a big cunt to you?" and he said "Now that you bring it up it does seem pretty easy to get into" and I said "Because I had children or maybe it's my mother's or one of my grandmothers' or theirs but what makes the dif? Doesn't unless it hurts. Either way. And we seem to be a good fit." He said "Then my question did seem immature to you" and I said "There's nothing to comment about. It's average." "My penis?" "Question and penis. Average." "Both length and girth?" "Listen. As far as pricks go you're average." "Okay. Glad I asked. Maybe penises begin to shrink once they've reached full physical maturity or after twenty or so years of being there or you just happened to have known slightly larger than average penises. Anyway now I know something more about you and you know how dumb I can become" and I said "You mean more than I already knew though maybe we're a good fit there too" and that was that. Several months later though I said to him in bed or when he was dressing or right after his morning pee or doing his daily early exercises with the lights on or in daylight but when his prick was visible to me I mean and at least semierect "You know? You do seem to have a bigger prick than the rest." "You mean before you did just happen to have bigger than average penises and now you don't?" "Could be or else I just forget what they were like before you or they never registered in my head. Even with Myles for so many years I've no recollection what his was like except for the extra labia or maybe that's only what I remember I know or the others after him till you first brought the subject up." "Want me to speak the truth for change? I'm not suffering or mad." "I knew it would both displease and please you and now for all time let's kick this theme." "Not before I try and find out from you whether there are any advantages to you in my having a bigger than average penis" and I said "Either you, we or I haven't taken advantage of the advantage or because I never noticed or commented about it before I already answered it but inquiry closed" and he acquiesced. Then we had sex my diary notes. Later he said "I'm just like the rest. Just like the rest. Just like the rest just like the rest."

Newt doesn't like the movies I like. Even going much to movies which I like. Or my music which is heavy rock, dance or flute music and plays without people or scenery on stage. Or even most of my friends or me his friends and what they do and books. He doesn't like my books. Doesn't even like my having so many bookcases of books or that I've so many more bookshelves to put up and boxes of books. He likes to cook though and I don't or can't or won't cook much except for my Middle Eastern burgers and bananas with spiced rice which he likes. We both like radio though different kinds of radio and I'm more interested in politics and economics and all kinds of reform than him and don't like television much but he can't even stand the low sound of it when Linetta listens to it after school while she reads, builds, bakes, macramés, homeworks or sews. All that trivia keeps couples together I think which is my root point. We don't trivia together enough or do much of anything well or otherwise together but trade quips and unzipper zips and sleep snuggy and snoreless in each other's arms for a nightful and in three years we've never been on a beach together or any other park but Prospect and Palisades and Central parks together and never been in Queens and nowhere but Riverdale in the Bronx once or out of New York and Jersey states. We do like to walk and occasionally he likes a long talk but he doesn't know how to use a phone or even own a phone while I can talk an hour a day straight on the phone and in walking he likes to walk further or farther than me or I and knows the difference between those first two and than me or I though I'm the regularly waged English teach gradually moving into films and we both like to bike. But he won't buy a bike and so is always borrowing my bike when we bike and I either have to use Lin's or if Tim's here then Tim's smaller than normal adult bike. He finds my favorite antique and junk stores seedy. My old clothes closets greedy. My fleeting ideas and disorderly home ways of avoiding reality. He plants and I pick. Eggs. Two a day I like scrambled or fried in margarine and with sausages or bacon while he likes unsalted butter but never eats eggs or much butter because of the cholesterol and won't touch my pig food for their nitrates and ites. His foot pads and hand palms are orange from too much carotene in the carrots or from just too many carrots a day while I can't even take one cooked or raw or carrotbread bite. But I have started to run and not because he likes to run and I do like to jog with him on our country or his park paths but don't like when he slows down for me or leaves me behind. And one day he grabbed my hand on a busy Sixth Avenue sidewalk and raced across the street with me being dragged behind him and I yelled "Stop the cars the buses stop the trucks the motor and bicycles stop the light's against us we'll get killed stop I'll fall bruise my knees bust my head my bag I'll lose my bag my life I'll never see my kids again stop" but he didn't and on the other side I went "Weee that was great" and hugged and swung him around and round on the spot. I don't know why I brought that last incident up. Except to say sometimes it was wild woozy fun and no matter what Newt might say I did love.

Newt I left you so many times I don't know how you could have come back to me or just be there for me when I went back to you those last three four or five times and now I'm sorry but this really is it it has to be it it just isn't working wasn't working was poor from the start poor timing a poor relationship we were just too opposite I don't know why but we were we couldn't've been can't be anything but the way we are and were so that's it Newt I'm sorry but that's it the end Newt it has to be will be is for right now and as far as I can see the end it is.

I started off telling stories about us and now I'm just talking to myself. That story at the grubsite. Maybe that's what put me off. Got me going on the wrong groove or track. I still can't get into that one though. And talking some more about it now I hope I won't lead anyone to any great suspense because they think it's any great or meaningful story because it's not.

There's nothing much more to say. I think no more stories to tell. One night in the park I blew him behind the backs of my kids. One Halloween in the dark we played hide and seek with my costumed kids and each scared the other three to smithereens. One Sunday afternoon he just creeped up behind me in his flat to drip he later said a drop of honey so he could lick it off my back and when I was smoothing out the end of his spread on his made bed I believe when out of nowhere he later said he got hard and slipped it in me from behind and in one minute flat and to this day neither of us knows how it was done we both reached heaven let's say. We had to confess. For either of us it's never been like that with anyone before or since including ourselves or even doing it to ourselves or at least I can say that now for myself but there was some superior break-through then and I only wish I had of it a videotape that was also hidden from my mind at the time so I could see if there was any way of duplicating what we did and later tried to do in the same positions without the honey and making of bed a dozen more times. But that's all done. He's all over. Though a gorilla that Newt. Big, strong, hairy and playful as one too just as I'm strong, hairy and playful and both of us we've said a little smelly in the right places and amounts too. But all done and over and now it's nice not seeing Newt but three different men at different times usually separated by a day and not having him around to put me down for this variety pack and make me guilty for not seeing him enough and every weekend. And nice having that variety in the head and mouths and surroundings and also because one likes the front most and another most from the back and the third likes me to sit on top most and what do I like most but to sit and get it from the back and not the front so much but every so often when I'm really feeling cuddly with the sit and back men and also want to kiss I ask them or move them and they do. But is anything missing not having just one? No I don't think so though those two months it was nice with Newt just living here and being here when I came home from school and even teaching in the same school with him when he came to sub and having lunch and sneaking in free feels and hugs in the base-ment office like a bunker cell and always the smell of the English department's burning coffeepot. And Linetta liked it better with just one because he was like a second father to her and the new three like second cousins or distant uncles but can't live for my kids. Two have their own divorced kids. Timon doesn't like the new three because they are three so they don't see much of him because they don't want to and Timon is beginning to distrust the affections

of all men excluding Myles. But I always come back to sex don't I?
Despite all Newt's other talents maybe that was the case. He once
said to me at least we can always make love if everything else fritzes
and I said that would be nice but I think once the love in a close
relationship goes the sex soon follows and he said "Nah not so or by
much" but last few times with Newt when I had little to no feeling
for him I just about felt repulsed by his presence and touch. That's
tough saying but tougher happening but the communal truth
might be but might not five to ten years from now or sooner in this
age of frivolousness is a man can almost do it anytime if he's fairly fit
and normal while his fairly fit and normal woman almost can't. But
what was it with him in bed? Not his words which outside of I love
you shut the door you weren't encouragement for much. Way he
rubbed my dugs? Three fingers and always the thumb. That alone
could make me come. And his tongue. Even his toes. Also his nose.
Never his chin though he tried couple times or his elbow which he
tried just once. But his fingers. This little piggy went to mark her
and so did this one and the other fat fellas as well. Our perfect posit?
Newt in my front from behind me while one of his hands fingering
me and other hand brushing from breast to breast and face screwed
around mine and slashing our tongues while slapping lips and gums
but kissing and sucking whatever parts of us we could reach and
Newt often in my ear which doesn't excite me as much as other
parts kissed and tongued but my rear raised just so I forgot and
maybe my hand mixed up with his under us playing with his balls
and cock but if it was my lips or neck being kissed or feebly bit it was
best of all. Each man has his own way I found and some almost none
and same way around I'm told and with each it can usually be good
if I feel for him and he can just keep it in there at least semierect and
with each sometimes great. What I didn't like that much with Newt
was when he'd suddenly hoist me off the bed without slipping out of
me and I'd find myself facing him and us doing it standing up. Or
really just Newt standing up and me sitting on his palms in his arms
with him bouncing us back and forth like a seesaw or I'm his
saxophone he's blowing hot and though I soon felt myself floating in

air I could never completely blot out my fear of falling and so for me some of it got spoiled. But he never let go and then so fagged out and winded from this acrobat act he'd collapse back onto the bed and once rolled off it with me with our groins still interlocked and there we were laughing away like that on the floor. Once when he lifted me I saw over his shoulder on the trail behind the house a woman looking at us while jogging by with her dogs. Then we fell and I saw her at a party a while after and we started guessing where we'd seen one another before before it hit me and I said. "Whole show for the neighborhood I'm afraid" and she said "Excuse me but I couldn't sleep that night thinking about it. First I thought he was victimizing you. Man off the road. Our bicycles are being stolen and ripe beans and squash vandalized. Who knows? Then I realized it was only slightly unorthodox coitus between a strapping young couple who for some reason left the shades up and it got me so stimulated thinking of it that I nudged my husband but he was too tired to then so that's why I couldn't sleep." Two of us have since become friends and I think she must have told her husband what she saw and the performers because he's made these eerie elastic eyes at me and forward trepidatious remarks about my pretty buttocks and nicely arched back but I think he's a dunce and don't hone for friends' husbands and will always put them off unless they separate or divorce. But Newt. Last time I saw him was when he said "Okay, goodbye, and let's make this the last one" and stormed out the house and then intentionally missed the hourly bus to the city and climbed back up the hill and said he couldn't go as he'd forgotten his toilet articles and that I'd have to drive him to a closer bus stop. So I drove him and parked at the bus station and in the car he said "I guess my love became too boring for you" and I said "Your love boring for me? That and that 'Let's make this the last one' are such corny things to say" and the bus came and he said "So I love you" and I said "And I loved you" and he said "Loved me? Loved me? Where'd it go, Mary? What happened to this summer's great love when you were creaming all over me and phoning your friends about it and just last week last month? You mean it just goes

goes goes like that?" and he snapped snapped snapped his fingers
and grabbed his shopping bag and typewriter and rushed for the
bus he'd missed before that was about to stop. Through the rear-
view I saw him wave without looking at me as he stepped into the
bus and I thought why does he think he'll even be seen or is he just
flapping his hand disgustedly at my last past tense? I waved back
though and driving home I of course cried as I hated to see anyone
so hurt.

I liked the way he played with Linetta. At first she didn't like him.
Thought him funny looking. Said her father and grandfathers were
better looking. Hair stood out on his sides. Bozo the clown she said.
Thin tuft in front like Charlie Brown's she said. Also the bull neck
and bulbous nose and pudgy face. I said "Would you believe some
women think Newt handsome?" and she said "They lie." But they
warmed. Played cards. Nonstop double solitaire which she was
invariably faster at and won. Stood on his sitting thighs. Didn't
demur anymore from his eagerness to kiss her head and caress. Also
a piggyback to bed whenever she wanted one and because she
knew both her parents thought her way past the age and for me
weight and height, Linetta almost as tall. But she had said to him
"Why can't you ever be serious to me?" which I thought an honest
gripe. "Okay" he said, "I will." This at the dinner table and "How's
school?" and she said "School's cool" and he said "Good. You've
homework for tonight?" and she said "I do but I'll do it" and he said
"Good. Now get to sleep. Finish your dinner. Eat your omelet. It's
got lots of protein to help you grow. Each piece of meat should take
a minimum of twenty-two chews. Your hands aren't that clean. You
come to the table with grimy fingernails and an unscrubbed neck?
Go to the bathroom and rewash them. Pardon me. Say you're sorry.
Don't interrupt your elders when they're speaking. Children
should be seen and not heard. You want to leave the table you say
'May I please be excused?' Now finish your dinner and drink all
your milk. Children are starving in India. In Africa. Southeast Asia
and Latin America and the America of these states. No you may not

be excused from the table till you get in bed and fall asleep and turn all your lights off and everything's been eaten up and we've had our salad and dessert." She said "That's not being serious. I want you to be serious like you're serious with things that are serious to you and Mom and me." He said "All right. What should we talk about? Why must we always have something to talk about? Say, there's a serious enough subject to discuss—why we always have to have something serious or unserious or just something to talk about." She said "Forget it" and to me "He can't be serious" and I said to him "Linetta has an honest gripe" and he said "I know. I can't. You're wrong. I agree."

At the interment I looked at Newt standing behind waves of unfamiliar faces but his swimming with tears and swollen from before and I thought Newt I love you Newt want to have a child by you and one's incubating inside me I think in spite of my device and if it isn't spun out by it soon I want to call it Louise or Louis Rose after my adopted sisser, all right? and he nodded as if he'd heard me and maybe he did as some recent news articles seem to say. Never told him though and few days later my coil aborted our blastoderm and substitute mommy for sisser before and so of course it wasn't my mother on one knee but me, wanting to be on two, feeling like fall. Mother. I loved her. Not as good as I miss her for sisser but this way I get to keep both rhyming lines in and the feeling's real and symbolism seems apropos, so in one swoop out- newting Newt himself.

Newt didn't like my group. I got him invited for a session so we could speak about our mutual problems before the group and hear what they and Dr. Glen and his two apprentices had to say. All in a circle in a small comfortable livingroom. "Where do I sit? Next to you, opposite you?" and I said sit anywhere you like. "No, that seat's always reserved for Glen," a grouper told Newt. Coffee. Cupcakes. Even diet soda and apple cider in Glen's icebox. Then Glen arrived. Always a little hurried and late. Once only in businessman's suit and tie and cordovans and conservative haircut. Now after a month's transformation we've asked him about but he refused to discuss, zippered up boots and flared jeans and western shirt unbuttoned to his navel and bracelets and pirate's earring in a pierced right ear and shaggy tailored hair. Glen began by asking progress reports on some of the groupers' problems from last week and month and year: impotency, frigidity, promiscuity, bisexuality, fears of inferiority, crowds, subways, elevators, alcoholism, dope addiction, emasculation and postoperative regrets to remove layers of fat from what she said both sexes made her feel were her too large and alluring breasts and financial, professional, marital, parental and artistic unsuccess. After the coffeebreak Glen said "As you all know we've a strange face with us today who I also understand tried to take my throne" and everyone laughed. "Newton Leeb by name. Stand up and take a bow for the folks, Newt." Newt stood and clasped his prizefighter hands. Hi and Hello and Nice to have you the groupers said and one "Want some more coffee, Newt?" and he said yes and the man got up to get it for him. "Now. We're getting late. So what do you think are the main difficulties in your relationship with Mary?" Glen asked Newt, "since I'm sure that's why she wanted you here. You're not doing an exposé on us, are you?" "No. First of all I want you all to know I love Mary very much." "Why'd you think you had to preface your comments with that confession. Newt?" someone else said. But since there'll be several people speaking here I'll do it in what I suppose is the traditional prose form, though correct me if I'm wrong.

". . . all to know I love Mary very much."

Preface remark.

"Because I want you to know that no matter how difficult and oscillative our relationship might be— That word relationship again. It just doesn't fit what Mary and I have."

"Yes, we all know and have to put up with it," Glen said. "But there it is. Accept. So?"

"So my most basic feeling for Mary is one of a deeply rooted and sometimes overwhelming and exhilarating full love. Now what else is new?"

"Have you ever told Mary this?" Glen said.

"Of course I have, you kidding?"

"All right. Don't jump on me. Antireacting so vehemently like that, someone else might think you're trying to press a point on us that you yourself might not completely feel or believe."

"Well I've told her hundreds of times. She can tell you. Maybe thousands."

"Maybe you tell her too often," Stu, one of the apprentices, said, "and that could be the cause of one of the problems you two might have: that she feels emotionally claustrophobic sometimes with all this intense admitted love spouting out of you."

"Has she told you that?"

"What's the difference? You can ask her later. But my point is—"

"No, let him ask her now," a grouper said.

"Yes, I've told them," I said.

"Okay. No problem," Newt said. "Just wanted to know. And I guess you've told me before too."

"My point before," Stu said, "is that many women and men and children even don't want to be reminded that often about how much they're loved and to what great or excessive depths and sacrifices by their loved object or parent, as it makes them feel guilty that they can't reciprocate in a similar or effusive a manner, or something like that."

"No, that's a good point, Stu," Glen said.

"Look. I tell Mary I love her when I feel like it or when I'm uncertain how she feels about me and would like her to answer she loves me too, though naturally not when I think it's what she wants to hear least. Though sometimes this feeling of love gets so welled up in me for whatever unaccountable but powerful reasons as far as I can see that I have to tell her I love her immediately and to tell her how much and sometimes to just yell it out to her—to SHOUT, like that—even if it's the last thing I know she wants to hear at the time. Though I'm also aware of the consequences of expressing this strong feeling in this strong way and that she might hate hearing it and instead of remaining neutral or bending a little to a lot to me, retract. Usually she responds positively with a I'm glad or Good and we kiss or hug or whatever. Or she could even laugh, which she's done out of nervousness or because it was so funny to find that just when she's feeling nothing for me and even wants to break it off again I'm choking back tears and sputtering on almost inexpressibly about this mighty King Kong feeling of love for her, and she doesn't think life should be that ironic or two people so antipodally aligned, all of which might sound ludicrous to you all."

"No, don't apologize," Glen said. "It sounds good. And if you are as you say willing to accept the consequences of so openly exposing yourself, which also means Mary foreseeably leaving you because she can't face up or meet the challenge of your love, then good too. I mean it."

"What I think," Stu said, "is one, he is hostile about this subject and of even Mary bringing him here to discuss it—that's a fact, Newt, no shaking of heads. There's a lot of repressed anger in you and I wouldn't put it past you that you'd like to deck me out right here for saying it."

"Not true. I wouldn't."

"It's true. Don't try to control it. C'mon," and he jumped up and pulled Newt's chair away and Newt stood and Stu grabbed him in a bearhug from behind and said "Okay. Get me off. Tear yourself out of my hold. Scream for me to let you go. Really rage. Get those goddamn deep bad uptight hostile feelings of yours out now" and Newt said to Glen "Call him off or I'm going to leave" and Stu said "Not before you pull me off you, Newt" and Newt walked to the door with Stu hanging on around him with his feet dragging behind and Glen said "Stu. Forget it. Sit down, will ya?" and Stu and Newt sat down. "You know it's true," Stu said, "no matter how placid you pretend to be, and two, you want to live in this world, you either got to grow your own food or pay the man who grows or sells it. Which means that maybe occasionally you don't have to make your love so manifest with words. You have to act out your elocution too. Or as the old saw goes, put your money where your mouth is or shut up."

"But I do put it where it is. And no pun and not just in bed

either, which is okay, isn't it, sweetheart? We've no real com-
plaints."

"No. It's very good," I said.

"And you know, we like to hug, touch, kiss and massage and hold
one another and help one another out. Though of course sometimes, just like everyone—"

"You're speaking? Speak for yourself," Stu said. "Don't sidetrack
to the universe."

"Sometimes I can be quite cynical and stupid with Mary. Jeal-
ous, abrasive, offensive, unreasonably insensitive and angry and
this awful still to me mysterious moodiness and melancholy I can
project that's been with me since I was two and which I know
Mary loathes as much as I do and the rest, but none of those that
periodically I think."

"Why?" Sarah, the other apprentice therapist, said.

"Why? All that?"

"Because you're now talking about the roots of what could be
your side of the problems between you two, not that we're sure
what they are. And by roots I don't mean the superficies of excessive screaming assertions of love and constancy and orgasmic roars
and yaps and all that physical crap, not that they're useless crap,
but the roots—the causations and determinants are what I mean.
Yes, why?"

"It's too complex. Can you answer why I'm like any of those,
Mary?"

"Let's stick with you, Newt," Glen said. "Mary sort of works
here. She'll get her turn. To rephrase Sarah and what I can almost
feel is a growing soupçon of skepticism on everyone's part here
regarding what you say, is you admit to jealousy and anger and
probably untenable reproaches and criticisms and so on to Mary.
Is it you don't like what she does or the way she does it or just is?
Her job, dress, interests, attraction, magnetism, mannerisms,
ideals, and what we've also seen is her occasional superior atti-
tudes and flippancy and overgenerous pride. Any of these really
tick you off? You two have broken off so many times that there's

got to be some good reason why. For example, just the way she can so immediately cut you off must piss you off."

"I don't love everything she does or is all the time but almost."

"You're lying," Stu said. "He's lying," to Glen. "Nobody believe his shit."

"Mary and I like being together and like having individual lives. We also have tiffs, rifts, knockdown brawls and permanent break-ups, but so far nothing that can't or hasn't been resolved. Her tendency to me sometimes has been to say hello boom I love you boom I loved you boom goodbye. While mine maybe because of almost no close head over heels associations for the three years before I met her has been to hold on after she goes and be there if she comes back. Or at least it takes a couple of weeks of letters and postcards and phonecalls on my part and midnight to four A.M. fantasies that she's suddenly going to ring my downstairs bell and jump in my bed and make love while we cry and apologize, before I really feel we're through, which we really have been but ended up not being yet. I also wanted to have a child by her, get married, so on, but she doesn't, has two, been married, so on and okay okay. I got her letter. I understand. That may come in time we think though we're not saying it must. But all in all it stays pretty good for me so long as it stays pretty good for us and I see her a couple of times a week each week if she's really not doing anything she can do without me or wants to be alone and now and then she says she loves."

"That last statement doesn't bother you?" Sarah said.

"No. Because what do I have to complain about? She's been good copy for me for one thing and never complained about it. And I also know that because of her immediate and contemporary history, what we have now is all she's capable of."

"Then neither of you," Glen said, "deny to the other when you're feeling shitty or angry or uncared for? Or when you don't like what the other person's saying or doing or get accumulated repressed feelings of hurt because you didn't say what you wanted to say?"

"He used to," I said. "But you see how he is now. I can hardly turn him off."

"Then what's your big problem then? That's what puzzles me. Why's he here?"

"Because Mary said I've a bad impression of group in general from a single experience in California where they just sat around me in a circle screaming at me and belittling my mustache then. And that it'd be worthwhile my coming here to meet you all and because she's spoken so much about me to you, for you to meet me."

"Mary hasn't spoken so much about you," someone said. "It's Myles. Their divorce and effects of it on her girl and boy. Christ, I've been here as long as Mary has and didn't even know your name was Newton or Newt till Glen introduced you."

"Listen you two," Glen said. "Compared to the rest of us including yours true, you got it made. You like each other and yourselves. You like what you're doing with your individual lives and where it's heading and you approach your mutual problems more openly, honestly and maturely than most. And when you do split you know you always tie up together again and each time you seem to strengthen your relationship a whit and learn something more. So what else you want from life—money, worldwide popularity and power and movie star bodies and looks?"

"Yes," I said.

"Then go out and get it, baby, but you got to be ready to work your ass off. Now hey. Time's running out so I want to go into what's happening with Andrei and Jane since his stomach ulcer and her miscarriage and operatic tour."

"I think someone should ask Newt why they don't live together," someone said.

"All right," Glen said, "let's say you asked."

"Because I'm a city person, she's a country. Because I find twice as much substitute teaching work in the city than where she lives. Because we've tried twice and so far it went well for two to three months and then didn't. And right now I think we agreed we need more room around us, right, Mary? That the last time got too intense with my not really knowing anyone up there except Mary and Linetta and Linetta's friends and the librarian, so we went back to our every weekend and every now and then extended weekend till we'll perhaps become dissatisfied with that and maybe think the reverse will work or former or some other change."

"Besides," a grouper said, "it might be the wrong time for Mary to settle down with only one person. And definitely in my opinion should she not get married and have a child by one when it's not even been two years since her divorce and where she's finally on her own and found her own career and so many new interests and friends apart from her mate's, which seemed her main mistake before. Am I not right in assuming all this from everything she's said here to now?"

"We can't go any further into it," Glen said. "Quitting hour has pretty near gonged. All I want to say to Mary is Mary, don't put all your eggs in one basket, got me down right? Because, baby, that's not where you are now. Okay. Quick. Andrei and Jane. What's been cooking with you two lately and how come out of any couple here, neither of you said a word through all this?"

So what more is there to tell? I meet his family in his talk and dreams. He has only photos of me. I go out to their cemetery plot and there's only one grave there, headstoned but vacant. He reads a prayer from a prayer book so small it seemed he had to have gotten it out of a Cracker Jack box. He collects house plants people abandon in garbage cans and gives them new life. He won't pay more than a penny per person at any of the voluntary contribution museums and can't stay there for more than half an hour. He makes his own yogurt out of yesterday's yogurt, has the exact same breakfast and does the exact same exercises every day, ignores sports, disdains games, devours his daily paper daily, thinks one of man's greatest inhumanities to man is not paying the fine on your overdue library books and mine to him is to malign his forty year old recalcitrant typewriter, isn't open and often is openly hostile to astrology and metaphysics and parapsychology and personal transformation through meditation and better nutrition or any new technology or fad that's there just for a laugh, all of which I think would get mighty tiring. A few days after my mother died he wouldn't hold me, so scared was he of my outrage, breakdown and screams, though he knew I needed help and had to be held. He can be a big prick and has a big prick and is very hairy and has hairy balls. When he was so sick that day he stuck his lips up to me above the covers and I said "What, kiss the sweaty meatball of death?" and I think that time we laughed hardest. He once said "You'll have other future love affairs other than with me but rarely will you find such a schmo with so much to sew who'll also have the insensitivity to put up with us." And yesterday he called. Said as a leader "You find that book and manuscript I left behind and asked you to send in the self-addressed stamped envelope I sent with sufficient stamps and right return and forwarding addresses?" and I said "Yeses as I told you before and as I wrote you before you didn't have enough stamps so they were sent back to you book rate." He said "Thanks, Mary, and how you been doing?" and I said "Mary's doing swell." "I got a new bed today. Want to help me test it out?" and I said "Don't be stupid, Newt" and he said "Yes, don't be stupid, Newt. They go well and you're so right again. But I still love you considerably, so that was a fairly understandably stupid remark considering everything you have to consider about the very nature of considerable love and what we don't know about it and what we don't know" and I said "Okay, but I don't love you. I'm sorry but that's the way she blows." "I've fixed up my apartment." "So?" "But you'd like it. Very colorful. Not bright primaries. Not even secondary elections or tertiary or triquarterly even selections but very odd pastels. Unusual combos. Even my ceilings are being replastered and painted several different yellows. Whole shebang. Stove fixed. You can now sit. And also make toast. And got a plumber in and so the shower really flows now though it still takes twenty minutes to get the water lukewarm. And new desk. Lamp. Desk lamp. New clothes. Shiny new shoes and two pair of sox too. Hair styled. From a fashionable hair stylist. Record player even. Even a record. Ferns and hanging ivy that hide me from the outside. You'd like it. But especially the bed. No split down the middle highriser. A double for a queen and king. Be my queen for a night, Em? Then princess and paup. For an hour. Half hour then. For a quarter and I'll stay the entire time in the bathroom sitting amidst my ivy and fern. I still love you." "I don't ditto you." "I do undon't ditto you." "Don't." "Can't top tinking of you." "Do." "Can't stop dop dinking dove due." "Stop." "I tried. I'll try. I try. I'm trying, Mary, this very moment right now." "Good. See you then, Newt." "One more thing." "Yes?" "No. If I say it I've said it and that'll be my one thing and we'll hang up and that's not what I want to do." "But I do." "Darling?" "Don't call me that. Makes no sense." "How's Linetta and Timon?" "That your one final fling?" "No. How are they?" "Great." "Myles?" "What's he to you?" "I don't know. He's nice." "Then call him if you like and find out just how so." "Rick, Mark and Bryce?" "Who are they?" "You still don't know?" "Yeah, but how do you?" "I still have friends around your way." "Henny the librarian and her books. A big mouth. I'm going to talk to her." "No, don't. She'll feel bad. I pumped her. Scout's honor. Phoned to say why my overdues haven't arrived and that they never will till she passes my quiz." "All right. And so I see three men. Wild hot stuff, honey." "You do it with them?" "Stupid Newt again?" "Get my letter?" "Yes. Now is that your last thing?" "I also got a steady job." "You did? Doing what?" "You're interested?" "Yes I'm interested. Doing what?" "Will be doing what. Working in a department store." "Not again. What about teaching and your evening homework?" "Had to give it up. Paid well but kids killing me and I want to live." "You were never a teacher anyway and so even subbing for one I thought was a dishonest way to survive. But I got to go." "Don't you want to know what I'll be doing in the store?" "Same thing, right? Selling. Little Boys Shop." "But this time selling little boys. Same shop. Start next week. Drop by. Give you a good deal and maybe a trade. If I'm not on the floor, go upstairs to the co-workers' cafeteria where we used to caf and co last Christmas season last. I can get you discounts. For Linetta and Timon too. Ten percent off on everything. Twenty percent on clothes I might wear in the store and Timon's almost my height. Bring him in." "I don't think so." "Too bad. It would be nice seeing you." "No it wouldn't." "Nicer if you smiled while seeing me and nicer than nice if in the shop you shook my hand and slapped my back and said Hi kiddo? and kissed me and nicer than nicer than nice if you meant it too." "I wouldn't. I can't. I won't. I'm sorry." "Mary?" "Yes." "Just wanted to say your name. Remember when I used to say it? Mary Mary Mary." "Yes yes yes. So? It's done. Now it's other men." "No." "And I'm sure for you other women." "Not really." "Then other men." "No. And I've seen someone else. Wasn't fun. Barely could come. Didn't." "For you that's a miracle and a half and for her I'm sure a grave disappointment." "Am I getting old? Nah. It's because she wasn't you and you." "I really don't want to hear about it. Though I'm sure your problem won't last long." "It might." "Big deal. I'm going." "Whereto?" "Off the phone. Noplace special. Papers to grade, kitty litter to pour." "Meet me for supper tomorrow night?" "Won't." "Night after tomorrow night?" "No." "Say when." "When." "You mean when?" "I mean nothing not now or then. I mean not again. That's what I mean. Never again. Look. Let me be straight one last time. I see other men. I like seeing them. I see three and I might see four and I might be dropped by one or drop one and then see three again or only two if I'm dropped or drop before I got my fourth or I might add two and see five. But you're not going to be fourth or fifth. Not sixth or any ordinal. I don't want to see you. I've seen you. We saw one another. We tried. It didn't work. It almost never worked. We were crazy for trying so long. It should have ended after the first month. And then ended during that first spring and then that summer. It was bad timing—remember? Bad timing. See someone else. Others. More than one. Believe me it can be fun." "Fun and one. I like those." "It's good for your ego. Good for you and yours. Maybe we didn't work because I'm the one person who knows I can't be with just one person and you're the one person I know who doesn't know that about me yet. But that's it for me. It might not always be so but I feel it will be for you with me. I also feel that's the way you really are too. You've always gone with just one woman, correct? And every one of them went strong for a while and then fizzled." "Yes. Always one. Never two. Surely not three. Though once I did make love to three women in one day. First one very early in the morning after a date. And that afternoon I met a woman I know on the street or on the street a woman I knew and we went to her place and eventually made love. And that evening—I was young and proud then, you see—just to make it three in one day which I'd never done before and thought would be something to boast about, I called the one woman I knew who liked me almost so much as to sleep with me anytime I asked when she didn't already have someone there or coming over. Well she answered and said it's late, what do I want? I said I'd like to come by and she said all right, but get over here in fifteen minutes as she's sleepy. I said I have to as it's now eleven-thirty and I want to make love to her before twelve. She forbore the pumpkin joke and I went over and she opened the door yawning and I said come on, you're tired, let's go right to bed and we got in bed two minutes to go and awful as this must sound to you, I came before the stroke of midnight." "How do you know her clock was right?" "I brought my own pocketwatch." "How do you know your clock was right?" "I dialed Nervous just before I left my place." "You look at your watch right after you two did it or more likely just as you did it?" "No. I checked her bed clock with my watch right before we went to bed and fixed her clock to correspond with mine." "You made it then. Hurray. Three cheers. Another story for the boys. But do it again. At least three different women in a week. You'll like it. And you'll get to know there are much better and more appreciative women for you than me and you'll forget me. You won't want me. You'll find I'm ridiculous." "I've already forgotten you. What's your name again? Who am I speaking to, sir? Goodbye, Mary." "So long, Newt." "No, wait." "What?" "Don't go yet." "Okay if you have something more to say to me but wait. But make it the last, please?" "My one thing to say is I order you not to go yet. Damn. Now I've said it and that wasn't what I wanted to be the last thing. But because I ordered you, you can't go till I release you." "Release me? What am I, some dog just out of training school who's gotten a command?" "I don't understand." "Sure you do. You're the one who said it. But you're just wasting time now and I'm falling for it. I'm going." "Linetta in?" "Why?" "So I can speak to her." "Why?" "To talk to her. Come on, we became friends." "Call her some other time, not now." "But there's no harm. She doesn't want to speak to me, that's fine. And this was the last thing I wanted to ask you." "Swear?" "Last." "By the way. I've written you a postcard about sending my own Newt and Mary story around. But I won't if you don't want me to and you think it conflicts with your own." "Do what you want. But at least send me a copy." "I will." "And if I can get it placed somewhere for you, would you want me to?" "I do. And if there's money in it, even better. Lin?" So she got on the phone and they spoke. He made her laugh. She him. He said "Hey, if you're ever in the city then we have to meet, okay?" She said he had no phone. "I got one," he said. "I've joined the human race." "Good," she said, "then I'll call you." She took down his number. He said "I'm sorry about your mother and I breaking up and one reason because it means I don't see you anymore." "Don't worry," she said, "it was the best thing." "You really think so?" "Best for Mo," she said, "though maybe not for you." Then they said goodbye and she told me what they talked about though most of it had been clear to me from her end of the line. That was yesterday. Half an hour ago he called and Linetta told me who it was. I said "Tell him I'm here but not in" and she did in those words and he said "Your mother shouldn't be using you as an intermediary like that. She should tell me herself." Linetta said "She already has. Plenty of times." He said "I guess so" and then "I hope you call me one day soon, Lin" and she said "Thinking everything over, Newt, I decided maybe that isn't too good an idea too, all right?" and he said "No it isn't all right" and she said "Well it will just have to be" and he said "Anything you say then, sweet face, and goodbye" and they hung up. I think that's enough. This is the end. Maybe I can't do it as well as you, Newt. But I'm through.

Prolog

I was going to be so good about it. I wouldn't write or call her
again. I already said that in my last letter to her in answer to her
last letter asking me to promise that. I said "Okay all right. Got me
ears dewaxed so your message came in clear. No more." I haven't
written or called since. Been a good boy. Haven't heard from her
in any way for a month. Every day I think of her many times
though. I'm always passing places we've been to and had some
good or bad times at but times at. She once said one of those last
times we came together again so soon after we split up seemingly
forever again "I found out during this break that everyplace someone wanted to take me to I'd been to with you. Every Chinese
restaurant, museum room, movie theater, coffeehouse and almost
every cafeteria for a snack." I put on one of my records and it of
course reminds me of her because that's why I put it on. Modern
clarinet and piano piece I play most and like best and the piece
I last played with her in the dark on my bed when I said "You have
to at least listen to the last band of this duet before you fall asleep."
When it was over she said "It's beautiful, lovely, like two Brazilian
birds, like two sweetspeaking quivering sleeping pills, but I think
it's finally for the night put me to rest, yes." Chair she'd flop into.
Toilet seat I've caught her on. My one and only washrag she'd give
herself before bed her quick C and A cleaning with. Walls remind
me of her too. That stain there on the wall above the bed where
she read on the right is hers. Left one's mainly mine and only an
inch higher. Bed doesn't remind me of her much. Bed I mostly
bought because she said she couldn't take the split down the middle of my highriser because the two of us couldn't sleep with our

feet twined and her head on my shoulder comfortably like one. My last night with her we slept on that bed for the first time together but never sort of consecrated the host. No, that's how I've become. Corny she might say "in an early age forty sort of way." I don't think so though maybe but horny you can bet. And I've tried rationalizing her away. Said to myself and aloud "She's gone, good, that's it, just forget, so I've seen you for the last time, cookie, you and your old shoes and socks, and no bringing her back, ain't caveman days, even if it was, other cavemen maybe know kung fu, so viola, c'est rien or almost, nothing you can do about it so why make yourself into a bigger fool, take it on the man, a good little boy when he's lost his best toy, go to the corner then and cry there if you have to cry, ah, don't be upset, no sweat, plenty of other marys you can bet, might get, oh you SOB, you little bastard and big bitch with the low bottom bulging behind, you're dead to me now, you hear, and make sure you know that from now on I'm dead to you for all time too." Corny she might say again "and this time not in the least attractive middleaged way. Your overemotion's exposing itself my dead, I mean my dear. Your baldness. Your supposed nonbitterness. Your belly of beer." Ah, the hell with her.

But how? Drinking of course. Drinking as the only course. That "Say, have another drink, me good friend. Already had four? Then have a fifth. What now? You've had bock beer, mixture of light and dark beer, bourbon, white wine, so what about a crème de cacao or Punt e Mes? You got to mix your drinks you know. You want to get sick?" Shit where is she? I've walked and biked around some parts of the city a dozen times on the days I thought there'd be the best chance she'd be in the places I biked or walked around: Tuesday nights when she takes her mime class for kicks. Didn't spy on her, from across the street—oh look she's walking hand in hand but isn't holding her own hands—no, just around the West Village where her class is, thinking I might accidentally bump into her before she goes into her dance studio. And on Friday and Saturday night at the movie theaters I thought she might most want to go to, for in two years I got to know her movie tastes. Niente. Bought tickets. Stood on how many freezing lines of movies I didn't want to see and paid too much for and walked out of each time. And every day I enter my building—ten times a day I'd say, not intentionally leaving just to enter again but because I've become very edgy and restless of late and must get out to walk, bike or run or find someone on the street I know to talk to—I think I'm going to see her car doubleparked out front and she somewhere inside my building. The vestibule. Hey beautiful old vestibule I once found her leaning shoulder and head against thinking should I shouldn't I dingaling him to see if he's willing to start the whole thing all over again? Sitting on the first steps of the first flight of stairs. In my apartment after leaving what she wanted to leave behind and about to go. Or gone and she heading downstairs while I'm racing up to get there before she tries slipping out through the roof or me the premeditatively slowpoking pup hoping to meet her halfway. Because I still have plenty of things at her place upstate that I said I don't need and she or the thriftstore there can have but which she might want she and her county to finally get rid of because she's finally rid of me and she also still has my keys. Hey, the keys. Mail back my keys, I could write if I wanted a rational reason to write, sending the note with a cryptic self-addressed stamped envelope only big enough for the keys. Never out front or in my building anywhere of course. So always a minor disappointment not seeing her. Minor even when I don't expect her. Minor.

My apartment used to be part of one apartment that my landlady had split up thirty years ago but never got two bells. So both vestibule bells to these apartments ring both apartments and though there's a tickback bell in each apartment neither of them ticks back. So my nextdoor tenant and I must walk down two flights to let in or speak to whatever friend or solicitor rang though we're never quite sure who the ringing's for. We do have a system —not a very good bell system but a bell signal system, two for him and one for me because my tenancy precedes his by three years.

The tenant before him was one ring to my two because he'd been living there for twenty years when I moved in, though I understand he was once a two too. But our landlady's always peeling off our two and one signal system stickers from our mailboxes where our bells are because she thinks they deface what she's called the one major building improvement since she split that apartment into two: the new aluminum mailbox with bell system attached, installed ten years ago. So we share bells, this newtant and I. No, I was the newtant, Mary said, "but way back when you moved in, while he's just a new tenant unless his name's Newt." "It's Ben, which I guess makes him a benant." Tenant before this benant hardly ever had visitors, deliveries or postage due, so I'd say that nine out of ten times the bell rang, which meant about eighteen or nineteen bell rings, it was for me. Now it's the reverse, almost exactly, maybe worse. Mary almost always rang my vestibule bell because she usually drove in from upstate or after one of her downtown classes and her car would be doubleparked and since it usually took a long time to find a parking space around here and she hadn't seen me for a few days, she'd want to find the space with me. For a while she had her own bell signal: one dot and two dashes for EM. But then both the previous tenant and I would meet in the hall, so Mary changed it to two dashes and two dots for her daughter's nickname for her, MO, but he found this excessively grating, so Mary went back to ringing me just twice. The benant and I recently agreed to allow as many individual personal bell signals as possible till it becomes too confusing for us, but by that time Mary had stopped ringing and so far he has none. I also told him that the EM signal was reserved but the MO he could have, but he asked if we could switch those around as the woman he thinks he's going to be getting close to is named Marie. So she'd ring, my Mary, and I'd go downstairs holding my shoes if I thought it was her, since that's how I walked around my place, without them, and we'd get in the car, chattering about what's been happening, pausing for a little reunion snuggling perhaps before setting out for a parking space. Then we'd take a walk, for breakfast maybe buy her cream cheese, wholewheat bagels and eggs, stop before some building we never architecturally discussed, some new shop or street sight or just stumble upon even another city location where we hadn't yet seen the Empire State Building from, and then probably end up at our favorite restaurant and bar: with luck at the one semicircular table and which perfectly fits the cubicle's niche, our favorite table once they built the enclosed patio that took away the semicircular window space. We'd have beers, Mary her blue cheeseburger and me the attendant fried onion and three pickle slices which she hates, and then go to my apartment and always make love if we haven't seen one another for a few days and then go to sleep, Mary's head almost always on my right shoulder, her new home, she once said, "My old rest home," she later said, "If we ever split up you have to give me one of those shoulders," she said, "Preferably the right one, though if I'm the one breaking up with you I'll settle for the left," she said, "And if you ever go on a long vacation or trip alone you have to leave behind one of your shoulders," she said, "And if you do sleep with another woman," she said, "which I'm not discouraging you to do, just promise you won't let her rest her head for the night on your right shoulder, since I don't want it to get even a little bent out of shape."

But where is she? this ex-Mary, late at night, Saturday night, in bed, round two, yes in bed, the time sir is two, arms around one of the three or four menfriends she was seeing when we stopped seeing, or maybe some new special man she recently met, just met, tonight at a bar or someone's house let's say, a blind date, "I know so and so who knows so and so who knows you and he said that I should or she said that we might or they said that they would, if you're interested, they gave me no assurances, great, I'll be wearing a red spittoon in my lapel," her head on his dildo, him in her mouth, him or he in her she mouth, really ravishing and lavishing it up to bring it all back there, hey lovey? she might say if she saw this as she said about some of my other pieces she saw about us, or sweetpea, chickadee, dearie, yousie, mysie, piesie, big

schmo, schmucko, funny fellow, my fine funny figure of a furry
fellatioable fellow, Newtie, Newtie the tootie, the loupie, the new-
tease, bluesqueeze, all those, she also most of those, swapping
endearments we also swapped, naked of course, in bed, hands,
mouths, he at the other end watching her as I used to love to do,
eyes usually closed: hers, and if opened only half open though
looking gratefully stoned, "That's it, that's it, the one thing you
can't stand most and which I can almost tolerate about you least
is the idea of someone sticking it in me, right?" and I said "Almost
right, for the actual sight of it might be worse," "Well you'll just
have to accept and even expect that I'll do with my body what I
please" and I said "If you do then I'll just have to leave thee" and
she said, after three years "If only we could just have a casual
relationship, because you remember what I said Jung said, about
the main desiderations and tensions between women and men I
mean?" naked of course, arms, legs, her room, his tomb, has to be
light on for him to be watching her end, those cute little nummu-
lar dribs and drams of him and Mary saying his consistency's so
much similar to one of the last men she knew, "Last man who?"
he might say or she stopping him when he senses he's about to
explode or just her jaws ache so no more or she stops so she can
enjoy her own blanks and then shifting around and in transit
wiping their faces on the sheets and he gets on top or side by side
or she atop or on her knees or he on his tibiae or she flat out on
her front and he in from behind or maybe in her poop for their
first time which I could never do first, last and always though once
almost wanted to, but no nothing either of us said we much liked
though maybe he fits better than me or double-quickly he wiz-
ardly comes up with a squish of vaseline or spit and she goes oh
oh oh no, really with the rumpus while he's cockadoodling Mary,
oh Mary, my Mary, my Emmy, Em, Emiline, Em of mine, em-
bryon, empyrean, emulsify me emulsion mine, perhaps talking too
much for her and with more word sense or nonsense than she can
take at such a time, and then the big wail, new man suddenly
swallowed up by that wail of wails and it's over, she's finished and

whichever heaven he's in it's beginning to hurt her so she pulls
away or has to unbolt and unchain them and maybe he isn't done
which would be fine for he tries slipping it back in but she says no
and moves away again and he understands or doesn't or gets mad
or doesn't or turns aside or doesn't for she explains and he understands again or doesn't and she says "Screw off, already, for it was
fun but sometimes it doesn't work for one or both of us and if it
did for me and didn't for you don't blow it, there'll be other times
if you just don't get too pissed off and pushy or touchy like the last
one" and he might say "What last one who?" or "You mean that
Newt?" and "Gee I really am overfeeding my ego and depreciat-
ing your own" and that'd satisfy her and she'd pat his cheek perhaps and tweak him or maybe go for a snack or water or milk if
he's got milk or something to drink because she's thirsty or he
might and she might say "As long as you're up can you get me
something to munch on and drink?" and he might ask what and
she "Anything you think I might like" or she might be more
specific or say from bed "I'm tired and would just like to sleep
right through tomorrow—say, how about us doing that, I've got
nothing to do, no papers to grade, no place special to be except
home around six when my daughter arrives" and he might want
to or who knows he might have a date with another woman
around noon and she might say "Break it?" and he might say no
or who knows he might say "Great, with a lot of loving and fun and
whatever—reading, even" and she'd say yeah and they'd snack or
drink or both or just go to sleep or first pee or all three before they
go to sleep or he might get up to brush his teeth and she'd say
"Don't, I hate the taste of toothpaste" and the light or candle
would be put out and maybe they'd first have to kick the Sunday
papers off the bed partially to unread and they'd say sweet dreams
and she'd be making a new impression on his shoulder and holding
his hand to her lips and he saying how much his shoulder likes the
new impression her head's making on it and his hand where his
hand is and a little kiss goodnight of course and maybe he'd get
an erection or the one he had never dropped off and start poking

her with it and she'd say "Who's that knocking knocking on my door?" and he'd answer and she'd say "Well whatever it is, I got plenty right now so I don't want any more" and he'd keep knocking or maybe try and come in through the window or maybe she'd eventually let him in and it'd turn out to be the best of her life and from the simplest position possible where they didn't even have to move from where they'd said goodnight from and for him too which would sort of seal it for them in a way and he might talk about it afterward and she might say "Sure, what do you think?" and he might say "So you feel we have a future, no?" and she might say "If we do split up very soon or just don't like one another's personalities anymore, no reason why we couldn't just do it together when we wanted to, since we really wouldn't have known one another long enough for there to be too strong an emotional tie to prevent us from that yet" and he might say "You bet" or "Say that again?" or "I'm for that if it so sadly has to come to that" and touch her again, discovering her nipples and with more fingers than she's used to and his technique you can betcha is better than ever and do something tricky with his tongue and she might say "This is crazy, Bill, Bob, Biff or Ben, but I want to screw all over again" and he might say "Hey, what do you know, me too" and they do in one of those previous positions or sitting whichever way in each other's laps or on a skin rug or in a chair someway or warm bathtub or with a bunch of pillows systems analytically emplaced by the man to make them feel as if they're doing it on cumuli and this time it's even better than before for them both and she might say "Never never never have I ever done it twice in a row like that so soon after a more than superior first normal and never would I ever be so greedy to expect to do it again like that with anyone including you" and he might say "You just might and I'm going to take a chance here and say chances are more that you might than just just might" and she might say "Horray" and they'd kiss and he might say "Want anything else?" and she might say no and he "Neither do I, then goodnight, Mary" "Goodnight" and they'd fold together again and fall asleep and maybe an hour from now one of them might get up for some water or the bathroom and unintentionally wake the other and they might sleepily start doing it again and it might turn out to be better than the rest or as good as the third or only a little worse than the second but still superior to the first superior normal and she might then say "I love you Bob, Biff, Bick or Ben, and it's not just the sex speaking" and he might say "I love you too, Emsky" or some other new name and she might say "I like my new name and me new fella and what he just said" and he might say "And I like that she likes my new name for her and what I said and that she calls me her new fella" and she might say "You know, I promised myself I'd never again plunge in so fast with anyone after Newt, but what can I say except I've never felt so strong or good with any man so quickly or maybe ever including my husband, Newt, Rick, Bryce and whatever that third one's was, and even though what I'm going to say now may put you off, everything's begun to revolve around you" and he might say "Me too with you and never have I felt so close with anyone including your husband, Newt, Brick or Rice" and they'd laugh and maybe cry and maybe turn the light on so they could see each other laughing and crying and they might make love again but I don't think so but if they do it won't be as good as before because she hurts now but maybe not or he hurts but I don't think so and they either might stop partway done or she might say "Do it in me without my coming" and he might say "No, it's not important" and she might say "Don't be silly, it is, and I'd assume the same from you if our tables were turned" and he does with her help and the traditional accompanying grunts and noises so loud he could break glass as someone said or I only read and where his neighbor next-door if they're at his place turns up the radio or raps on the wall and she says "We're not making too much commotion?" and he "It's okay they're used to me by now" and she might laugh or express nothing and he might say "I was only kidding" and they'd kiss and hold each other through the night, past sleep, till morning, past the time one of them's already awake, getting up, having fun, breakfast outside or in, bike ride if tomorrow's nice, tomorrow's supposed to be cold and rain, good, that'll keep them indoors, no, bad, no, all of it's all right, no, typing about it makes it all all right, no, Mary I'm so in love with you I could plotz, no, Mary I'm so mad at you I could phone, no, don't plotz, don't phone, do get up for one more drink but don't drink, no drink but water with two aspirins as I've drunk too much as it is, and as I stood at the kitchen tap I looked at her photos above the stove, two I have of her, one sullen, one smiling, both unframed, one smiling I painted stars around it on the wall and many of the streaking and bursting symbols associated with fireworks and sullen one sunlight rays sallying out of it and blue clouds and afternoon quartermoon and while I was standing two gondoliered balloons with my pen, but now back at my desk, where I can barely type, hardly write, ready to crawl to bed on my unconcentrated head instead if I have to, "Mary" I say, "Mary" I speak up, "Mary" I scream at my top, "I loved you but it was always bad timing in the end my friend and now it's over and there's nothing more to say" and my neighbor that young man named Ben who moved in just a when a few months ago with his fifty-seven out of sixty vestibule bell rings, a nice guy, going for his Ph.D., also teaching English to under-privileged children in a parochial school he says under Title III three times a week, raps back on the wall to me, fact following fiction somewhere I wrote or read of someone else, fiction follow-ing fact following fiction I think it said, and maybe not only for my screaming but loud typing so I try to type lighter but can't so I type goodnight.